WILD STALLION

"A Romance Novel is all about the Gal and the Guy...
It's their Journey. It's their Story."

ISBN-13: 978-1514625538
ISBN-10: 1514625539

WILD STALLION

First Printing, 2015

Printed in the United States of America

https://www.valeriewestromance.com

WILD STALLION

Valerie West

To all those who are horse lovers,
whether you ride professionally
or whether you ride for pleasure,
this book is dedicated to you...

Standing in the winner's circle with family, friends and her winning horse was an experience all too familiar to her...

Not this time.

She thought she had done everything she could to prepare him for that special race.

But something went wrong...

ONE

Ryan Hollister removed a DVD of one of her favorite winning races from a stack of videos on top of the dresser.

She sat down on the foot of her bed, holding the empty case, staring at the video playing on the TV.

There was a faint scent of leather in the room. Not the fragrance of perfume one would expect in a woman's bedroom.

Numerous cups and ribbons were displayed in a trophy case standing against one wall.

"I want to find work on another ranch, but how can I tell mother and daddy?"

Ryan's thoughts were interrupted by a knock on the door.

"Hi, daddy. Come and watch Easy Money's video with me."

"Ya did such a good job with him, Honey. I'm so proud o' ya. By-the-way, how'd that filly do in the exercise ring today?"

"Desiré did good, daddy. She's gotten used to the lunge line work-outs. She'll make a fine brood mare someday."

"I noticed ya were exceptionally quiet at supper tonight. Is anything wrong, Sweetheart? Anything on your mind ya wanna talk 'bout?"

Ryan twiddled with the DVD case, flipping the lid open and closed. She put the case on the bed beside her and looked at her father.

"Umm..."

"C'mon. Ya can tell your dad," her father said, putting his arm around her, pulling her close.

Ryan took a deep breath.

"I think I'm ready to go out on my own, daddy. To find work on one of the other ranches around here."

"Well, this is not a big shock to me. I've been expectin' to hear ya tell me this. I know ya have a wish to have your own place someday. Are ya ready to do that? To look for work on another ranch, I mean?"

"Yes. I am. Working on another ranch would be an opportunity for me to see how others run their ranches. I've never said anything about it to mother, though."

"If ya leave, I'd be short-handed 'round here, Honey. Ya've been my right hand for a lot o' years."

"I know, daddy, but—"

"I'd have to hire maybe… two guys to take your place."

Her father grinned and winked.

"Two guys to take my place, daddy? You're kidding, right? You're the best daddy in the whole world," she said, throwing her arms around him and kissing his cheek.

"Well, if ya feel you're ready an' ya wanna find work at one o' the other ranches 'round here I'll help ya. As for your mom, I'll let her in on our little talk tonight."

"Thanks, daddy."

"It's late. I'm gonna turn in. I appreciate ya tellin' me what was on your mind. I'll see what I can do an' don't worry 'bout your mom."

Ryan followed her father to the door. They gave each other a hug. He gave her a kiss on the cheek.

Her father opened the door, then turned to her.

2

"Ya'll always be my little girl. I love ya. See ya in the mornin'. G'night."

"Thanks, daddy. I love you, too. Goodnight."

Ryan turned the TV off, undressed and laid down.

She looked up at the saddle mounted on the wall above the headboard.

It was given by her parents on her sixth birthday and was a constant reminder of her dream and her passion all these years to have her own place someday.

"I hope mother will understand."

TWO

Ponderosa Pine was a small community of several thousand, nestled in the high desert about fifty miles East of Albuquerque, New Mexico.

It was horse country.

McKenna ranch was ten miles East of town.

Chance McKenna was greeted by Carmen Martinez when he walked into the dining room.

"Good morning, Mr. McKenna. Please, sit down. There's coffee on the table. I'll bring your breakfast right over."

"G'mornin', Carmen. Thanks."

Chance poured his coffee from a decanter.

He removed a letter from an envelope he took out of his shirt pocket. It showed signs of having been wadded up and crumpled.

The letter was signed by Mr. R. A. Lopez. Mr. Lopez' demands for a meeting were becoming more frequent. More persistent.

Chance McKenna continued to make excuses to avoid a confrontation with Mr. Lopez.

There was another problem facing Chance McKenna.

The ranch and the horses demanded all his time. He had hired a couple of top hands during the past several years, but they all moved on to work at other ranches leaving him scrambling to find someone with the experience he was looking for.

The worried look on his face did not go unnoticed by Carmen when she brought Chance his breakfast.

"Is something wrong, Mr. McKenna?"

Chance looked up after a few seconds staring at the plate Carmen had just put in front of him.

He quickly stuffed the letter into the envelope and put it into his shirt pocket.

"Uhh... no, Carmen. It's fine. Not to worry. I was uhh... I was just thinkin' 'bout what to do. I need to find a top hand to help out 'round here, that's all. I'll be goin' into town for feed after breakfast. Call if ya have any problems before I get back."

"I will, Mr. McKenna. Don't worry. I'm sure you'll find someone. Eat your breakfast now before it gets cold," she said, in a motherly tone of voice and with a reassuring smile.

THREE

S cott's Western Wear, Tack and Feed store was located on one of the high-traffic side streets in Ponderosa Pine.

The building was a wooden structure typical of those in the old West.

A sheet metal overhead covered the front porch.

Two steps led up to the porch from a wooden boardwalk on either end of the porch.

Goods and merchandise included Western clothing, horse supplies and accessories and livestock feed.

Julie Scott purchased the business a couple of years ago and her business picked up when she added apparel for men, women and children. Her store was the only place in Ponderosa Pine to buy Western style clothing.

It was mid-morning.

Julie was busy putting up inventory in the children's clothing section.

The small copper bell hanging above the door announced someone was entering the store.

Chance McKenna closed the door behind him.

"Good morning, Mr. McKenna. I've not seen you for a while. You okay? Do you need some feed?"

"G'mornin', Miss Scott. I'm good, thanks. Yeah, I need some hay an' some grain, but first I wanted to ask if I could put this ad up on your bulletin board over there?"

"Sure. What is it you're selling, Mr. McKenna?"

"Well, I'm not sellin' anythin'. I need to hire someone to help out 'round the ranch. Sam moved on 'bout three an' a half weeks ago an' now I'm short-handed. Breedin' season's just 'round the corner an' I need some help. Someone who knows horse ranchin' an' has top hand experience."

"I wondered why Sam hadn't been in lately. I'm sorry to hear he quit. So... a top hand, you say? You know, Mr. McKenna, I have a friend with years of experience. I could get—"

"Knows horses, does he? All right then, get in touch with him if ya wanna, Miss Scott. I'm up against it, though an' I need help. Like, right now. In the meantime, I'll stick this ad on the board if that's okay."

"Sure, go ahead, Mr. McKenna, if you can find a spot. The board's getting pretty cluttered with ads."

Chance found an empty spot and stuck the ad onto the cork board with a pin he took from a row of colored pins sticking in the board.

"Okay, Mr. McKenna, pull your truck around back and let's get that feed loaded."

FOUR

Morning chores were finished. Mixing grain would take up the rest of Ryan's time until lunch.

There was an eight months old colt she wanted to start breaking in the afternoon. He was going to be her next choice to train for the race track. He showed a lot of promise.

Ryan's cell phone rang.

"Jules? Is something wrong?"

Julie spoke in a hurried, rushed, nervous tone of voice. Unlike her. She was usually calm and collected when she called. It was always just a friendly chat between two, longtime, childhood friends wanting to catch up on the latest gossip at both ends.

"Nothing's wrong. I'm... I'm good. Uhh... listen. Just listen. Okay? One of my customers came into the store this morning. He left just now. He put an ad on the bulletin board. He's looking for a top hand on his ranch. I told him I knew someone who could—"

"He's looking for a top hand? Jules, you do know what a top hand is on a ranch, right? There's a heck of a lot of responsibility that goes along with that job. You know that."

"I know. I know. Listen. You can do it. This could be the opportunity you've been hoping for. His name is Chance McKenna. He's not like the other ranch owners I've told you about before who said they were looking for help, but they weren't that serious about hiring someone. He's different. This one's different. He needs some help now."

"Different? What do you mean, different?"

"He's the first rancher who came into the store and put an ad on the board."

"Well, I guess that does mean he's serious, doesn't it?"

"Just pack your things and get out here, Liz. I've told you before you can stay with me. Okay? Once and for all, just do it. Tell your folks you're coming out for a visit. It is a visit, right? Then go talk to Chance McKenna and see if it works out. Okay? I have a good feeling about this."

"I don't know. That's a long way to go. New Mexico? Let me think abou—"

"No, Liz. No. There's no time to think about it. You need to get out here."

"Can you tell me any more about Mr. McKenna? What's he like?"

"He seems nice. He's always polite. He comes to the store several times a month for feed. His top hand left and he's serious about needing help, Liz. That's all I know."

"That's it? Well, I finally did have a talk with daddy last night about wanting to look for work on another ranch. He agreed to help me, but we were talking about ranches around here, Jules. I don't know how he'll take it when he finds out it's for a job out there. I'm more concerned about mother, though. She'll be terribly hurt, I know."

"Just talk to them. It's time they both knew about your dream. Talk to them."

"Okay, I'll talk to them about this tonight at supper. I'll say it's a visit. I won't say anything more about it than that. I don't know anything more anyway, so that part would be the truth, right? If they're okay with it, I guess I'll try to leave tomorrow morning. They're going to wonder why the rush. It would leave daddy short-handed. Wow! This is happening all of a sudden, Jules. This is really a short notice."

"I know. I know it is, but I called as soon as Mr. McKenna left the store. Don't back out and don't waste any time making up your mind. Mr. McKenna could hire somebody else before you get here. I'm excited about this. It's been a long time, Liz. I miss my best friend. I'm sure your parents will understand. Tell them both I love them. Okay?"

"I will, Jules. I miss you, too."

"Call me tomorrow morning before you leave, will you?"

"Oh? You've got me leaving already? Okay, I'll let you know how it goes tonight. All right? Either way, I'll call you in the morning. Thanks for calling. Love you."

"Love you, too."

Ryan's thoughts were spinning around in her head after she hung up.

Could this be the chance I've been hoping for?

FIVE

Ryan struggled mentally with the words she would have to say to her mother and father. How would they react to her desire to leave? Moreover, would they be sympathetic to her desire to leave the following day?

Working with that young colt in the afternoon helped take her mind off the evening meal.

~~~

Supper time.

Ryan put her fork down half way through the meal.

She glanced, one at a time, at her parents.

"Umm… mother. Daddy."

"There's something I want to tell you both."

"That sounded serious, Honey," her mother said. "What is it?"

"Jules called me this morning. She wanted me to come out for… a visit. She's been out there a couple of years now. I told her—"

"A visit?" her father asked, looking at her from under his eyebrows. "Does this have anythin' to do with what ya an' I talked 'bout last night, Ryan?"

Ryan's father could read her like a book. He always knew.

"Well... yes, daddy. It does. It's a—"

"Sooo... we're talkin' 'bout more than just a visit, right?"

It was too late to back out of the conversation now. The hint of a smile on her father's face supported her self-confidence.

Ryan avoided her mother's gaze.

"Yes, daddy. It's... it's about a job out there."

"A job, Honey?" her mother asked.

"Your mom knows, Ryan. She an' I talked 'bout it last night."

"Yes, mother. A job. It's about a job on a horse ranch in Ponderosa Pine."

Her mother continued to stare at Ryan a few seconds longer, lightly tapping the fingertips of one hand on the table. Ryan could see in her mother's eyes the hope the words she was hearing from her daughter were somehow not true.

"This decision seems terribly sudden, Honey. Not a word. Not even a hint about it, except to your father last night. I'm wondering... does it have anything to do with... with Rob Morris?"

"No, mother, it doesn't. It has nothing to do with Rob Morris. It's about me and the choice I need to make about being on my own. I hope you understand. It's about me and my choice."

Ryan turned to her father. She sensed he was more sympathetic to her decision to leave and was more understanding than her mother was. Especially after the conversation she and her father had the night before.

"We do understand, Sweetheart. Your mom an' I made our choices in the past an' now it's your turn. If this is what ya wanna do, your mom an' I have agreed to support ya. It's not that far away, right? It's not that far. Hell, I could throw a stone from Tulsa to Ponderosa Pine."

Their laughter at her father's comment lightened the moment.

"We'll be sorry to see you go, Honey," her mother said. "You'll always have a home here if things don't work out. Your room will always be yours. We'll leave everything in there as it is. We love you very much and we'll miss you very much."

"Thank you, mother. Thank you, daddy. I'll miss you, too. I love you both. Very much. Thanks for understanding."

Now comes the difficult part. Here goes...

Ryan took another deep breath.

"There's just one more thing I need to tell you. I know this is a very short notice, but... I should leave in the morning. Jules said that rancher needs someone right now. He put an ad on the bulletin board in her store. I'm hoping I can get there in time to talk to him. It's about a twelve hour drive from here."

Ryan's mother and father turned to each other with bewildered looks on their faces.

"You want to leave tomorrow morning, Sweetheart?" her mother said tearfully. "Well... you're right. This is a short notice. Why so soon?"

Ryan needed to console both her parents and let them know how important her decision was to her.

"I have to get out there as soon as possible, mother. Jules told me about a couple of jobs before this one. I didn't tell you and daddy about those jobs. Those ranchers weren't serious about wanting to hire someone. This time it's different. I want to go out there and talk to the owner of the ranch."

Ryan paused for a moment, then turned to her father, expecting some comment from him after hearing the news of her departure in the morning. He said nothing. The surprised look remained on his face.

"I know you'll be short-handed for a while, daddy, but this could be the chance I've been waiting for. It's what we talked about last night."

The concerned looks on Ryan's parent's faces disappeared slowly and turned into reassuring smiles. Ryan knew she had stilled their worry and their surprise.

"Ya can tell that ranch owner he can contact me if he has any question 'bout your experience, Baby Girl."

"Thanks, daddy. Thank you both."

It was done.

The conversation with her parents went a lot more smoothly than Ryan thought it would.

They continued with supper.

There were some lighthearted moments during which Ryan's mother and father recalled treasured memories of Ryan's childhood, occasionally causing her to blush.

Those moments softened unspoken thoughts of Ryan's departure the following day.

Ryan helped her mother with the dishes.

Ryan tried to steer the conversation away from their goodbyes in the morning. She sensed her mother was on the brink of tears several times and in fact, so was she.

It was a difficult end to the evening, but it was the outcome Ryan hoped it would be.

Ryan set her alarm for an early hour. There was not a lot to pack. She would do it in the morning.

It was not easy going to sleep. Ryan tossed and turned. She replayed the phone call with Julie over and over in her head. She thought about the conversation with her parents at supper. A hundred thoughts kept racing through her head.

Suddenly, one thought in particular pushed the others away. The realization this could very well be the last night she would sleep at home. In her own room. In her own bed.

SIX

After they finished breakfast the following morning, Ryan's parents helped her load her things into her pickup truck.

It was her mother's request that Ryan leave some of her things in her room.

When everything was loaded into her truck, Ryan, her mother and her father stood looking at each other in silence. It was an awkward moment.

Time for the goodbyes.

This would be the first time Ryan would be away from home for any length of time. It was a very difficult time for Ryan and her mother. Ryan and her father would go away together for a day, or two, whenever they had a race to go to, but they would always return home. Her mother understood those times, of course.

This was a more permanent goodbye and the tears could not be helped. Ryan and her mother were very close emotionally. There was even a tear or two showing in her father's eyes.

Time for the hugs and kisses.

"It's time to go. I love you both. I'll call you from the motel tomorrow night and as soon as I get to Jules' house."

"You'll do just fine out there, Honey," her father said. "Don't forget... ya know horses an' horse ranchin' as much as, or more than, any man an' ya have a lot to offer someone needin' help on his ranch. Just remember all I taught ya. All ya learned. Just give it a hundred percent like ya always do. You'll do just fine. Drive careful on the way out there."

"Yes. Take care of yourself, Sweetheart," her mother said, wiping the tears from her eyes, "and be careful driving. Call us from the motel and as soon as you get to Julie's place—"

"I'll be careful, mother and I promise to call. Thanks so much for the sandwiches."

"and Honey," her mother continued, "take some time off out there. For yourself, I mean. Away from the ranching. Enjoy some socializing. Maybe Julie could help in that department? With some introductions? It's been a long time since you and—"

"Elizabeth," her father said, shaking his head.

"Mother. Please. I do appreciate your concern for my social life, but I'm going out there for a job. I won't be looking for a boyfriend."

"Well, I'm just saying," her mother said.

Smiles followed and helped to lighten the moment between Ryan and her mother.

"Give Julie our love, Honey."

"I will, mother and Jules sends her love to you and daddy."

One last kiss and hug each for her mother and her father.

Ryan got into her truck and waved a final goodbye to her parents.

~~~

"Are you ready for a roomie, Jules?"

"For real? You're coming?" Julie blurted out.

"Yes. I'm at the gas station."

"Yaaay!. How did it go last night?"

"It went well. Mother and daddy were heartbroken at first, but they understood."

"Liz, I'm so excited. Your bedroom awaits, M'lady."

They giggled heartily.

"Thanks, Jules. I'm excited, too. I can't wait to get there. I won't call again unless there's a problem on the way."

"Be careful driving."

"I will. See you soon. Love you. Bye."

"Love you, too. Bye"

One final peek at the items under the tarp in the back of the truck.

Ryan tugged on the rope holding the tarp. Her father had tied it securely.

She entered Julie's address into the GPS unit mounted on top of the dash.

Ryan turned the key in the ignition.

"Mr. McKenna... I'm on my way."

She drove to Interstate 44 and headed West.

SEVEN

Ryan was uncertain about, but confident her meeting with Mr. McKenna would go smoothly and she would leave with a job offer.

She put the window down and took in the surroundings.

Hanging by chains from a wooden crossbeam supported by wooden poles on each side of the entrance were crooked, wrought iron letters that showed signs of weathering and disrepair.

The letters spelled 'McKenna'.

A slight breeze was blowing. The letters banging into each other sounded like a gigantic wind chime interrupting an otherwise eerie silence.

Mounted on a cement post and standing guard outside the gate was a call box.

Suddenly, Ryan was having second thoughts. Should she press the transmit button or should she turn around and go back to Julie's house?

Being here and hopefully getting the job would be a stepping stone on a path to realizing her dream.

Her dream was the reason she had come all the way from Tulsa after all.

Ryan recalled her father's words. His words gave her strength. She was on her own now. It was time for her to take that first step.

She pulled up to the call box, hesitated briefly, then pressed the transmit button.

Ryan had the feeling she was being watched even though there was no sign of a camera.

There was a short pause, then a voice came from the call box speaker.

"What d' ya want?"

The voice sounded irritated. Abrupt. Not the slightest hint of any interest in speaking to her.

Was that Mr. McKenna?

"I'm Ryan. Ryan Hollister. Julie Scott's friend? She told me the owner of the ranch was looking for a top hand. Would that be you, Sir?"

There was another period of silence.

"D' ya own a telephone, Hollister?"

"Well... yes, I—"

"Then why didn't ya use it before drivin' all the way out here?"

"Uhh... I was in the neighborhood," she said, thinking a little humor might take the edge off the conversation.

"I'm real busy, Hollister an' furthermore—horse ranchin's a man's game."

"What an arrogant so-and-so," Ryan said, under her breath.

That remark raised the hackles on the back of her neck. The feeling of taking on the challenge welled up inside her and gave Ryan the confidence she was looking for to deal with the situation.

There was only one card remaining in Ryan's hand that might get her inside the property. She put it on the table.

"A man's game, is it? Well, Sir, if it's a man's game, then I've probably played it at least as long as you have and I probably have as much experience working with horses as you have. If you're Mr. McKenna and if you're serious about needing a top hand then you need to talk to me."

If that doesn't cause some sparks to fly at the other end nothing would.

She waited.

There was only an absence of sound coming from the call box speaker.

If the unidentified voice was that of Chance McKenna had Ryan jeopardized her opportunity to meet with him?

She checked her watch.

Eight fifteen.

She waited.

Minutes passed.

She waited.

Ryan looked at her watch again.

It was just past eight twenty.

Six minutes.

That did it. She had waited long enough.

Ryan started to back out onto Ponderosa Pine Road.

The silence was broken by the rasping sound of metal scraping against metal.

A chill ran up the back of her neck.

She drove forward. Slowly.

In her rear view mirror, Ryan saw the gate closing.

EIGHT

R yan was in a forest of ponderosa pine trees. The smell of manure
was barely discernible beneath the scent of butterscotch and
vanilla.

Paddocks on either side of the driveway were divided by wooden
fencing and resembled squares on a checkerboard.

Several horses were grazing on lush, green grass and clover.

The paved driveway ended in a cleared parking area.

At the base of a medium-sized hill was a Southwestern-style ranch
house with a wide porch.

A pickup truck, a late model SUV and an automobile were parked
beside each other in front of the house.

Located a short distance from the house was a large horse barn.

Between the barn and the paddocks were a number of corrals holding a few mares with foals by their sides.

A small cabin was nestled among ponderosa pines between the
house and the barn.

Visible behind the barn was a tractor parked beside an equipment shed along with two horse trailers.

The buildings and the landscape on this part of the property were very well kept in contrast to the shabby condition of the sign above the main gate.

Ryan parked her pickup truck near the barn.

Two startled doves flew from a small bush nearby.

A soft whinny was heard inside the barn.

There was no one in sight.

Ryan opened the door, stepped out and stood beside her truck.

She reached down and petted a dog that came running up to see who the visitor was.

Ryan could not see him, but she could feel his eyes touching her from the shadows inside the barn.

Seconds later he emerged from the breezeway.

There was an unmistakable cockiness in the way he carried himself.

A feeling of uneasiness coursed through Ryan's body.

"I'm Chance McKenna."

He raised the brim of his hat revealing finely chiseled, Grecian, god-like features that caused Ryan's heart to skip a beat. He was tall. Slim. His piercing brown eyes seemed to look right through her. There was a stubble of beard showing. Even though the temperature was in the low sixties his shirt was unbuttoned. His bare chest showed a ripple of tanned muscles. He was wearing a pair of faded jeans.

Chance McKenna was a lot younger than she expected.

Despite his cavalier demeanor, the man standing in front of her could make Ryan forget her reason for being here.

She shook her head slightly, trying to shake loose the thoughts racing through her mind.

"As much experience with horses as I do, huh?" he said, greeting her with that same aggravating and annoying tone she heard coming from the call box.

"Well... I'm happy to meet you, too, Mr. McKenna," she replied, with a bit of the same sarcasm she had received from him. "Yes, I stand by what I said about my experience. I'm here to talk about what I can do for you and your ranch."

"That sounds a bit presumptuous, Hollister. I usually give a test when I hire someone."

They stood looking at each other in silence for a few seconds.

Ryan could not believe what she just heard. She collected her thoughts. Any anxiety or uneasiness she felt earlier disappeared. She was not about to be talked down to by Chance McKenna. It was time to protect her self-esteem and take charge of the conversation.

"Are you serious, Mr. McKenna? A test? What in the world are you talking about? I've been around horses and horse ranches all my life, Sir and I've never heard of such a thing. What sort of test? Wait… before you answer that let me say this—I've worked on my parent's horse ranch in Oklahoma since I was thirteen years old. That's fourteen years, Sir. My experience brings with it a lot of hard work, many successes and some heartaches along the way."

Chance McKenna said nothing. He could only stand there. Speechless.

Ryan Hollister was not finished.

"What's more, I'm a licensed, racing Quarter horse trainer. I have no intention of taking an aptitude test at a common horse ranch to prove I'm capable of working with horses. If you need further proof, Mr. McKenna, you can contact my daddy and ask him about my experience and you can check my record of winnings on Oklahoma racetracks."

Chance McKenna stood with his hands on his hips. No woman had ever talked to him that way before. Especially when the subject was horses.

Without further words, Ryan stepped into her truck.

She grasped the steering wheel and fixed her gaze straight ahead.

"Excuse me for wasting your time, Mr. McKenna. Will that gate be open when I get out there?"

"Yeah, but—"

Ryan Hollister touched the brim of her hat and forced a polite nod.

23

"Good day, Sir."

Chance McKenna watched with a startled expression on his face as Ryan's pickup truck disappeared.

He was dumbfounded. He stood for a few moments staring at the empty driveway before heading back to the barn.

"Did she say, 'a common horse ranch'?" he muttered.

Chance McKenna was in desperate need of help. He preferred to hire a man.

The ad he posted a few days ago on Julie Scott's bulletin board did not yield any calls from anyone asking about the job.

The only response so far was Julie Scott's friend, Ryan Hollister, who showed up unannounced just now at the main gate.

She sure was easy on the eyes. Nice figure. Loved that long, blond hair. She didn't look like a woman who spent her days throwin' tack on a horse or exercisin' one on the end of a lunge line.

"I'm curious. Could she do the job?"

NINE

Ryan Hollister and Julie Scott were like sisters. Ryan was the old-est by a couple months. They grew up on neighboring ranches outside Tulsa.

Julie was a kidder. She was always after Ryan about something. Anything to needle her friend.

Ryan, on the other hand, was the more serious one most of the time.

However, when it came to being the one to offer support to the other, it was Julie who came forward for her friend. Ryan always relied on Julie for support and now that Ryan was away from home that sup-port mattered more than ever.

~~~

Julie hurried home after closing the store.

"So… tell me all about it, Liz. Did you get the job?"

"Didn't I hear the words 'He's always polite' come out of your mouth when you told me about Chance McKenna on the phone the other day?"

"Yeah, that's what I—"

"Well, he was anything but polite. He was really irritated when I showed up, Jules. Why didn't you tell him I was a woman?"

"I'm sorry, Liz. I thought if I told him you were a woman he would've told me not to bother calling you. If it doesn't work out with Mr. McKenna we'll find another rancher around here who needs your experience and isn't hung up on hiring a female. Too bad. Chance McKenna doesn't know what he's missing if he doesn't hire you."

"I really unloaded on him. I told him about my trainer's license and track winnings and I told him if he needed more proof he should call daddy. Daddy would set him straight for sure."

"You're right. Your father would. For sure. So, how did you leave it with him?"

"When I headed for the main gate I saw him in my rear view mirror, standing where I left him, with his hands on his hips. I don't know what he was thinking or what he'll decide. He was speechless when I told him what I thought about his hiring methods. He wanted to give me a test, Jules. Can you imagine me taking a test, whatever that means, to get a job on a horse ranch?"

"He wanted to do what? Give you a test?"

"Yeah. That's what got me going. Maybe he said it to see how I'd react. I let him have it. I'm so disappointed. I wanted that job. It's a perfect location and the property—you should see it. It's like being in a forest. It's beautiful out there and there's this sweet smell in the air. I don't see him wanting to hire me after what I said to him, though. He's not a woman hater, is he? I wonder, after the way he acted toward me."

"I don't think he hates women, Liz. I just think he probably has personal issues with a woman working on a horse ranch and he wasn't prepared to see you at the main gate. I'm betting you're the first woman who asked him for a job. I'm sorry. If I would have known that, I wouldn't have told you about the job."

"I know. Look… maybe we can make some calls tomorrow? Calls to some of those other ranchers? Now that I've come all this way, I might as well try to find work around here. I'd feel a bit ashamed and embarrassed going back home. How would I explain it to mother and daddy? Especially daddy."

"All right. We'll see if we can get you hired somewhere else and by-the-way... you can use me as a reference, Liz. I'll tell them an ear full."

TEN

Ryan was in Julie's store the morning after her meeting with Chance McKenna. Julie told her so much about the store during their phone conversations. Ryan was anxious to see it for herself and do some shopping. It would take her mind off Chance McKenna.

"I really like your selection of boots, Jules," Ryan called out, holding up a pair of dress boots. "I'm going to have to buy a pair of these."

"Those just arrived a few days ago. Pretty cool, huh?"

The telephone on the counter rang.

"Good morning. Scott's Western Wear, Tack and Feed. This is Julie. May I help you?"

A surprised look came over Julie's face.

"Uhh... just a moment, please."

Julie cupped her hand over the mouthpiece.

"Liz, come over here."

"What is it," Ryan asked, still admiring the boots.

"You need to take this."

Ryan put the boots down and hurried over to take the phone from Julie.

"Hello. This is Ryan Hollister."

There was a pause.

A smile came slowly to Ryan's face. She gave Julie a wink.

"Thanks. Thanks very much. I appreciate that."

Another pause.

"Oh. Okay. I understand."

Another pause.

Ryan leaned against the counter and listened intently.

"Uhh... just a moment," she said, picking up a pencil on the counter and motioning to Julie for a piece of paper.

Ryan hurriedly wrote something down.

"All right. Got it. I'll be there in about a half hour. Thanks for calling, Mr. McKenna. Bye."

Ryan put the phone down.

She was smiling ear-to-ear.

"Well, what did he say?" Julie asked excitedly.

"He wants me to come back out to the ranch. He said he thought we should start over. He gave me his cell phone number," Ryan said, waving the piece of paper in the air.

She folded the paper then put it into her shirt pocket.

"He wants to start over? That sounds encouraging, doesn't it?"

"It sounded like an apology. Actually, he did say he was sorry for yesterday. Well, we'll see."

"I'm so happy for you, Liz."

They gave each other a hug.

"I know you're going to get the job. I just know it."

"Thanks, Jules. I hope so. I'll tell you all about it tonight."

ELEVEN

Ryan stopped outside the main gate. She felt no anxiety or uneasiness. No tension this morning.

She had the feeling this was going to be a much more pleasant meeting with Chance McKenna than the one yesterday. She was looking forward to it, in fact.

Ryan removed the piece of paper from her shirt pocket and called the number.

The main gate opened.

~~~

Chance McKenna was standing in the driveway in front of the house when Ryan pulled up.

He walked over to meet her. She put the window down and remained in her truck.

"G'mornin', Miss Hollister. So, ya do own a telephone," he said, with a sly grin on his face.

"Good morning, Mr. McKenna."

Chance opened the door and helped Ryan out of the truck.

He led the way to the house.

"This is a beautiful property, Mr. McKenna."

The initial attraction Ryan felt for the man walking beside her burrowed its way into her thoughts.

Once again, Ryan had to shelter herself from any romantic inclinations. This was not the time or place to be having them.

"It smells like a bakery out here," she said.

"Oh, that? It's comin' from the ponderosa pines on the property. Dew forms in the cracks o' the bark overnight an' gets heated by the sun in the mornin'. There's an invisible mist that settles over the whole area. Sometimes it's butterscotch. Sometimes it's vanilla. It takes away the smell o' what the horses leave behind, if ya know what I mean."

"Yes, Sir. I know what you mean. It certainly is refreshing."

They entered the main house through a side door and walked through the laundry room.

The sound of a vacuum cleaner could be heard in another room.

Chance explained his housekeeper was cleaning the front part of the house.

The kitchen was large. In the middle was an island with stools around one side. All the appliances were stainless steel. They added a reflective, modern touch to the Western decor.

The dinning area was also a large area with a rustic, wooden dinning table that could seat at least a dozen guests.

A chandelier made from an old wagon wheel hung above the table. It held twelve black-wicked candles in iron holders.

"D' ya drink coffee, Miss Hollister?" Chance asked, taking two cups from a cup holder above the counter.

"By the bucketful," Ryan said, grinning.

"There's a plate with some donuts there on the table, if ya'd like. D' ya take cream an' sugar?"

"Just a bit of cream, thanks."

The atmosphere was made more cordial while they enjoyed a cup of coffee and a donut each.

Chance explained further some of the requirements of the job, but acknowledged his comments only served to review what Ryan undoubtedly already knew.

Chance was just filling in time before getting to the real matter at hand. Offering the job to Ryan.

Ryan Hollister was on pins and needles.

"Okay, Miss Hollister. I won't keep ya waitin' any longer. I've decided to offer the job o' top hand to ya. I'm sure ya can handle any situation that comes up. Sooo… are ya interested?"

Ryan could not wipe the big smile off her face. These were the words she wanted to hear.

"Uhh… yes, Mr. McKenna. Yes, I'm interested. I'm curious, also. What made you decide to hire me?"

"Well, after ya left yesterday mornin', I realized if ya didn't have the experience ya said ya had, ya wouldn't 've made those claims an' ya wouldn't 've told me to check 'em out. I knew ya had to be tellin' the truth, but if it was goin' so good for ya back in Oklahoma, Miss Hollister, why'd ya come out here?"

"I have a dream, Mr. McKenna. A dream to have my own racehorse training stables someday. I decided I had worked for my parents long enough and it was time to go out on my own and find work on another ranch. They agreed it was time for me to make my life's choices."

"I hope your dream comes true, Miss Hollister. For now, you'll be a big help to me. I'm glad you're here. Welcome to McKenna ranch," he said, offering an outstretched hand.

"Thank you, Mr. McKenna," she said, shaking his hand.

Ryan managed to contain her excitement. She didn't want to seem too anxious. There was a big smile on her face.

Chance said he would make the contract for three months to see how it worked out. Ryan agreed on a trial period.

Chance handed Ryan a piece of paper with an offer of salary written on it and told her it was preliminary and was negotiable.

Ryan managed to conceal her surprise at the amount.

"This is very generous, Mr. McKenna. I accept. Thank you."

There was a remote control and a key ring with several keys on the table.

"The remote control is a bit tricky until you get used to it. It is only used to open the main gate when entering the property. Otherwise, the gate closes automatically after entering and after leaving. It opens automatically when leaving the property. Got that? You'll get used to it, Miss Hollister."

"It won't slam shut when I'm driving through, will it?"

"No."

They had a good laugh.

"My veterinarian, Dr. Brown, has a remote if he needs access in case of an emergency. Carmen also has a remote."

"These keys are for a cabin located a short distance from the main house," Chance said, picking up the keys. "Ya can stay there if ya want. Rent free. The cabin has always been used by the top hand on the ranch. I must warn ya, though, it will need some serious cleanin'."

"I noticed the cabin yesterday. I'd like to take you up on your offer to stay on the property, Mr. McKenna. Thanks."

"You're welcome."

Ryan took the keys and the remote control. Chance also gave her a list of the important telephone numbers she would need.

It was time to show Chance a tangible piece of information which should put his mind at ease about her qualifications.

Ryan reached into her handbag and handed Chance the document.

"I wanted you to see that."

Chance looked intently at the document, read it and noted it was current. He handed it back to Ryan.

"Ya didn't have to show me your trainer's license, Miss Hollister."

"I know. I just—I wanted you to see it," she said, putting the license back in her handbag.

"I'm impressed with your trainin' an' racin' background. Most o' the ranches 'round here have operations similar to this one. Breedin' the brood mares an' sellin' the yearlings each year. That's pretty much it. They're not really interested in racehorses. They don't have the facilities to train 'em for one thing. However, there's a neighborin' ranch, the Hills, that had a young colt. The Hills couldn't do a damn thing with him. He's not even green-broke. Not only that, he hates men messin' with him. He's wild. He did trailer okay, though, when I brought him home. It's just the up close handlin' he doesn't like. I bought him last month. He's eight months old now. I intend to use him for stud service when he's ready. He's got racin' bloodlines. You'll see him in a few minutes when we go out to the barn."

It was as if Chance mentioned the part about the colt's racing bloodlines as just a passing bit of information, but it got Ryan's full attention.

"Do you have his papers?"

"Yeah. Ya can take a look at 'em if ya want to. I'll give 'em to ya before ya leave. Well, I think we're finished here, Miss Hollister. C'mon. I'll give ya a tour o' the barn an' ya can see that colt."

TWELVE

The barn was twelve stalls with a breezeway separating six stalls on each side. Two large doors at each end of the breezeway allowed main access for feed delivery, removal of manure and bringing horses into and out of the barn. There was a door on one side of the barn to enter and exit if the breezeway doors were closed.

"You could hold a banquet in here, Mr. McKenna."

They couldn't keep from laughing.

"Yeah. I try to keep it clean, Miss Hollister. Sometimes we have buyers come in wantin' to see the horses in a settin' other than a corral or a paddock."

Chains dangled from large eye hooks on either side of the breezeway. They were used to cross-tie a horse so buyers would have a better chance to see a horse outside its stall.

Halters and lead ropes hung neatly on wooden pegs outside each stall.

They started walking through the breezeway.

When they approached the far end of the breezeway, Ryan saw him.

His muzzle was poking out from between two vertical rods of his stall door.

They walked up to the stall.

Ryan let out a gasp.

There in front of her stood the most beautiful horse Ryan had ever seen. A pitch black coat with no markings except for a small, white star barely visible under his forelock. He let out a whinny when he saw Ryan. It was as if it was a special Hello to her.

"Miss Hollister, this is Flyin' High."

"Flyin' High? Is that his registered name?"

"Yeah."

"Hello, Flyin' High. Hello, boy. He doesn't look wild to me, Mr. McKenna. He's beautiful. He's gorgeous. His color. His conformation. I've never seen such a perfect looking horse as he is. I want to give him a nickname. Let's see... how about... Midnight? What do you think, Mr. McKenna?"

"I'm not quite sure what to think, Miss Hollister. Ya certainly are excited over 'im. Are ya okay? I've never seen anyone so ga-ga over a horse before."

"I'm fine. I'm okay," she said, laughing.

"Yeah. Midnight sounds like it's prob'ly a good nickname for 'im," Chance said. "It suits 'im. His color an' all. Yeah. Midnight. Good nickname, Miss Hollister."

"All right, then. Can we go into his stall?"

"I don't think that's a good idea. I wanna move 'im out to one o' the paddocks in a month, or so, when I know he's settled down. You'll be able to see him better out there."

"Fine. Let me know when you're going to move him. He's gorgeous."

Both laughed at Ryan's little-girl reaction to the stallion. She wanted to stay at Midnight's stall a while longer, but there was more of the barn to see.

Ryan said Goodbye to the stallion.

Next, they headed to the tack room.

Chance pointed to a small audio horn mounted outside the tack room doorway and told Ryan the horn would sound if someone pressed the call box button at the main gate.

They went into the tack room.

Chance took two cups from a cup rack and poured their coffee.

"A sink? Electric hotplate? Mini fridge?" Ryan said, taking in the surroundings. "All the comforts of home, Mr. McKenna."

Suddenly, something ran from behind a saddle tree and out the door.

"What the heck was that?" Ryan asked, with a startled look.

"That was Calico, the cat. She's the barn mouser. This is her territory. She keeps the grain room free o' mice an' rats. Did she scare ya?"

"No. Not really. I wasn't expecting to see a cat in here. Calico? Appropriately named. She has a beautiful coat, what I was able to see of it. Uhh... what's up with that, Mr. McKenna?" Ryan inquired, pointing to a cot and bedding against one of the walls.

"The cot? Well, in case Carmen throws me out o' the house. No... it's for sleepin' out here if a mare's likely to drop her foal at night so someone can be with her. While we're on the subject o' foalin' mares, Miss Hollister, have ya ever had occasion to help a mare if the foal was—"

"Have I ever had to turn a foal around? Is that what you're asking, Mr. McKenna?"

"Yeah."

"I have a pair of rubber gloves that go up to the shoulders, Mr. McKenna. Like those hanging over there. I had to wear them once. It wasn't a pleasant job, but it was necessary to save the foal and the mare, and I did it. Daddy said I did everything just right. According to the book, daddy said."

"Miss Hollister, I don't know what to say. I'm impressed. I've never had to go in an' turn a foal 'round. I've talked to a couple o' ranchers who have. Nasty job. I'm sure ya made your father proud."

Chance showed Ryan how to operate the call box monitor and the intercom. He turned the monitor on to show the main gate, call box and immediate road area around the main gate.

"Is this where you were watching me yesterday morning?"

"Yeah, it is."

Chance didn't want to talk about seeing Ryan at the main gate on that first morning. He didn't make any further comment and Ryan didn't want to push it. He turned the monitor off.

"Ya can keep your tack in here if ya want. It'll be safe. No one'll bother it. The coffee's ready, Miss Hollister. There's some creamer in there," he said, pointing to the mini fridge.

There was one last item in the tack room Chance wanted to show Ryan. He reached for the on-off switch on what appeared to be a radio and CD player combination setting on a shelf above the bench.

"I usually keep this on at night an' turned down low, if there're horses in the barn. 'Specially foalin' mares."

Chance turned on the music system.

The sound of a Mozart symphony filled the barn. Ryan stood looking at him not knowing what to say.

"It comforts the horses an' they seem to get a better night's sleep," he continued, trying his best to keep a straight face.

"Are you kidding me? Is that for real?"

"Yeah. It's for real. Ya noticed I didn't change any knobs when I turned it on didn't ya? The horses prefer classical music. Mozart mostly. I tried Country an' Western, but they don't fancy Country an' Western much."

"Classical music. In a horse barn. The next thing you know the horses will be wanting to do the minuet with each other out there in the breezeway, Mr. McKenna."

That brought a laugh from Chance.

"However, I must admit, it does have a calming and soothing effect," Ryan said. "I like some classical myself once in a while, but I never thought about playing it for my horses. I'll be sure to turn it on at night, especially when there are foaling mares in here. I'm impressed with the barn. Very clean and very efficient. Not to mention the music system. Anymore surprises, Mr. McKenna?"

They stopped outside the grain room for a few moments.

Ryan mentioned she mixed all her own grain for her horses. Chance told her she could do the same here if she wished. He put Ryan in charge of the grain room. He told her she and Calico would become good friends.

At the rear of the barn Chance showed Ryan the exercise ring and the six-horse hot-walker.

Just then Ryan's cell phone ring tone signaled a call. She saw it was Julie and let it go to the mailbox.

"Ya need to take a call?" Chance asked.

"It was Jules. I'll call her at the end of the driveway on my way out."

"Is that song a favorite o' yours? Your ring tone, I mean."

"Uhh... yes. It's 'Together Again'. I know. I know. It's mid-seventies, but I love that song by Emmylou Harris. What's one of your favorites, Mr. McKenna?"

"I go back even farther than that. 'Easy Lovin' is one I like."

Ryan had just been handed another surprise by Chance McKenna. One of his favorite Country and Western songs was a love song.

"You're right. That one is back there," she said. "I know that one, too. I like those Country and Western songs from the fifties, sixties and seventies the best. Not so much yelling and screaming."

"Okay, We're through out here for now, Miss Hollister. Oh, I almost forgot. I'll get Midnight's papers for ya. I'll be right back."

It pleased her Chance called the stallion by the nickname Ryan just gave him.

Chance returned with Midnight's papers in a manila envelope and handed them to Ryan.

"I guess I should call Miss Scott an' tell her to take my ad off the bulletin board."

"I'll tell her tonight."

Chance walked Ryan to her truck. He opened the door, took her hand and helped her in.

"Thanks for the job, Mr. McKenna. I appreciate it. You won't be sorry you hired me. I'll be out bright and early tomorrow morning to move into the cabin. Thanks again."

"See ya in the mornin' then. G'day, Miss Hollister," he said, touching the brim of his hat.

Ryan headed for the main gate.

In her rear view mirror she saw Chance waving to her.

Ryan sounded her horn in response.

She stopped outside the main gate and left a message in Julie's mailbox.

"Hey, Jules. I'm just leaving the ranch. There's a lot of news to tell you."

THIRTEEN

It was four o'clock in the afternoon. Julie was anxious to hear all about Ryan's second meeting with Chance McKenna. She closed the feed section early, leaving Rosalynn in charge of the main store.

~~~

Ryan had supper on the stove when Julie walked in the door.

"How'd it go, Liz? I thought about you all day."

"I got the job, Jules. I got the job!" Ryan exclaimed, rushing over to Julie, hugging her.

"Liz, that's wonderful. I'm so happy for you. I knew Mr. McKenna would hire you. I just knew it. So, tell me all about it."

"Well… we chatted a short while in the kitchen. He told me how the main gate remote control system works. Then, he offered me the job. I showed him my trainer's license. He was impressed, Jules. We took a tour of the barn. That is the cleanest barn I've ever seen. Chance put me in charge of the grain room."

"Wow! That sounds like quite a tour you had, Liz."

"Get this—one of Chance McKenna's favorite Country and Western songs is a love song. He told me after he heard my ring tone."

"A love song? Seriously? It sounds to me like your man has a softer side after all."

"My man? Jules, Chance McKenna's my boss now."

"It was just a slip of the tongue. So what happened next?"

"Let's see. Oh, yes. I forgot this. There's a little kitchen area in the tack room and there's a cot in there."

"Wait a minute. Did you say a cot? Like—a bed? Did he make a move?"

"Geez. It's for sleeping in the barn if a foaling mare needs to be watched at night, Jules. That's what it's for. Chance was surprised when I told him I'd turned a foal around once. He'd never done that. Also, there's this beautiful, calico cat that's a mouser in the grain room. Its name is Calico."

"It sounds to me like Mr. McKenna's taken a real interest in you, Liz. Anything else?"

"There is. I saved the best part til last. Chance told me about a colt he bought from a neighboring ranch. He said it came from a racing background. It's an eight months old colt. Never been broke. I have his papers. He's in the barn and he's the most beautiful looking horse I've ever seen. He's black as ink. I nicknamed him Midnight. Can you believe it, Jules? A racehorse on McKenna ranch?"

"Liz, are you thinking what I think you're thinking?"

"I probably am. I can't wait to go online and look at his charts. So, that's it. That's pretty much all that happened this morning. When it was time to leave Chance walked me to my truck. He took my hand and helped me in. He also helped me out when I arrived. What a difference. huh? So arrogant yesterday. So sweet today."

"Oh? Sweet? Are you sure there are no feelings starting to happen for this guy?"

"Uhh... no. There aren't. No feelings. I can't let myself get involved with him now or later, Jules. I need to show him I know what I'm doing working on a horse ranch. I need to show Mr. McKenna I can play the game."

Julie looked at her friend with a mischievous smile on her face. Ryan recognized that look. It always meant there was more digging to follow. Julie kept it going.

"Is he not handsome, or what? You can almost see the testosterone oozing from his pores," Julie said, winking, with a devilish grin on her face.

"Enough already, Jules. You know, I was having second thoughts on the way here from the ranch. I know it's the opportunity of a lifetime. I know that. It's what I thought about a lot when I was home. The chance to work on a horse ranch and have some real responsibility. And now, I have that chance. The chance to show Mr. McKenna what I can do for him and the ranch. There's a lot riding on this job, Jules. What if I'm not up to it? Back home there was always daddy to lean on. But now—"

"Now, you've got me, Ryan Elizabeth Hollister and don't you forget it. Stop with those negative thoughts. You have so much experience to give to Chance McKenna and his ranch. He needs your help. He must realize your ability or he wouldn't have hired you. So, put those thoughts out of your head and do what you do best, Liz. Horse ranching."

"Thanks for your support, Jules. I appreciate it."

"One more thing—Chance offered to let me stay in a cabin on the ranch. Rent free."

"Really? That's great, Liz. So, you'll be leaving from here then?"

"Yes. I'll move into the cabin tomorrow morning. Thanks so much for letting me stay here, Jules."

"Don't even mention it, Sweetie. I'm so happy for you."

"Oh, before I forget, Chance said you can take his ad off the bulletin board."

"I'll take it down."

They chatted during the rest of their supper.

There was a lot more to catch up on.

Details of the past two years that could not be talked about during their phone calls.

This was a very happy time for both of them.

Best friends together again.

"I want to get up early and pack my things so I'm going to take a shower and go to bed. Love you, Sweetie. Good night."

"Love you, too, Babe. I'm so happy it's all working out for you. Think positively, okay? See you in the morning. Good night."

FOURTEEN

Ryan was anxious to tell her mother and father the good news before going to bed.

"Hello, mother. There's good news from here. I got the job. Is daddy there?"

"Honey, that's great. I'm so happy for you. Brian! Pick up the phone. It's Ryan," her mother said, calling to Ryan's father from the kitchen.

"Hi, Baby Girl. How are ya?"

"Hi, daddy. I'm good. I was just telling mother... I was hired this morning as a top hand. It's the job Jules told me about. It's on Mr. McKenna's ranch. I'm so happy and so excited. Mr. McKenna's letting me live in a cabin on the property. Rent free. The place is really beautiful out here. It's like being in a forest. Ponderosa pine trees everywhere. Mr. McKenna breeds and raises registered Quarter horses. Show horses."

"Wonderful, Honey. That's great news," her father said. "I told ya not to worry. Ya can do the job. Great news. We're both so proud o' ya."

"That is such good news, Sweetheart," her mother said.

"There's something else, you guys. Mr. McKenna bought an eight months old colt a few weeks ago and he has racing bloodlines. I have his papers. I'll let you know more about him after I go online to look at his charts. He's all black. A small white star under his forelock. Otherwise, he's all black. He's beautiful. His registered name is Flyin' High. I nicknamed him Midnight. He's never been broke, though. I'm hoping I can work with him."

"Ya nicknamed him Midnight? Sounds like a great name to match his coat. So ya don't know anythin' more 'bout him yet? His sire or dam? He's never had tack on him, ya say?"

"I haven't checked his charts yet, daddy, but I'll let you know when I find out more about his background and no, he's never been under tack yet. I'm hoping I'll be able to break him. We'll be breeding some of the mares soon. Mr McKenna wants to see how I handle that. It's getting late so I'll say Goodnight for now. I love you both and miss you both."

"Wonderful news, Sweetheart," her mother said. "Email some photos of your new home, the cabin and of course, some photos of Mr. McKenna, too. We love you and miss you, too. Goodnight, Sweetheart."

"Yeah, Honey an' maybe ya could get a picture o' that colt, too," her father said. "I'd like to see him. Don't worry 'bout the breedin' job. Ya've done it hundreds o' times. Love ya, Baby Girl an' remember, we're just a phone call away if ya need to talk. G'night."

"Thanks, mother. Thanks, daddy. Talk to you soon. Good night."

Ryan went online to look up Midnight's lineage before going to bed.

She was ecstatic and overjoyed at what she found.

FIFTEEN

A couple of months had passed since Ryan signed on as Chance McKenna's top hand. Day by day, she was assuming more responsibility, more often than not, on her own. This did not go unnoticed. Chance liked what he was seeing from his new top hand.

Daily, when doing chores in the barn or mixing grain, Ryan would spend time at Midnight's stall, talking softly to him and giving him apple or carrot treats. Midnight always gave her his special Hello. A soft whinny. She longed for the day when he would be moved out to a paddock.

It was early December. Breeding season on McKenna ranch.

"I wanna breed a few mares tomorrow mornin', Miss Hollister. It's time to get started with that job. I'm wantin' to see how ya handle that. I know everyone has a different way o' doin' it."

"I'm looking forward to it, Mr. McKenna. Do you use a teaser on the mares?"

"I just let the stallion do his thing."

"Back home we had a mule we used as a teaser."

"That sounds a bit cruel, Miss Hollister. Mules are the end of the line and can't do anything with a mare."

"I know, but Leonard seemed to enjoy it," Ryan said, with a grin on her face.

"Leonard?" Chance remarked, smiling.

After the morning feeding and watering was finished, Ryan called Julie to give her an update.

"We'll be breeding some of the mares tomorrow morning, Jules. Chance wants to see how I handle that."

"Breeding some mares, did you say? Maybe that will put a few ideas into his head. Okay. Show Mr. McKenna how horses do it, Liz."

"Jules, you're unbelievable. I'll let you know how it goes," Ryan said, laughing.

~~~

Chance woke up early and decided to do the chores by himself.

When he finished he went to Ryan's cabin and knocked on the open door.

"Come in, Chance."

"I already fed an' watered. Let's go breed some horses, Hollister. Ya ready?"

"Yes, Sir, Mr. McKenna, I'm ready."

They entered the breezeway and walked to the far end. On the way, Ryan called out to Midnight. He gave her a soft whinny. Chance took notice, but made no comment. Again, he wondered if that horse and his new top hand had a thing going on.

They went to the exercise ring. The ring was one-hundred fifty feet in diameter. Large enough to lunge a horse without damaging its legs.

"I usually do the breedin' here, inside the exercise ring. I been thinkin' 'bout buildin' a couple o' stanchions outside the ring so we could tie the mares to 'em. Better than one person havein' to hold the mares, but I haven't gotten 'round to doin' that yet."

"That's what we had at home. Uhh... Mr. McKenna, is there a bucket and some soap in the tack room? Some twine string, too, maybe?"

"A bucket? Soap? Twine string? Ya're not gonna tie me up an' give me a bath, are ya, Hollister?"

That brought hearty laughs from both of them.

"I could do that. I mean... no. No, I'm not going to give you a bath, Mr. McKenna. You said you want to see how I breed horses and I'm going to show you. I always wash the mare and the stallion before-hand, then I tie the mare's tail."

"Really. I'm glad ya cleared that up. I've heard o' doin' the washin' thing, but I never bothered with it."

"Given the value of the stock you have on this ranch I suggest we start doing it. It makes the process a bit more sanitary. It makes perfect sense and doesn't take up a lot of time. When I'm involved in the breeding process that is how we'll do it, Mr. McKenna. You okay with that?"

"I guess so. From now on, we'll do it your way, Hollister. I think there's a bucket in the tack room an' some soap an' towels an' a ball o' twine string on the bench."

She's already takin' charge o' the breedin'. This is gonna be an interestin' mornin'.

Chance went to get the first mare. He brought the mare to the ring and tied her lead rope to a rail.

Ryan returned with a bucket of soapy water and some towels.

"We'll use that bay stallion over there," Chance said, pointing to a nearby paddock. "Today we'll breed Ginger an' a couple o' mares in those corrals over there."

Ryan washed Ginger and waited for Chance to lead the stallion into the ring. It didn't take long for the stallion to be ready. Ryan used the opportunity to wash him while Chance held him and looked on, with dumbfounded curiosity.

"This is a first for me, Hollister. Ya did that like ya've done it a hundred times before."

"I have. Hundreds of times. Now, lead him up to her and if I have to help him do his business, then I've done that before, too, Mr. McKenna."

"Hollister, you're amazin'," he said, leading the stallion up to cover Ginger.

The breeding went fine with no problems the rest of the morning.

Ryan tied each mares tail. She washed each mare and stallion while Chance held the stallion. It wasn't necessary for Ryan to help either of the stallions do its job.

Chance let Ryan take full control of the breeding of all the mares. After each mare was done Chance took her back to her corral.

He was beaming with pride at the way Ryan handled the job.

"Ya say ya've helped a stallion enter a mare when he had trouble coverin' her?"

"That's right. Many times. My daddy taught me all about breeding horses. Sometimes the stallion gets too eager and has trouble finding what it is he needs to find, if you get my drift."

"Yeah, I get it. Ya know, the first time I saw ya, Hollister, I never guessed ya for a horse breeder. I learned somethin' from ya today. Ya've satisfied my curiosity. What other horse ranchin' secrets are ya keepin' from me?" he asked, with a big grin on his face. "Good job!"

"Thanks, Mr. McKenna," Ryan said, smiling, knowing she had pleased him.

"It's almost noon. We can go to the house an' have a sandwich an' somethin' to drink if ya'd like. I already gave Carmen a head's up we might be comin' in for lunch."

"Lunch sounds good. I'm getting a bit hungry. I did notice, though, a couple of the mare's feet could use some trimming. I could do it if you have a file and a clippers. I usually carry a hoof pick when work-ing around the horses," she said, retrieving a hoof pick from her back pocket, waving it in the air.

"Why am I not surprised ya'd be workin' on a horse ranch with a hoof pick in your pocket? Call Tim if ya want or else ya can do the trimmin' yourself. There's a file an' clippers in the tack room. Let's go have lunch."

Plans were made to repeat the breeding the next two days on the same mares. It's usually a three-day process to make sure the breeding was successful.

"Uhh… I have a question, Miss Hollister," Chance said, after they finished lunch, "Uhh… I wanna ask ya—what's your favorite color?"

A curious look came over Ryan's face. It was an unusual question and seemed a bit out of place. It had nothing to do with horse ranching or horse breeding. After considering for a moment, she answered.

"My favorite color? It's, umm... yellow. My favorite color is yellow, Mr. McKenna."

SIXTEEN

O n the final day of the breeding there was a knock on Ryan's open door in the afternoon.

Chance was standing on the step with a big smile on his face.

"What's up, Chance? What is that?"

Chance handed Ryan a gift box secured with a yellow ribbon. A large, white bow was stuck on one corner of the lid.

"I stopped by Miss Scott's store an' asked her to help me pick out somethin' for ya. A small gift for the job ya did breedin' those horses the past couple days."

Ryan removed the greeting card slipped under the ribbon.

To Ryan,
for a job well done!

"Thank you, Chance. You shouldn't have, though. I was just doing my job."

"I know, but ya taught me a few things an' I appreciated it. Go on. Open it."

Ryan carefully coiled the ribbon around her fingers and stuck the bow to the ribbon.

Inside, between several layers of wrapping tissue, was a mini-skirt with buckskin fringe on the hemline, a shirt with pearl buttons, a vest and a neckerchief.

The mini-skirt, shirt, vest and neckerchief were yellow and white.

"Oh, Chance, it's a sweet gift. Thank you so much."

Ryan put the box on the couch.

She walked over to Chance and put her arms around him.

Chance held her close.

That was the first time Ryan felt Chance's arms around her. After all, she had been on the ranch only a short time. Not long enough to be involved. Surely not long enough to expect to be in the arms of her boss, but it felt good. It felt right.

Chance pulled away slowly.

They looked at each other and smiled.

A moment to share. A moment to remember.

"When I was in Miss Scott's store this morning she apologized for not tellin' me the whole story 'bout ya. 'Bout ya bein' a woman an' all. I told her not to worry. I said ya're more than qualified for the job an' ya'll do just fine. In fact, I'm gonna tear up that three-month trial period contract. Ya're a permanent employee now."

"Thank you, Chance. Gee, I'm so happy to hear you say that. Thank you so much."

"Ya've earned it. All right. I'm goin' back to the house an' fill out some o' the paperwork on the mares an' stallions we bred this season. I'm guessin' ya know how to do that, too."

"Yes. I know all about the paperwork part of the breeding process. Thanks again for the gift, Chance. I love it and thanks for making me a permanent employee of McKenna Ranch."

Ryan was not thinking about Chance McKenna being her boss or his decision to make her a permanent employee. She was thinking about the gift he just gave her and the embrace they just shared.

I want to wear this outfit for him, but when? It will have to be up to him.

Ryan read the note again and took one more look at the clothes before hanging them in the closet. She would try them on later when she was sure Chance would not be coming to the cabin unexpectedly.

Ryan's cell phone rang.

"Liz, you haven't called. How did the breeding go?"

"Sorry, Jules. I just got busy with work. Breeding. Trimming hooves, etc. Sorry."

"Well, I'm calling now because Chance came into the store this morning an—"

"I know, Jules. I know. He just gave me a—"

"A gift, right? What did you think of it? He said it was a surprise for doing such s good job. Of course, I assumed he was referring to the breeding sessions."

"I was so surprised Jules. I almost cried when I read the card. You know, he asked me when we finished the breeding what was my favorite color. I wondered what the heck that was all about. No man ever gave me clothes before."

"You're on Chance McKenna's mind, Liz. Everything should fit. If it doesn't bring it in and I'll exchange it."

"Thanks, Jules."

"What made Chance want to buy that outfit for you anyway, I wonder? Really. I mean... besides you doing such a good job breeding those horses and all."

"Jules, where are you going with this? I did a good job. Chance liked it. That's all it was."

"If you say so."

"Actually, Chance did say he learned a few things from me during the breeding chores. He let me take charge of the whole process, Jules. He said from now on we'll do the breeding my way. Wasn't that nice? He also told me my employment status is permanent. I don't know if I'd mentioned this before, but Chance hired me for a three-month trial period. Today he ripped that up."

"He did? You must be happy about that, huh? He knows what he's got. I'll say it again, Liz. You've made an impression on Mr. McKenna."

"Jules, after we finished with the breeding this morning, I felt like... like I was home. Like... McKenna ranch was my home. Is that weird?"

"No, it's not weird, Liz. It's called settling in. Settling in to the new job. That's all. It's good, though, that it feels like home to you. It is your home now. Right? You're Chance McKenna's number one horse breeder."

A moment of laughter together.

"I know, but being a top hand is a lot different from breeding a few horses. I don't know, Jules. I just don't know if I can—"

"Listen, Ryan Hollister. Listen to me. Don't bring up those feelings of doubt again. Just remember what your father told you and taught you all those years. Okay? I don't want to hear you talk that way any-more. Just do the job and continue to show Mr. McKenna he made the right choice when he hired you."

"I will. I love the job. You know, I'm thinking a lot about Midnight. I want to break him, Jules. I saw his charts online. He's got all the qualifications to be a winner. You'll have to come out here and see him."

"I'll come out soon. The way you're carrying on he must be some-thing special. Let me know about the clothes, Sweetie? Love you. Bye."

"Thanks, Jules. Love you, too. Bye."

SEVENTEEN

Chance received another call from Mr. Lopez a few days after giving Ryan the gift. The letters had turned into phone calls and the phone calls were coming more frequently lately.

Chance had run out of excuses.

It was time to face Mr. Lopez in person.

~~~

Ryan and Chance finished the morning's feeding and watering chores.

"I should be back by noon, or a little after. Take care o' the place, Ryan. If ya have any problems, give me a call. All right?"

"I'll take good care of everything, Chance. Don't worry."

Ryan went back to the cabin. She finished up with a bit of cleaning she wanted to do in there then went to the closet.

"Chance isn't here to see me in this outfit. Now is a good time to try it on."

Everything was a perfect fit. Julie knew Ryan's size in clothes. They had always gone shopping together. When they were younger they even traded their clothes with each other.

Ryan took off the clothes and hung them back in the closet.

She was putting her jeans on when she heard a disturbance coming from the barn area.

A horse was screaming. Horses don't scream that way unless they were fighting or they were hurt, or both.

Lady, the collie that greeted Ryan the morning of her first meeting with Chance, began barking.

Something was terribly wrong outside.

~~~

Two of the mares, Lily and Dawn, had their butts pointed at each other and each one was kicking the other one. It looked like Dawn was getting the worst of it.

Lily had somehow opened the gate between the two corrals and was in Dawn's corral.

Each mare had a foal at her side. Ryan looked for the two foals. She made sure they were not where they would get hurt. Lily's foal was still in its corral. Dawn's foal was standing at the far side of her corral.

Ryan managed to separate the two mares. She put Lily back into her corral then secured the latch with the chain Lily had unwrapped to open the gate.

It was Dawn who was screaming. Ryan saw a tear on her hind quarter. A bleeding gash no doubt put there by one of Lily's hooves.

Ryan immediately called Dr. Brown.

"Dr. Brown's office."

"Hello. This is Ryan Hollister at the McKenna ranch. There's been an accident between two of the horses. One has a gash or tear on its hind quarter and it's bleeding. Can Dr. Brown come out now?"

"Chance McKenna's place? I'll let Dr. Brown know. He's out on a call right now, but he should be there shortly."

"Thanks. Hurry."

"I'll get in touch with Dr. Brown immediately, Miss Hollister."

Ryan went into Dawn's corral to comfort her. She thought about calling Chance, but what could he do at this time? The damage was done.

~~~

A short time later an SUV came up the driveway.

It was Dr. Brown's van.

Ryan motioned for him to drive to the area near Dawn's corral.

"Hi. I'm Dr. Brown and this is my assistant, Miss Susan Potter."

"Hello, Doctor. Hello, Susan. I'm Ryan Hollister."

"Nice to meet you, Miss Hollister. Now, let's have a look at that mare."

"She's that one over there, Doctor," Ryan said, leading the way into Dawn's corral.

Dr. Brown was a man in his middle thirties, stocky build, brown hair and eyes. He had the look of someone who spends a lot of time out doors. Tanned.

Susan Potter, appeared to be just out of her teens. She was in her first year of veterinary medicine studies. She had been interning with Dr. Brown since enrolling as a student at the academy.

Dr. Brown asked Ryan to hold Dawn's halter while he took care of the wound. He gave Dawn a shot of penicillin. Susan handed Dr. Brown a stitching needle, stitching thread and numbing compound after Dawn's wound was cleaned.

"It's not that bad, Miss Hollister. A few stitches should do the job. Hold her now."

The tear required a couple dozen stitches. Dr. Brown applied some medicated salve to the wound. There was no way to apply a bandage to the area.

Dr. Brown left some cleaning solution, some medicated salve and some cotton balls with Ryan and asked her to clean the wound and apply the salve at least two or three times a day. He suggested it might be best to put Dawn and her foal in the barn until the wound healed.

Ryan's thoughts shifted to Chance. What would he think when he returned home?. He had left her in charge of the place and now this. She would tell him exactly what happened. It was not her fault. She handled the situation as best she could. Surely he would understand.

A few minutes later there was the sound of a vehicle in the driveway.

Ryan turned to see Chance arriving home.

Chance hurried over to Dawn's corral when he saw Dr. Brown's van.

They shook hands.

"What happened here, Doc?"

"There was a fight between two o' your mares, Mac," Dr. Brown said. "That one got the worst of it," he said, pointing to Dawn. "It's not serious. Just a tear needing a few stitches. It should heal in a week or so. I told Miss Hollister you should put the mare and her foal in the barn while the wound heals. I gave Miss Hollister some medication to put on the wound several times each day. Okay? Call if you need me, Mac."

"Thanks, Doc. Thanks for comin' out. I appreciate it."

Dr. Brown and Susan got into the van and headed for the main gate.

Chance turned and stared at Ryan. He said nothing. He just stood there looking at her with those piercing brown eyes.

"What're you looking at, Sir?"

"I thought I could trust ya to watch over the place when I'm away. I thought ya could do the job. How'd Lily get that latch open? Were ya in her corral this mornin' after I left?"

Ryan had heard enough of the accusations and the innuendos directed towards her and decided to speak up in her own defense.

She returned the stare.

"Are you blaming me, Mr. McKenna? No, I was not in Lily's corral this morning."

"Why didn't ya call me?"

"Why didn't I call you? You couldn't have made it back here in time to make any difference. That's the reason I didn't call you. Lily had already done the damage to Dawn. My immediate responsibility was to get Dr. Brown out here to tend Dawn's wound. That's exactly what I chose to do. This accident was not my fault, Mr. McKenna. I will not take any of the blame for it. Do you understand? Do not yell at me. Do not blame me. If you want to hire someone else to do this job, then go right ahead. Hire someone else. Put your ad back on Julies' bulletin board. What's it going to be, Mr. McKenna?"

Ryan gave Chance McKenna a choice. Take back what he said to her or look for a new top hand. She would quit rather than be accused of doing something she hadn't done. Chance could hear that in her voice. He could not afford to lose her. With her experience Ryan would have no trouble finding work at one of the other ranches. Chance knew he needed to smooth things over with her. He had the feeling she would walk out if he didn't apologize.

"I didn't—I wasn't accusin' ya, Ryan. I'm sor—"

"You weren't accusing me, Mr. McKenna? What do you mean you weren't accusing me? What do you think you just said? You accused me of having something to do with Lily opening the gate between the corrals. Like I left that gate latch open or something. That's what you accused me of, Sir and furthermore, may I remind you, Mr. McKenna, it was you who fed Lily and Dawn this morning. Not me. You. Did you check the gate latch on the gate? Did you check it? May I also remind you that when a horse discovers it can open a gate it will keep trying again and again to open that gate. Horses are not stupid. I am not the one to blame for this accident and no matter my boss or not, don't you dare blame me without some proof."

Chance was speechless.

Ryan was showing the same strength of character she showed the first day she came to the ranch. Once again, Chance McKenna was on the defensive.

"I don't wanna hire anyone else, Hollister. Yeah. I guess I was the one who fed Lily an' Dawn an' I thought all the gate latches were secured. I didn't mean to yell at ya."

"You guess? You guess, Mr. McKenna? Well, I intend to show you proof Lily knows how to open that gate. I'm not sure how or when, but I'll get you the proof."

"Okay. You win, Hollister. Let's get these two in the barn," he said, walking into Dawn's corral.

Chance led Dawn into the barn. Ryan made sure her foal followed its mother. They put Dawn and her foal in one of the foaling stalls.

Ryan turned to Chance after they finished the evening chores in silence.

"Let's forget about what happened between us today, Chance. I don't want to argue anymore. Arguing is not about who wins or who loses. It's about resolving differences and making sure those differences don't get in the way again.

Damn, a horsewoman and a philosopher. Guess I'd better watch what I say to her from now on.

"I agree. All right, Hollister. I'm goin' back to the house. Don't stay out here too long. G'night."

"Good night, Mr. McKenna."

EIGHTEEN

Chance decided to do the feeding and watering by himself the next morning. He didn't want an encounter with Ryan. Not just yet. Let a few days pass so they could both cool off.

"Why are the breezeway doors closed? They were open last night."

Chance entered the barn by a side door and opened the breezeway doors on the end nearest the house.

He saw her in the light shining into the breezeway.

Ryan was asleep on the cot from the tack room. She was covered with a couple of blankets. The cot was in front of Midnight's stall.

Instead of waking her immediately, Chance opened the doors on the far end of the breezeway.

He did the feeding and watering of the horses inside the barn without waking Ryan.

Chance went to the tack room and made a pot of coffee.

When the coffee was ready Chance added some creamer to a cup.

"Ryan. Ryan," he said, softly, shaking her gently.

Ryan stirred and rubbed her eyes. She looked up at Chance.

"Where am I? What—what time is it?"

"It's 'bout nine o'clock in the mornin'. Did ya sleep out here all night?"

Sleep was still in Ryan's voice and in her eyes.

"Uhh... yeah. I did. I closed the breezeway doors an—"

"I saw ya closed 'em. I told ya not to stay out here too long last night. Ya'll catch cold. Why didn't ya go back to the cabin?"

"I wanted to make sure Midnight was okay," she said, still trying to shake off the sleepiness. "Is he okay this morning?"

"Ryan... what're ya talkin' 'bout? That horse has been in here since I brought him home. He's fine. Ya should've gone to the cabin. Here. Here's a cup o' coffee. I hope I got the creamer right."

Ryan sat up. She took a sip of the coffee, looked first at Chance then at Midnight. The stallion was eating his hay.

"Thanks for this. The creamer's just right, Chance. Well, I guess we can put this cot back in the tack room. It's pretty comfortable actually —for being a canvas mattress," she said, getting up.

Ryan folded the blankets. Chance carried the cot and Ryan carried the blankets back to the tack room.

"I need to go to Julie's store an' get some hay an' grain. I didn't pick up the feed yesterday. The mornin' chores are finished 'cept for muckin' the stalls. Will ya take care o' that?"

"Yes, Chance, I'll muck out the stalls after I tend to Dawn's wound."

Ryan walked over to Dawn's stall to see how she and the foal were doing. Dawn was eating her hay. Her foal was nursing. Dawn and the foal looked just fine.

Chance hesitated outside Midnight's stall.

"Ya know, I'm thinkin'... this might be a good time to put Midnight in a paddock. Ya ready?"

Ryan was more than ready. She didn't need to be asked a second time.

Chance reached for the lead rope hanging outside Midnight's stall.

Ryan took hold of his arm.

"Wait. Let me lead him out. Don't worry, Chance. I've handled a lot of horses. Remember?"

"Not like this one ya haven't."

Chance could see Ryan was going to react like a little girl. Pouting if she didn't get her way.

"Oh, all right, but be careful."

Chance opened Midnight's stall door just wide enough for the two of them to enter.

Ryan hooked the lead rope to Midnight's halter, talking to him and petting him..

"He didn't move an inch, Hollister. Interesting."

Ryan looked at Chance and smiled.

Chance opened the stall door.

"C'mon, boy. C'mon, Midnight," Ryan said.

Midnight followed Ryan into the breezeway.

Chance gave Ryan a big grin and a thumbs up.

~~~

They put Midnight in a paddock close to the barn. Next to the driveway. Away from any mares.

The stallion seemed to enjoy his new freedom. He galloped away, stopped, turned to look at them, then began grazing.

"Midnight looks magnificent out here in the paddock, Chance."

"Yeah. He does."

"I'm so glad we moved him."

"When the time comes, maybe we should work with him together. Might be safer," Chance said.

"I'd like that. I think it would be better if both of us worked with him. Together. He looks docile enough, but why take any chances. Right? I'm looking forward to breaking him, Chance."

"Well, that takes care o' that. I'll be back in a while. Ya have my number," Chance said, walking to his truck, grinning, as if to remind Ryan to take good care of the place and call him if there was trouble.

Ryan stayed at Midnight's pasture until Chance was out of sight.

She called Julie to tell Julie what happened with the two mares and how she and Chance had gotten into a heated argument the day before.

She told Julie Chance was coming to pick up feed and asked Julie to find an inconspicuous way to keep Chance in the store for a bit longer than it would normally take him to pick up feed.

Ryan hurried to the cabin.

A plan to redeem her self-esteem was forming in her head.

NINETEEN

Back in her cabin, Ryan took a quick shower and changed into a clean shirt and jeans.

She took her video camera and went to an area where she could see Lily and the corral gate, but Lily could not see her.

Ryan watched the mare for some time. Lily did not approach the gate. Ryan waited and watched. She was hoping Lily would try to open the latch before Chance returned home. Ryan wanted the proof Lily opened the gate by herself.

A short time later. Lily walked slowly to the gate. She began to rub the latch with her nose.

This was what Ryan was waiting for.

Lily was going to try to open the gate!

Ryan aimed the camera at the gate and waited.

Lily began to play with the chain Ryan had wrapped around the latch yesterday when she put Lily back in her own corral. Lily used her nose to brush against the chain.

Lily kept trying.

Finally, the chain dropped to the ground. Lily used her nose again to push the latch up until it cleared the corral post.

The gate swung open.

All the corral gates had spring hinges that allowed the gates to open by themselves when they were unlatched.

Lily walked into Dawn's corral.

Ryan was beside herself and overjoyed with excitement. She captured Lily opening the gate. She had the whole thing on video. She had the proof.

Ryan put Lily back in her own corral, closed the gate and wrapped a piece of baling wire around the latch and the gate post.

There was no time to spare.

The sound of a vehicle in the driveway meant Chance was arriving home.

"Everythin' okay, Ryan? No problems?" Chance asked, getting out of his truck.

"No problems, Chance. Not this time. Everything's fine here. C'mon, I'll help you unload the feed," she said, trying her best to conceal the surprise.

They unloaded the hay and grain, laughing and joking together. Both were in a much different mood than the day before.

"Let's go into the tack room for a minute, Chance. I have something to show you," Ryan said, when they finished unloading and storing the feed.

Ryan took the video camera out of her pocket and turned it on. She handed it to Chance without saying a word.

Chance watched the video several times, but said nothing. Finally, he looked at Ryan with a forced grin on his face.

"I'll be damned. Ya're right, Hollister."

"I told you she'd try it again. Now we have proof of how Lily opened that latch, Chance."

"Ryan. Ryan, I wanna—"

Ryan put a finger up to her lips.

"Shhh. No more apologizing, Chance. We know what we need to do. We need to come up with a different way of securing the latches on all the corral gates. It was Lily this time. It could be one of the other horses next time. It could even be Midnight if he's ever put in one of the corrals."

"I know. Yesterday was the first time it happened, but you're right. It could happen again with any o' the horses. I'll think 'bout a way to secure the latches."

"I already wrapped a piece of bailing wire around Lily's gate latch."

"Thanks."

Chance handed the video camera to Ryan.

"I'm goin' back to the house," Chance said, not wanting to say any more about their argument the day before or the video he just watched.

Back in her cabin, Ryan thought about how she had managed to get the evidence she wanted.

Her intention was not to embarrass Chance or shame him, but rather to redeem her own self-esteem.

Ryan did that.

She felt vindicated.

All was right again between Ryan Hollister and Chance McKenna.

TWENTY

There was a knock on Ryan's door a couple days later. She opened it to see Chance standing there, saying nothing, looking at her with a sheepish grin on his face. She assumed his demeanor had something to do with his feelings related to the video he saw of Lily opening the gate.

"You're not going to say you're sorry again are you, Chance?"

Chance stood in the doorway, saying nothing.

"Well, are you?"

"No. I mean… no, I'm not gonna say that again, Miss Hollister. It's just that—well, on the way home from pickin' up feed the other mornin' I was thinkin'—will ya… would ya… go out?"

There was an uneasy pause as Chance continued to stand there, rocking from side to side.

"You mean, like—a date?"

"Yeah... I guess so."

"What brought that on, Mr. McKenna? C'mon, tell the truth. Is this an apology date?"

Chance didn't answer. He just continued standing there, looking at Ryan with that silly grin on his face.

Ryan wondered if she should encourage him. Did she really want to give in to her feelings? In her mind, Ryan answered her own question.

She thought she better help Chance or he may never get the words right..

"Well? I'm listening. Are you going to ask me? Proper like?" she said, waiting for Chance to get his nerve up.

"Yeah, I guess... I guess I am. Will ya go on a date with me, Miss Hollister?"

That silly, sheepish grin turned into a boyish one.

Chance was nervously rocking side-to-side with both hands clasped behind him. Ryan felt a bit giddy herself. Like they were both in high school and the boy standing in front of her was trying to get his nerve up to ask her to go to the senior prom.

Ryan knew she had feelings for Chance McKenna, but she kept pushing them aside even though Julie would remind her of it almost every time they talked to each other.

She wondered if any relationship between her and Chance would ever get past the employer and employee stage, but with Ryan constantly denying her feelings for him, how could it? This time, though, against her better judgment, she gave in to those feelings.

She turned on her little girl charm, pretending to be shy, letting Chance McKenna know he wasn't the only one who was inadequate when it came to asking for, or accepting, a date.

She began twirling a strand of hair around her finger, twisting her body in a slow, rotating motion with a coy, girlish look on her face.

"Uhh... I don't know if we should, Mr. McKenna," she said, fluttering her eyelashes.

They was a momentary pause in their conversation.

It was all Ryan could do to contain the laughter she felt building inside her.

Chance put a serious look on his face. He raised his eyebrows.

"Miss Hollister, ya're body language is tellin' me somethin' different."

They burst into several moments laughing. Giggling. Looking at each other.

"Umm... all right. I'd... I'd love to go on a date with you, Mr. McKenna. Thanks for asking."

That did it. Chance stopped rocking side-to-side. His ear-to-ear grin told Ryan he had his self-confidence back.

"Thanks, Miss Hollister. Thank ya. Is Friday night okay for ya?"

"Umm... let's see. Uhh... yes. Friday's fine," she said, pausing with a grin, still playing the shy little girl. "I have no other plans for Friday night."

They laughed together. That seemed to ease the nervous tension they both were feeling.

"Thanks. I'll pick ya up at—seven o'clock?"

"Seven it is. I'm so looking forward to Friday, Mr. McKenna. Thanks again for asking me."

Chance tipped his hat, turned and went back to the house.

Ryan's immediate thoughts were of Chance asking for a date and her agreeing to go on a date with him.

Spending time away from the ranch with Chance McKenna was something Ryan thought about many times since accepting the job. She managed to put those thoughts and the feelings that went with them out of her mind until today.

Now, she was ready to explore those feelings further.

TWENTY ONE

F riday night. Date night. Ryan anxiously waited for this night for several days. To be alone with Chance McKenna. Away from the ranch.

She had the perfect outfit to wear.

The Western boots Ryan bought at Julie's store matched the clothes Chance gave her.

She wore her hair down. She knew Chance liked it when she wore her hair down.

On this night, especially, she wanted to please him.

"Tonight, I'll pretend we are just two kids on our first date. Well... it is our first date, isn't it?"

There was a knock on the door at seven o'clock sharp.

Ryan opened the door to see Chance standing there, holding a single, long-stemmed, yellow rose.

Her heart skipped a beat just like it did that first day she saw him emerge from the breezeway.

She felt her knees go weak.

My god! He's gorgeous!

"Chance, you look so handsome. You're right on time. I'm totally impressed. Please. Come in."

"Thank ya, Miss Hollister. Thank ya. Wow! Look at ya. Ya're beautiful. Ya clean up real nice for a gal workin' with horses all day long. Look at that outfit!"

"Thank you, Chance. That was sweet. Thanks again for getting the clothes for me. I love them."

Chance handed the rose to Ryan.

She went to the kitchen and put the rose into a glass of water.

"Ya've got legs, too, Miss Hollister," Chance said, when Ryan returned to the living room.

"My legs?"

"Yeah. I've only seen ya wearin' those jeans 'round here. It's refreshin' to see ya wearin' a skirt for a change."

"Are you a leg man, Mr. McKenna?"

"Uhh... yeah. I am. Yours are the best I've seen. Those white boots sure go good with the outfit, too."

"Geez, we're all done up in yellow and white tonight, Chance."

"Yeah. Miss Scott helped me pick out the neckerchief the other day an' I chose the color so we'd match. I told her it was for a special occasion," Chance said, giving Ryan a wink.

Chance reached into his shirt pocket. He handed Ryan a turquoise ring for her neckerchief.

"I want ya to have this, too. For your neckerchief."

"Oh? What a sweet gift. Turquoise. I don't have any turquoise jewelry. Thanks, Chance."

Chance helped Ryan put her neckerchief through the ring.

"Now, we really match," she said, "Are we ready? Oh, wait. The nights are still a bit nippy. I'll get my jacket. I have a white, Western hat also. Would that be too much? What do you think?"

"That sounds great. We'll match one hundred percent then. Wear it. This is our night, Darlin'. Let's go get 'em."

On the way to the closet Ryan almost burst out laughing at what Chance had just said. His self-confidence was definitely at its peak. He called her Darlin' again. A harbinger of things to come?

Ryan opened the closet door and chose her white, Western-style jacket with buckskin fringe on the sleeves and her white, Western hat. She seldom had occasion to wear either the hat or the jacket, but tonight was a very special occasion.

"Look at ya. I can't wait to show ya off," Chance said, when Ryan returned to the living room.

"So... where are we going, Chance?" Ryan asked, on the way to Chance's truck.

"You'll see. I'll ask, though... d' ya dance, Miss Hollister?"

"Yes, I dance, Mr. McKenna... if someone is leading."

TWENTY TWO

Even though Ryan kept pestering him on the way, Chance was not about to let on where they were going on their date. He was bound and determined to keep it a secret as long as possible.

"Eeee! The Dreamcatcher!" Ryan shrieked, when they turned into the parking lot. "Wow! This is a real surprise, Chance. Jules told me so much about this place."

"Darlin'… it's the only place in town."

"I know. I know, but it's still a surprise."

They arrived at the Dreamcatcher just in time to find a place to park. The parking lot filled up fast on Friday night. This was the only place with any action. Many of the locals came here on Friday night to eat, drink, dance and socialize.

The Dreamcatcher Bar and Restaurant decor was Native American throughout. Dreamcatchers adorned the walls and hung from wooden beam ceilings.

There was one large area inside with no interior walls. The restaurant seating was on one end of the room and the bar area was on the other end. A pool room was behind the bar. A band platform and dance floor separated the restaurant area from the bar area. There was an upright piano on the band platform.

Booths lined both end walls and the front wall of the restaurant and the bar. The booths had high wooden dividers with small, staggered, rectangular cutouts that provided a more private setting between them. Tables and chairs filled the remainder of the floor space in both the restaurant and the bar.

Wednesday night was Karaoke night. On Friday night a local Country and Western band played and there was dancing.

Chance opened the front door. He followed Ryan inside.

"Hey. Mac. How's that new top hand workin' out?" a voice called out, from behind the bar.

Everyone at the bar put their drinks down and turned to see who had come in.

"She talks, Hawkeye. Why don't ya ask her?"

Chance introduced them.

"Hi, little lady. Welcome to the Dreamcatcher. I'm Jake Hennessy. Everybody calls me Hawkeye. I'm happy to meet ya. Wow! Ya sure are pretty."

Jake Hennessy was the owner of the Dreamcatcher. He was part Irish and part Navajo Indian. Irish on his father's side. Navajo Indian on his mother's side. He was well liked by all the locals and he knew them all by name.

Jake was a muscular build, forty-five years old, five feet nine inches tall, with black hair and black eyes to match. His features showed signs of his heritage.

"Thanks, Hawkeye," Ryan said, shaking hands, "I'm happy to meet you, too. I've heard so much about your place from my friend, Julie Scott."

"Yeah, I know Julie. She an' her friend come in once in a while."

"To answer your question, Hawkeye... I'm working out just fine at McKenna ranch."

Ryan, Chance and Hawkeye laughed, then Hawkeye turned to Ryan with an eyebrow raised.

"Ryan, huh? That sounds like a guy's name. Ya sure don't look like a guy to me."

"I get that all the time, Hawkeye. My mother and daddy wanted a boy, but they got me instead so they gave me this name. It could be a girl's name or a boy's name. It fools a lot of people."

"Yeah. It fooled me," Chance said, somewhat under his breath, looking at Ryan and grinning.

"Well, whatever. Ya sure do look pretty in that outfit, though."

"Thanks, Hawkeye. Uhh... Chance got it for me."

Ryan could feel Chance's eyes on her. She bit her lip.

Hawkeye's eyebrows raised.

"Mac got ya that outfit?"

With a quizzical look on his face Hawkeye turned to Chance.

"Is somethin' goin' on out there at the ranch, Mac? Somethin' we all should know 'bout?"

"Nothin' that'd interest ya, Hawkeye."

All the customers seated nearby at the bar could not help but laugh at the exchange between Chance and Hawkeye.

"Ya don't look too bad yourself, though, Mac. All that turquoise? My people would be proud. You an' your little lady take the best-dressed prize in here tonight. For sure."

Hawkeye went back behind the bar. He motioned for a lady talking to a customer at the other end of the bar to come and meet Ryan and Chance.

An attractive woman who appeared to be in her early forties, average build, long, black hair in braids and wearing a headband with a feather in it, came over. Hawkeye put his arm around her.

"Ryan. Chance. I'd like ya both to meet my friend, Linda Silvernail. She helps me back here on Wednesday an' Friday nights. Linda, this is Ryan Hollister an' Chance McKenna."

Linda smiled and extended her hand. "I'm happy to meet both of you."

Linda, Ryan and Chance shook hands and after a bit of small talk between the four of them Linda went back to serving a customer at the far end of the bar.

"So, what can I get ya guys?" Hawkeye asked. "How 'bout you, little lady? Do ya want one o' those umbrella drinks in a fancy glass?"

"Umm... no thanks, Hawkeye. I'll have what Chance is having."

Hawkeye turned to Chance. "I like this one, Mac. All right. Two beers comin' right up."

Chance and Ryan thanked Hawkeye and took their beers.

Chance motioned for Ryan to follow him.

"Where are we going, Chance?"

Chance took her by the hand.

"Oh? Are we going to play some pool?"

"Uhh... yeah. I thought we'd play a couple o' games before we eat," Chance said, winking. "Are ya as good a pool player as ya are a horse woman, Miss Hollister?"

TWENTY THREE

There were two pool tables in the center of the room. Two white, half-globe shaped lamps hung from the ceiling above each table. The room was brightly lit. Not the typical dim, smoke-filled pool room with Tiffany lamps above the tables, as seen in some of the early-day movies.

Two guys were playing on one of the tables.

Chance and Ryan set their beers on one of the stand-up counters which were built against two of the walls. They each chose a cue stick. Ryan took off her jacket and laid it on a stool.

Chance put a quarter in the coin slot. He looked at Ryan and asked her which game they should play.

Does she know anythin' 'bout the game o' pool?

There was no hesitation in Ryan's reply.

"Eight-ball's fine, Chance."

They put chalk on their cue sticks. Instead of rolling their cue balls to see who had the first break, Chance racked the balls and offered Ryan the break.

Two solid-colored balls went down. Ryan had the low-numbered balls. She pocketed all her balls and then she sank the eight-ball.

Chance never got a shot.

Ryan won the first game.

Chance looked at her with eyebrows raised and an embarrassed look on his face.

Yeah. She knew somethin' 'bout the game. Oh well, maybe it was pure luck.

Ryan racked the next game and motioned for Chance to take the break even though it should have been her break. She gave him a big grin.

One solid-colored ball went down this time. His second shot put another solid-colored ball in a pocket. He missed his next shot. It was Ryan's turn and she proceeded to pocket all her balls and then she sank the eight-ball.

Ryan won the second game.

That wasn't luck. That was skill. This is embarrassin' as hell.

"Okay, Hollister. Ya cleaned my plow twice. Let's see if ya can make it three times."

Ryan smiled at Chance as he put another quarter in the coin slot. She racked the balls and told Chance to take the break shot again.

This time two striped balls went down.

Chance felt like he might have a chance to win this one. His first shot after the break missed and it ended up at the far end of the table. However, four of his balls were grouped together in front of the eight-ball.

If she makes all her shots and needs to sink the eight-ball, she doesn't have a shot.

Ryan had the solid-colored balls and pocketed all seven of them in succession. She needed to sink the eight-ball to win the third game, but she had a problem.

The cue ball ended up in a position different from where she wanted it to be with respect to the eight-ball. It came to rest directly behind that group of four balls that belonged to Chance. There was not enough room to try a cue ball jump shot because the eight-ball was too close to Chance's group of four balls. The cue ball might land on top of his balls. A bank shot was not possible either because of the cue ball's position and Ryan didn't want to give a shot away with a safety.

However, there was enough room for Ryan to try a shot her father had taught her. A shot she had practiced many times and became proficient at making. One of the most difficult shots in the game of pool.

Ryan studied the layout of the table for only a minute, then she made her decision. She was totally unaware of anyone else in the room. All that mattered at that moment was the shot in front of her.

She pointed to the pocket where she was going to sink the eight-ball.

She looked at Chance with just the hint of a grin on her otherwise stoic face. He looked at her and shook his head.

She's gonna try a massé shot. This I gotta see.

By this time the guys on the other table noticed Ryan's skill at playing pool and they were watching silently.

Ryan approached the cue ball with her cue stick held nearly vertically above it. She took aim. She needed to make sure she hit the cue ball at just the right spot to put the right amount of spin on it.

There was complete silence in the pool room except for an occasional bit of laughter and loud talking coming from the bar area.

A look of intense concentration appeared on Ryan's face.

Her cue stick came into contact with the cue ball. The cue ball started spinning and began moving in a curving arc around Chance's group of four balls. It was heading straight for the eight-ball. It struck the eight-ball at just the right place and the eight-ball headed for the pocket. The pocket Ryan had pointed to prior to the shot. There was a clicking sound as the eight-ball fell on top of other balls in the pocket.

Ryan won the third game.

Chance could not restrain himself. He put two fingers to his mouth and let out a whistle that could be heard throughout the entire bar and restaurant.

"Yeah! Yeah, Ryan!" he yelled, pumping his fist, cheering and whistling.

Cheering and clapping came from the two guys at the next table.

Chance rushed over to Ryan and congratulated her. They put their arms around each other. Chance held her close. She was feeling that same feeling she had felt when he gave her the outfit she was wearing. She was shaking. She gave him that great big smile.

"Damn, Hollister—that was amazin'! Ya've answered my question, Darlin'."

Chance took Ryan by the hand.

"Let's go have those steaks now," he said.

TWENTY FOUR

When Chance and Ryan returned to the bar, Hawkeye and everyone was waiting for them. The clapping and cheering continued as they walked to where Hawkeye was standing.

The customers at the bar stood up, applauding. No one knew exactly why they were applauding, but they knew something incredible must have happened in the pool room.

"What the hell was all that yellin' back there, Mac? The cheerin' an' whistlin' an' clappin' could be heard all over this place. I'm sure it wasn't for a shot you made."

Chance was still holding Ryan's hand. He raised it for everyone to see.

"Ya're right, Hawkeye. Uhh... y'all—," Chance said, turning to everyone seated at the bar and at the nearby restaurant tables, "I want ya to meet a real pool player. This little lady knows the game. She beat me the first two games an' if that wasn't enough, on the third game, she pulled it all out o' the bag with the most amazin' massé shot I've ever seen. It was sweet."

More clapping and cheering for Ryan.

Chance squeezed Ryan's hand. The hand he was still holding.

Ryan looked up at Chance with joy in her eyes and with that big smile still on her face.

"A massé shot, huh?" Hawkeye said. "I've seen a couple o' guys who come in here try one, but they didn't know what the hell they were doin' an' damned near put a hole in the felt on one o' my tables. I'll tell you what... to celebrate the little lady's winnin' shot let me give you guys a pitcher on the house—"

Turning to Ryan, "an' the next time ya try a massé shot little lady, let me know so I can charge admission."

That brought a big laugh, cheering and clapping from everyone in the bar. Chance's pride was showing. Ryan could feel it.

"I'll send Cindy over with a pitcher," Hawkeye said.

Ryan excused herself. That big grin was still on her face. She winked at Chance.

Chance watched her walk down the hallway to the lady's room. That mini-skirt was doing its job. He felt the excitement building inside him. Ryan stopped momentarily at the door to the lady's room, turned to grin and wink at him, then went inside.

"This is gonna be a good night."

The band members came in and started setting up their instruments. There was a banner hanging on the wall behind the band platform.

The Dreamcatcher presents
Country Express
Every Friday night 9 to 1
for your listening
and dancing pleasure
Requests are welcomed

Chance listened to the band members tuning their instruments while he waited for Ryan to return.

~~~

A short time later, Ryan reappeared, carrying her jacket. She looked at Chance with that devilish, coy grin on her face.

"Have you been waiting long?" she asked, with a wink.

Chance returned a big smile, took her hand and led her to one of the only remaining empty booths on the end wall.

A hush settled over the restaurant. Everyone stopped what they were doing and stared.

Chance and Ryan sat down. Ryan put her jacket and hat on the seat beside her.

"It seems you and I are the center of attention, Mr. McKenna."

"Well, I'd say it was you, Miss Hollister. These people prob'ly never saw the most beautiful horse woman in the world before—dressed to the nines."

The two of them could not keep from laughing out loud.

Ryan was so happy. She was exuberant and she was showing it.

A waitress approached the booth carrying a pitcher of beer and two glasses.

"Hi. I'm Cindy. I'll be your waitress for the evening. This is from Hawkeye," she said, pouring some beer into the glasses. "My, you two are having a good time. Have you decided?"

"Yeah. We are, Cindy. Uhh… I mean, yeah, we're ready," Chance said, looking at Ryan who was still laughing.

They ordered steaks with all the side dishes.

Then, in a more quiet tone Chance proposed a toast to Ryan.

They raised their glasses. Ryan's eyes were sparkling as she looked at Chance and listened to his words.

"A toast, to the most amazin' woman I've ever met. Ya know horses better than any man I know an' I learned tonight—ya're a heck of a pool player. I'm the luckiest guy in the world to have ya by my side, Miss Hollister. Thank ya for bein' here. Here's to ya."

Ryan was lost in the sound of his voice and the words he was saying to her. She fought back tears. Tears of joy.

Ryan realized she was having real feelings for the man sitting across from her. Feelings that had nothing to do with horse ranching or playing pool. Feelings she knew she should not have for the man who was her boss.

The sound of their glasses touching brought her back.

"Thanks so much, Chance. Thank you for bringing me here."

They enjoyed their dinner and talked while the band played the first set.

Ryan looked across the room and spotted Julie with a friend.

Julie waved when she saw Ryan and Chance.

"Look who's here, Chance. Hey—Jules. Come over here."

Julie took her friend's hand and they came over to the booth.

Julie introduced her friend as Bobby.

"Aren't you two handsome? Liz... you look fabulous, girlfriend," Julie said, turning to Ryan and giving her a wink.

The four of them chatted briefly.

"I'll stop by the store in the morning, Jules." Ryan said.

Julie and Bobby said their goodbyes and went to see a movie.

"So tell me, Miss Hollister, are there any other hidden talents I should know 'bout besides horses an' pool?"

"No. That's it, Chance. Horses and pool."

"Ya've always been interested in horses?"

"Yes. Always."

"I can picture ya as a little girl gallopin' 'round the yard straddlin' one o' those wooden horse heads on a stick. Am I right?"

"Uhh... no. Not quite. Daddy had me on a horse by age six and I was galloping around the yard on the real thing."

Chance could not contain himself and responded with a burst of laughter. Ryan joined him.

"Ya know, I can see ya on the back of a horse at age six. Your parents must've been so proud o' ya. Next question... I have to ask. When did the interest in playin' pool happen?"

"We had a pool table in a spare room and I can remember trying to hold a cue stick when I could barely see over the edge of the table. Daddy would stand me on a chair to make the shots. He showed me everything he knew about the game. He had won some trophies when he was younger."

"That awesome massé shot... when'd ya start learnin' that?"

"I must have been about ten or eleven when daddy showed me how to do it. I love that shot. I would practice for hours. Setting up balls and practicing. During high school I entered and won several regional and Oklahoma State championships. I have some trophies and a cup in my bedroom at home. I confess. I should've mentioned all this when you suggested we play some pool."

"No. No. I'm glad it happened the way it did. I was a lot more surprised when ya made that winnin', third game shot than I would've been if I would've known beforehand ya'd prob'ly make it. Amazin'. I really envy your skills on the pool table. I'm guessin' ya have your own custom-made cue stick hidden away. Right?"

"Umm... yeah, I do. I have several, in fact, but I didn't bring them with me."

"Why not?"

"Well, I didn't come out her to play pool, Mr. McKenna."

"'All work an' no play'. Ya've heard o' that, haven't ya?"

"I have, but how about 'A glutton for punishment', Mr. McKenna? You've heard of that, I assume?"

"Yeah, but I was thinkin' more along the lines o' ya teachin' me a few tricks rather than ya kickin' my butt game after game."

More laughter from the two of them.

"Oh, all right. I'll ask mother to send my sticks."

"Good. Next question, Miss Hollister—d' ya have any brothers or sisters?"

"Uhh... no. I'm an only child. Mother had a real tough time with the delivery. The doctors told her she couldn't have any more children. That's probably why my mother and I are so close. I guess it's also the reason I look at Jules as being a sister. Daddy was so pleased when I showed an interest in horses and the ranch."

"I'm sorry to hear 'bout your mother, Ryan. I must say, ya turned out all right."

"Thanks. Okay. Enough about me. How about you, Chance? Do you have any brothers or sisters?"

"No, I don't. I'm an only child, also. We have that in common. I was a typical boy brat when I was younger. I didn't care 'bout the ranch at all til I was in my early twenties. My dad inherited the ranch from his dad an' he owned it when he met my mom. The ranch has been in the McKenna name for a long time. Mom an' dad wanted me to go to business school so I could take over from 'em, but I had other plans an' ended up more or less driftin' an' workin' on various ranches til I was in my middle twenties. My parents left me the ranch. I soon realized I needed to get serious 'bout takin' care o' the place an' I put all my effort into it."

"Your property is one of the nicest in the area, Chance. I'm happy and proud to be a part of it."

Ryan wondered for some time whether or not Chance McKenna was in a relationship. This was her opportunity to find out.

"Are there any—girlfriends, Mr. McKenna?"

The matter-of-fact, unhesitating response from Chance somewhat surprised and reassured her.

"Uhh... no, Miss Hollister. No girlfriends. No. I'm what they call a loner, I guess. I've not met a woman who was that interested in horses or ranchin'."

"Does that mean you're totally committed to the ranch and you don't have—"

"Time for a relationship?"

"Yes."

"If the right woman comes along then I'll give it a shot. Now, it's your turn, Miss Hollister. How 'bout all those boyfriends waitin' for ya back there in Oklahoma?"

"Boyfriends? Uhh... no. Well... there was one. A long time ago. Rob Morris. He wanted me to forget about horse ranching and join him in his business world. Buying and selling stocks, bonds and hedge funds. Can't you just see me working behind a desk all day? Yacking on the phone with clients. That world is not for me, Chance. I'll stay with the horses."

"I'm glad ya did. Ya said Miss Scott wanted ya to come out here, but did ya also come out here to escape the guy? What's his name? Rob—"

"No. That relationship was over before I left Tulsa—long ago over."

"The band should be back from break soon. Wanna stick around for a dance, Miss Hollister?"

"Of course. You did ask me if I danced before we left the cabin."

"So I did."

TWENTY FIVE

The band returned from their break to start the second set. The leader, Sean Nelson, spoke into the microphone.

"Uhh... ladies and gentlemen, may I have your attention, please?"

Those in the room became quiet.

"Thank you. We'd like to start this set off by playing 'Together Again', from 1977 and made popular by Emmylou Harris. This is a dedication to Ryan from Chance. Let's hear it for the happy couple."

The undercurrent of chatting stopped. There was a moment of complete silence. Most of those in the restaurant and bar looked around to see who Ryan and Chance were.

The crowd seemed to be somewhat confused by the names of the couple.

Then, they saw who the couple was. Chance helped them by raising his hand. Everyone clapped for Ryan and Chance.

Ryan looked at Chance with an embarrassed, but happy look on her face.

"Chance. You remembered."

Chance stood up and reached for Ryan's hand.

"Dance with me, Miss Hollister."

Chance led Ryan to the dance floor.

He took her in his arms and held her close.

The dance floor quickly filled with other couples, but Ryan and Chance were alone with each other.

Alone in a crowded room.

The scent of Ryan's shampoo lingered in her hair. Jasmine.

The band started playing. Sheri Lang, the female vocalist in the group, came to the microphone and began singing.

Chance sang the words, softly...

Together again my tears have stopped falling
The long lonely nights are now at an end
The key to my heart you hold in your hand
But nothing else matters cause we're together again

Ryan looked up at Chance.

She felt the heat coming from his body. She smelled the scent of his cologne.

Those burning feelings began sweeping over her. Like a wildfire. She was lost in the moment. Lost in the arms of the man dancing with her and singing to her. Ryan was being swept off her feet. She was in a place she had never been before.

"Don't let it end."

Chance pulled Ryan closer. He could feel her heart beating.

It was then he noticed for the first time the scar on Ryan's left jaw. It was barely visible.

Ryan and Chance continued to dance.

Chance sang the entire song to Ryan.

There was clapping and cheering for Ryan and Chance from everyone on the dance floor when the song ended.

Chance touched the brim of his hat and nodded to everyone, thanking them.

Ryan and Chance stood holding each other for a few moments, looking into each others eyes.

Chance gently brushed Ryan's cheek with his fingertips.

They returned to their booth holding hands.

Chance asked Ryan to sit beside him this time. He wanted to be close to her. They sat down with Ryan on the inside.

Ryan's hands were on her lap. Chance took one of her hands in his.

"Thank ya for the dance, Miss Hollister."

"Thank you, Chance. Thank you for the dedication and the dance. It was a total surprise. You're a wonderful dancer and, I might add, a very good singer, too. You knew all the words. It was a wonderful surprise."

"I wanted it to be perfect, Darlin'. I wanted to take ya to a different place while we were dancin'."

"You did, Chance. You did. It was perfect. I was totally in a different place... and time. It was wonderful. Thanks again for dedicating that song to me and singing it to me. No man has ever sang a song to me before."

Chance rested one of her hand's on his leg. Ryan did not resist.

"Tell me 'bout the scar on your jaw, Ryan. How'd it happen?"

Ryan covered the scar.

"It was years ago. I was working on a horse's feet and it kicked me. It was a young horse and hadn't had its feet messed with very much. It took a while to get to a doctor's office and get it stitched, so the scar remains. I'm a bit self-conscious about it. Makeup doesn't do much to hide it."

"Ya needn't be self-conscious, Darlin'. You're a beautiful woman. It's barely visible an' not noticeable at all unless someone was as close to ya as I was just now. I never noticed it before, but I wanted to know how it happened."

"Thank you, Chance."

They finished their drinks.

"We should prob'ly call it a night, Darlin'. It's back to work tomorrow. Work on a horse ranch never stops. Not even on a weekend."

"I know."

Chance put Cindy's tip under the pitcher.

They went over to the bar, paid the tab, said good night to Hawkeye and thanked him for the beer.

Hawkeye thanked them for coming in and said they shouldn't be strangers.

~~~

On the way home Ryan put her head back on the headrest, closed her eyes and thought about the evening just shared with the man next to her.

It was the most wonderful date I ever had.

TWENTY SIX

Chance was having mixed thoughts on the way home. Thoughts of the evening just spent with the woman beside him, resting her head on his shoulder. Thoughts of the nagging problem he was having with Mr. Lopez.

Ryan had to be told about Mr. Lopez. But not now. Not tonight. Chance was not going to spoil what had been a perfect evening. He would wait for a more appropriate time to tell her.

~~~

Chance parked the SUV near the barn. He didn't want to wake Ryan, but they couldn't sleep in the SUV all night.

"Hey. Sleepy head. We're home", he said, softly, stroking her hair.

Ryan opened her eyes.

"Oh. Sorry, Chance. I dozed off. Let's check on Dawn. I cleaned her stall and put fresh straw down earlier."

Dawn was lying down. Her foal was lying beside its mother.

"Everything looks good out here. C'mon, Darlin'. I'll walk ya to the cabin," Chance said, taking Ryan by the hand.

Chance held Ryan's hand when they were in the Dreamcatcher. That was different. They were on a date in a public place. This hand-holding on the ranch was something new.

On the way to the cabin, they expressed feelings about the date and how much they enjoyed each others company.

The area around the cabin door was illuminated by a small light Ryan turned on before they left.

A light breeze was blowing the leaves of nearby trees.

Shadows were dancing all around them.

Ryan looked at Chance.

The light was just enough to show him the longing in her eyes.

Chance took her in his arms.

He pulled her close.

"Ryan," he whispered.

This was the moment Ryan was waiting for all night.

I want him. I want him, but—

There was a battle going on inside her head. She realized she must not let herself act on the emotions she was feeling. Those feelings were more intense now than ever before. Especially after the evening they just shared.

She whispered, "Chance—"

"I know, Darlin'. I know. I thought 'bout this moment all the way home. I was thinkin' 'bout this moment all night long."

Ryan felt his arms closing around her. Strong, yet gentle. She felt secure. Safe. She looked up at him. Those feelings inside her were overwhelming. They were driving her crazy. She could resist no longer.

With her lips parted, she raised her mouth to meet his.

"Kiss me, Chance."

He pulled her closer. His mouth touched hers. Softly.

She could not resist.

She closed her eyes.

Ryan had never felt a man's kiss the way Chance was kissing her now.

She could feel the passion building inside her. It took her breath away. It had been such a long time. She went limp in his arms.

Time stopped.

The kiss ended slowly. Chance held her for a few moments longer. They opened their eyes and looked at each other. They both knew they had just shared something very special.

Ryan wanted this moment to last forever.

She was still in his arms.

In the shadows Ryan could see the look of desire was still in his eyes.

"Chance—"

His lips and mouth covered hers. More intense this time.

Chance pulled her closer. He kissed her with a passion Ryan had never felt from any man before. Her head was spinning. The kiss ended after what seemed like minutes.

Chance looked into her eyes. He stroked her hair and smiled.

"I had a really wonderful time tonight, Darlin'," he said, softly.

"It was wonderful for me, too, Chance."

"G'night, Darlin'," he said.

"Good night, Chance."

Ryan chose to not speak aloud about the feelings those two kisses brought her. She did not want to spoil the moment with words.

She watched Chance walk down the path toward the main house.

~~~

Ryan brought the glass of water and the rose into the bedroom.

She picked up the glass and smelled the rose. She would save it. It would remind her of him, but Ryan knew she would never need to be reminded of this evening with Chance McKenna.

She placed the turquoise neckerchief ring in a small jewelry box on top of the dresser, undressed and hung her outfit in the closet.

Lying in bed, Ryan thought about their date and all her feelings for Chance McKenna. The passion she felt when they danced and the kisses they just shared.

Their relationship was on a new path after tonight.

Ryan wondered how far it would go. How far should she let it go?

Chance McKenna was her boss.

TWENTY SEVEN

R yan stopped at Julie's store the following morning. She was anxious to tell Julie all about the night before.

"You and Chance looked amazing, Liz. That outfit looked great on
you. You looked so happy. So... c'mon, dish it out. What happened
when you two went home last night? Tell me all about it, Sweetie. I
want all the details."

"I'll get to last night, Jules, but first of all, before I left the ranch
this morning, Chance said something to me. He said, 'Bring me a six
pack, Sweetheart.' He never called me 'Sweetheart' before."

"He called you 'Sweetheart'? So... was that a bad thing?"

"Well... no, but the way he said the word 'Sweetheart' sounded—
well, it sounded like he meant it. There was an affectionate ring to it. I
don't know how to explain it any better than that, Jules. Maybe I'm
making more of it than it really was."

"Yeah. I think you're making too much out of it. I'm sure he meant it, though, or he wouldn't have said it. It sounds to me like he still had some lingering memories of the date, Liz. What about last night, at the Dreamcatcher?"

"Last night we played pool and had dinner. You were there when we were having dinner, Jules. You and your friend, Bobby."

"Pool and dinner. Sounds pretty dull to me so far," Julie said, grinning. "Is there more?"

"I'm getting to it, Jules. Be patient. We danced. He sang to me when we danced. When we got home, we kissed. That's all we did. That's it. Sorry, I can't give you any more details than those."

Julie thought she would try to change the direction of the questions she was asking her friend. More general questioning instead of the direct questioning she started out with. It was obvious Ryan was not going to get into the nitty-gritty details about the date.

"You kicked his butt on the pool table, didn't you?"

"I did. Yes."

Ryan wanted to talk about her winning massé shot in the third game. She went into great detail about how she made it and about the reaction she received from Chance and everyone in the bar. Julie listened intently, but she was anxious to get back to the more detailed questions she wanted to ask her friend and the answers she wanted to hear.

"Chance sang to you, you said? On the dance floor? I've never heard of a guy singing to his date while they danced, except in the movies, maybe. What was that all about?"

"It was a dedication song from Chance to me and—he sang it to me."

"That sounds so romantic, Liz. What happened when you got home?"

"Geez. I told you already, Jules. You don't give up, do you? We kissed. He kissed me. That's all we did."

"Well, at least that was something. Maybe he's noticing you're a woman after all and not just his top hand. Right? Was it good?"

Ryan's eyes took on their far away look. A look Julie had come to recognize as a signal her friend was going into her daydream mode.

"It was wonderful, Jules. Those were the most wonderful, most romantic kisses I've ever had."

"Oh? Kisses? There was more than one?"

Ryan looked at Julie, but she was not really seeing her friend. Ryan was lost in the memory of those kisses from the night before. She was staring off into space with a glazed look in her eyes. Julie realized she was right. Ryan had entered one of her daydream worlds. Julie snapped her fingers in front of Ryan's face.

"Ryan? Hey!"

Ryan shook her head and looked at Julie. She was back in the reality of the moment with her friend and she thought she had better try to answer the questions Julie was asking without giving away any sign of her feelings for Chance McKenna.

"So, that's all we did, Jules. Are you satisfied?"

"Kisses, huh? This morning he called you 'Sweetheart', you said. Right? To me, it sounds like that date and those kisses were still on Chance McKenna's mind."

"Okay, Jules. Let's leave it at that. Let's just leave it there."

That was the end of gossip about Ryan's date.

Ryan wanted to talk about Midnight. Breaking him. Training him for the racetrack.

"I just hope Chance lets me work with Midnight by myself, Jules. I hope I'm up to turning him into a racehorse. I know he has the qualifications to be a winner."

"We talked about this before, Liz. You're up to the challenge. Just remember your father's words. You broke a lot of horses back home and you landed on your butt a time, or two, as I recall. Midnight can't be any worse."

"Yes, I remember daddy's words. But Midnight's an eight months old colt and according to the Hills, his previous owners, has never had a bit in his mouth or a saddle on his back and he hates men. I hope he'll be able to tell the difference if I start working with him."

A good laugh between them took their minds off Julie's curiosity about her friend's date the night before.

Just then, Ryan's cell phone rang. The Caller ID told her she needed to answer it.

"Why would Chance be calling me?" she said, looking quizzically at Julie.

Ryan hurriedly pressed the Talk button.

Julie watched the color on Ryan's face turn pale.

After a few moments, Ryan hung up.

"That was Carmen. Chance had an accident."

Ryan put the phone back in her jeans pocket.

"Did she say what happened?" Julie asked.

"No. I need to get home right away, Jules."

TWENTY EIGHT

After he finished wiring all the corral gate latches, Chance went to the tack room, picked up his saddle, a saddle blanket, a lead rope and went to Midnight's pasture.

Chance stood at the railing watching Midnight eating grass.

"How can a horse tell the difference between a man and a woman? That's ridiculous."

What could be so difficult about working with that horse? Chance broke a lot of horses before. Ryan was not here now. It would be a perfect time to see if he could at least get a saddle on Midnight by himself. The bridle and a bit in Midnight's mouth would come later.

Chance hung the saddle and blanket over a rail.

Midnight raised his head and looked at Chance.

Chance climbed over the fence.

With the lead rope coiled in one hand, Chance walked slowly toward the stallion. When he was able to get hold of the halter, Chance fastened the lead rope.

At least that went more smoothly than the last time he tried to hook a lead rope to Midnight's halter.

Chance recalled how easy it was for Ryan.

Midnight followed Chance to where the saddle and blanket were hanging on the fence.

Chance looped the lead rope around the top rail of the fence.

Midnight stood still.

Chance picked up the saddle blanket and slowly laid it across Midnight's back.

Midnight stood still.

Chance picked up his saddle, hooked the right-hand stirrup to the saddle horn, and eased the saddle onto Midnight's back.

Midnight stood still.

Chance bent down slowly and reached under Midnight's belly for the girth strap, not making any sudden movements.

Midnight stood still.

Chance was about to take hold of the girth strap when, without any warning from Midnight, all hell broke loose.

Midnight let out a shrill scream. He began snorting and kicking. He threw his head from side to side, pulling on the lead rope, trying to get loose.

Chance tried to jump out of the way, but Midnight swung his hind quarters toward Chance and kicked with both hind feet.

Chance McKenna was in the wrong place at the wrong time.

A cracking noise could be heard.

Chance went down, clutching his right leg, yelling in pain.

"Help! Carmen! Help!" he yelled.

Midnight pulled on the lead rope, trying frantically to get loose. He managed to get the lead rope free of the fence rail and ran to the other side of the pasture with the lead rope hanging from his halter.

The saddle and saddle blanket ended up on the ground a few feet away from where Chance was lying.

Carmen had just finished a turn of laundry. She decided to hang the clothes outside to dry in the sunlight rather than using the dryer. The clothes line was in a location that allowed her to see Midnight's pasture.

Carmen heard the commotion coming from Midnight's pasture and watched him kicking and snorting for a few seconds, then, she heard Chance yell and saw him fall to the ground.

Carmen dropped the laundry basket and ran to the pasture.

"¿Qué ha pasado, el Sr. McKenna? What happened?"

Chance was trying to crawl to the gate, dragging his right leg.

"Hurry, Carmen. Ya need to call Dr. Alquist. I think my leg's busted."

Carmen didn't have her cell phone with her. Chance managed to get his phone out of his jean's pocket. He handed it to Carmen.

Carmen called the clinic.

Ms. Wilcox, the receptionist who normally answered the telephone, was on her lunch break

"Hello. Dr. Alquist?" Carmen said.

"No, Ma'am, this is Dr. Alquist's assistant, Nurse Higgins. May I help you?"

"Yes, Ma'am. My name is Carmen Martinez. Mr. McKenna's house-keeper. Out here at McKenna ranch. Mr. McKenna had an accident with one of the horses. His leg is broken, we think."

"Can you bring Mr. McKenna to the Medical Clinic?"

"Yes, Ma'am. I can bring him."

"Good. I'll let Dr. Alquist know to expect you."

Carmen hung up and handed the phone back to Chance. He motioned for her to keep the phone. He asked her to call Ryan to tell Ryan there was an accident and they were on the way to the doctor's office.

Chance asked Carmen to not say any more about the accident.

Carmen made the call to Ryan then handed the phone to Chance.

"I'll get my car, Mr. McKenna. Don't move."

TWENTY NINE

The Ponderosa Pine Medical Clinic was one of the newer facilities in Ponderosa Pine.

It was a one storey brick structure.

There was a separate emergency entrance for ambulances and other emergency vehicles. The clinic saved many patients the necessity to make the drive to Albuquerque.

Inside there was a main lobby with a waiting area and an admission's desk. In the rear of the Clinic, there were three patient examination rooms, a lab and an x-ray room.

The physician staff included Dr. Alicia Alquist, the chief resident, and Dr. Leo Winters. Both doctors alternated duty at the Clinic.

Dr. Alquist was the doctor on duty today. She was Chance McKenna's doctor.

Nurse Higgins was waiting for Carmen and Chance when they arrived. She had a gurney prepared with some warmed blankets.

Nurse Higgins was a Nurse Practitioner. She was a woman in her late twenties and average build. Reddish-brown hair and green eyes.

Nurse Higgins was waiting for Carmen and Chance when they arrived.

Carmen and Nurse Higgins helped Chance onto the gurney.

They wheeled Chance inside.

Nurse Higgins asked Carmen to wait in the waiting room. She took Chance to one of three patient examination rooms.

There was a bed in the examination room, but Nurse Higgins told Chance to remain on the gurney.

Nurse Higgins replaced the warmed blankets..

Nurse Higgins took Chance's vital signs; temperature, oxygen, blood pressure, heart rate. She recorded them for Dr. Alquist. She typed the results into the computer. She asked Chance what happened and made that entry into the computer.

"Dr. Alquist will be in shortly, Mr. McKenna. Try to relax."

"Make it quick, Nurse. I'm in a hell of a lot o' pain here."

Nurse Higgins left the examination room and closed the door.

Chance had no thoughts of Midnight in his head. No thoughts of Ryan in his head. The pain in his right leg was unbearable.

There was a knock on the door.

Dr. Alquist and Nurse Higgins entered the room.

Dr. Alquist was in her early thirties. Slender, blonde hair and blue eyes. She was five feet seven inches tall.

"What happened here, Mr. McKenna?" Dr. Alquist asked.

"Uhh... I tried to make friends with one of my horses, but—"

"But—it broke your leg. I'd say the horse was making a statement, Mr. McKenna. It didn't want to be your friend," she said, with the hint of a smile on her face.

"It hurts, Doctor."

"I know. Nurse Higgins will give you something for the pain in a minute. We're going to have to ruin those jeans, Mr. McKenna."

Dr. Alquist motioned to Nurse Higgins who was standing at the foot of the gurney with a pair of scissors in her hand.

"Do whatever ya need to do, Doctor. Just—hurry up."

Nurse Higgins cut off the right pant leg just above the knee. Dr. Alquist took a look at the wounded area.

"Before we take an x-ray, that wound will need to be cleaned. There is some abrasion and broken skin there. Also, Nurse Higgins will shave your leg around the area. Now you know what we women have to go through, Mr. McKenna," she said, with a wink and a smile to lighten the moment.

Chance managed a smile in return.

Nurse Higgins cleaned and disinfected the wound and shaved the leg while Dr. Alquist made some entries in the computer.

Nurse Higgins gave Chance a shot to ease the pain then wheeled him into the X-ray room.

X-rays were taken. Nurse Higgins wheeled Chance back to the patient examination room.

~~~

When the X-rays were developed, a technician brought them to the examination room.

Dr. Alquist studied the film on an illuminated light box.

"You're lucky, Mr. McKenna. It's only a fracture. Not as bad as it could have been. It's a stable fracture of the tibia. The larger of the two bones in your lower leg. The one most people refer to as the shin bone. Your fibula is fine. There is a large bruise and some laceration on the outer skin area of the leg. That suggests to me the flat, bottom part of the horse's hoof contacted your leg rather than the front edge of the hoof which would have caused a lot more damage."

"My tibia? My fibula? Whatever they are. Am I gonna need a cast, Doctor?"

"Yes, you are, Mr. McKenna. You'll need crutches, also. I'm going to apply a fiberglass cast to your leg."

Dr. Alquist tried to lighten the moment again. Much like asking a child what flavor candy sucker it would like after being stuck in the arm with a needle, she put a serious look on her face and asked the question.

"What color cast would you like?"

"What color cast would I like? Ya're askin' me 'bout a color for the cast, Doctor? Hell, I don't—"

Then, in a fleeting moment, Chance's thoughts turned to Ryan.

"Uhh... wait, Doctor. D' ya have a yellow one? A yellow one would be nice."

"Yes. We can make it a yellow one, Mr. McKenna."

Dr. Alquist and Nurse Higgins applied a mold to Chance's right leg, then put a fiberglass cast over top of it.

Dr. Alquist told Chance he would be on crutches for at least twelve weeks and he was not to put any weight on the leg during that time. He was to keep the leg elevated as much as possible during the early stages of healing to reduce the swelling.

Dr. Alquist also gave Chance a list of things to watch for during that time and told him to call her if there was an indication of any of the items on the list. Chance told her he would take care of the leg and would do what she told him to do. She told him to call if he needed more pain medication.

"Twelve weeks, huh? Seriously, Doctor?"

"Yes. At least twelve weeks, Mr McKenna."

"I hope I'll be able to take a shower during that time."

"Of course. The mold will be okay if it gets wet. No problem and the cast is fiberglass. Not like those old Plaster-of-Paris ones, so water won't affect it either. But, if you wish, you may put a saran wrap around the top of the cast while you shower to keep the water out of it. Just be careful in the shower, Mr. McKenna. We don't want to put a cast on the other leg now, do we?"

Chance managed another painful grin and shook his head in agreement.

"I want to see you again in six weeks. We'll take an x-ray at that time to see how things are progressing. If you have any of the symptoms on that list be sure to call me immediately."

Nurse Higgins went to a cabinet and took out a pair of crutches. Chance got up with the help of Dr. Alquist and Nurse Higgins and put the crutches under his arms.

Dr. Alquist went with him to the waiting room where Carmen waited anxiously.

Dr. Alquist told Carmen to put some pillows under Chance's leg when he was in bed to raise it which would help ease the pain.

Chance thanked Dr. Alquist.

He and Carmen headed to Anderson's Pharmacy to pick up the pain medication Dr. Alquist had called in.

~~~

On the way home Chance's thoughts returned to Ryan.

How was he going to explain to her what happened? How would she react?

THIRTY

Ryan expected to hear a siren and be lit up by red, white and blue lights coming up behind her on her way to the ranch. Obeying the speed limit was the furthermost concern on her mind.

Thoughts of the accident were running wildly through her head. She wished Carmen could have told her more about it. It must have been bad if Carmen was in such a hurry to get Chance to the clinic.

"What was Chance doing that caused him to have an accident? Was he doing something with the tractor? Did he hurt himself working in the tack room? Was he doing something with the horses?"

~~~

Ryan opened the main gate and entered the driveway.

When she approached Midnight's paddock the stallion raised his head.

A lead rope was dangling from his halter. There was a saddle and a saddle blanket on the ground near the paddock gate.

Ryan's worst fears were realized.

"Chance must have tried to get on Midnight's back. He must have been bucked off, but why would the saddle be on the ground if Chance had buckled the girth strap? Where was the bridle?"

Nothing about what Ryan saw in the paddock made any sense. She would have to wait to hear what happened from Chance.

Carmen's car was gone. Carmen and Chance had not come home yet.

Near the clothesline Ryan saw the overturned laundry basket and a few pieces of laundry on the ground. She gathered the laundry and set the basket outside the back door.

Ryan went out to Midnight's paddock and approached him. She was able to go up to him and remove the lead rope from his halter. She petted him for a few moments then picked up the blanket and the saddle and took them to the tack room.

She would wait in the cabin.

~~~

An hour filled with moments of anxiety and restlessness passed, then Ryan heard the sound of Carmen's car.

She ran out to meet them.

Ryan helped Chance out of the car. He was holding a pair of crutches. His right leg was in a fiberglass cast covering the leg from the knee to half of the foot.

Ryan and Chance looked at each other for a few moments without saying a word. Ryan just shook her head in disbelief, then she spoke with a straight face. Expressionless. Not smiling.

"That's a real sexy-looking pair of jeans, Mr. McKenna—and what's that thing on your right leg?" she asked, facetiously, still without any expression on her face.

Carmen opened the front door of the house. She and Ryan offered to help Chance into the master bedroom, but he motioned them away, walking on his own with the help of the crutches.

"I'm okay, ladies. I can manage by myself," he said, waving them away and hobbling into the master bedroom.

~~~

The master bedroom was large. A king-sized bed was against a wall. At the foot of the bed was a wooden chest the width of the bed with a folded quilt on top of the lid. A nine-drawer dresser with a large mirror was against a wall. A wooden three-drawer night stand was on each side of the bed. A four-bladed fan with a light was mounted in the ceiling above the bed. The floor was wood with several area rugs placed around the bed and dresser.

Ryan and Carmen helped Chance onto the bed despite his insisting he needed no help. They put pillows under his leg as Dr. Alquist ordered.

Carmen went into the kitchen to fix the pain medication.

"Hurry, Carmen. It hurts like hell."

Ryan was trying her best to remain outwardly calm. On the inside, she was steaming.

Ryan and Chance continued to stare at each other without a word between them.

It was Ryan who broke the silence.

"What happened after I left here this morning, Chance?" Ryan asked, speaking in a deliberately soft, unwavering voice, with an expressionless look still on her face.

Chance was not sure he should say what he was thinking, but he said it anyway.

"Midnight looked like he wanted some attention. So... I gave him some. D' ya like the color o' my cast, Hollister? I picked it out 'specially for ya."

Chance managed a half-heartened laugh even though he was in terrible pain. The pain shot Nurse Higgins gave him was rapidly wearing off.

"That was not the least bit funny, Mr. McKenna. I asked you once. I'll ask you again. What happened with you and Midnight?"

The level and pitch of Ryan's voice was starting to rise. It was obvious she was losing her patience with Chance McKenna and his attempt to make a joke of the situation. The look on Ryan's face and the sound of her voice told Chance he had better stop kidding around and tell her the truth about the accident.

Carmen returned with a glass of water and some pain pills and handed them to Chance. He took the pills, then spoke, looking down at the cast on his leg. He avoided Ryan's eyes.

"I tried to put a saddle on him, but I didn't get the girth strap hooked up."

There was a long, silent pause as they both continued to stare at each other.

It was Ryan who broke the awkward silence for the second time.

"I'm furious with you, Mr. McKenna. What in hell were you thinking? I gave you credit for having more damn sense than that. You said the Hills warned you Midnight was a handful. Why would you try to put a saddle on him when I wasn't around to help? We talked about that when we put him in the paddock. Remember? What in hell were you thinking?"

Chance had never heard Ryan swear before. Not even when they were having their argument about the two mares fighting, but she was swearing now. It was obvious she was more than a little upset. That was real anger aimed at him and he knew he had to deflect it somehow.

"Before ya start dumpin' on me, Hollister—yeah, it was my fault. I shouldn't 've tried it by myself. You're right. I shouldn't 've tried messin' with that s.o.b. by myself."

The stern look on Ryan's face gradually disappeared and in its place was a look of sympathy for the man lying on the bed. He was defenseless. Helpless. It was an opportune time to take advantage of his condition. This was as good a time as any to let Chance McKenna know exactly how they were going to deal with Midnight.

Ryan set her jaw, fixed her gaze and spoke in a calm voice.

"Okay, Mr. McKenna. Here's how it's going to be. Listen up. From now on, any work done with Midnight will be done by me, and me alone. I have years of experience breaking horses just like him. I'll break him and I'll do it alone. By myself. My way. Understood? Do you have a problem with that, Mr. McKenna?"

Chance just stared at her with his jaw dropped. He was not prepared to hear what he just heard from his top hand. She obviously meant business. His only immediate response was to point to the cast on his leg. He tapped it lightly with his finger tips.

"Look at this. Do I look like I'm in a position to argue with ya, Hollister? I'm lookin' forward to seein' just how ya handle that horse. From now on then, he's your responsibility. Do with him what ya want. That's what ya were hopin' for since the first time ya set eyes on him, ain't it? That's what ya've wanted all along, ain't it?"

"Yes, Chance. That's what I wanted," she said, her voice becoming softer and quieter now. "That's been my wish since seeing him in his stall the day you first showed him to me. My wish was to be the one to break him. By myself. My way. That wish has come true, but I didn't want it to happen like this, Chance. I'll break him. You'll see. I'll make you proud."

"I have the feelin' ya will, Hollister," Chance mumbled, under his breath, not showing his amusement at Ryan's self-confidence or the pride he was feeling for her determination.

Chance continued to look at her. Not responding. He knew she had the upper hand under the circumstances. There was no use arguing with her. He managed to put a smile on his face.

Chance called out to Carmen to come back to the bedroom.

"Carmen, uhh... Miss Hollister will be in charge, runnin' the ranch while I'm on those crutches. If ya need anythin' 'round here, on the ranch, please ask her. I know you'll give her any support ya can. D' ya have friends, Carmen, or d' ya know anyone, who'd be able to work for 'bout three months, or so, to give Ryan a hand 'round here? They'll need to be on the ranch from early mornin' til late afternoon. They'll be paid for their time."

"Yes, Mr. McKenna. I have two young boys in mind. Alfredo and Juan Gomez. Brothers. I know they have worked on some of the other ranches. I know their parents. We are good friends. They are good boys. They are good workers. I'll ask them."

"Thanks, Carmen. That's all for now."

Chance turned to look at Ryan, standing at the foot of the bed. He waited for her to say something about the responsibility he just handed to her.

"Thanks for putting your trust in me again, Chance. I'll take care of business around here. You'll see. Don't worry. If I need something from you I'll ask for it and I'll check on you everyday. I know Carmen will be a big help, also. How long did Dr. Alquist say you 'd be laid up?"

"'Bout twelve weeks, is what she told me."

"Twelve weeks, huh?" Ryan said, with a slight shake of her head, "It's getting late. I should get the evening chores started. I'll come and see you tomorrow, Chance. Get some sleep."

Ryan hesitated then turned and started to leave the bedroom.

"Wait. Wait, Ryan. Before ya go, there's one more thing I need to tell ya. Somethin' ya need to know. It's important."

An ominous silence fell over the room. Ryan turned and walked slowly back to the bed, looking at Chance with a curious look on her face.

"Tell me what, Chance?"

"I prob'ly should've mentioned this before now. In fact, I know I should've. I received a notice o' foreclosure on the ranch a couple o' weeks before I hired ya. There's an outstandin' balance due on the loan left by my folks an' I'm not able to pay it down. I received a call again today from the loan officer at the bank. I've been receivin' letters an' phone calls from him on a regular basis. There're only a few weeks to come up with a payment or else—"

"Or else what?"

Chance hesitated, hoping to find the words to ease what he knew would be devastating news. There was no easy way to say it.

"The bank'll take the ranch," he said, half under his breath.

Chance took his eyes off Ryan and stared out the window.

Ryan felt the blood drain from her face. She looked at Chance and shook her head, not sure she heard what she just heard.

She wondered what could be worse than the accident with Midnight. Well, this was worse. A lot worse. Chance's leg would mend, but the ranch could be lost.

Ryan stood looking at Chance with no expression on her face.

"When I told ya I was goin' to town that mornin' on business—the day those two mares got into it," Chance continued, turning to look at her again, "it was to have a talk with the chief loan officer at the bank. That meetin' with him didn't go well. Not at all. That was prob'ly the reason I jumped all over ya that day when I came back home. I wanted to take my anger out on someone an' ya were the nearest person 'round."

Finally. It was said. Now, Ryan knew about the foreclosure problem. Chance waited for her to say something.

"A notice of foreclosure? Why did you wait until now to tell me? Were you afraid I might not take the job? Why did you keep it a secret from me until now, Chance? When were you planning on telling me? When?"

"I don't know. I don't—I don't know, Ryan. The time never seemed right. Anyway, I told you now. Okay? I told ya 'bout it now. I'm thinkin'—maybe I can hold an auction out here an' sell some—"

"Sell what, Chance? You've got a pickup truck, two horse trailers and a tractor. That's it. That's what you've got. Surely you're not thinking about selling any of the horses are you? There must be another way to pay on the loan. Another way to delay the foreclosure. We— we'll have to find another way."

Chance's face showed stunned surprise at what Ryan just said. She had included herself in what he thought was his personal problem.

"We—Hollister?" he said, with raised eyebrows.

"Yes. We—Mr. McKenna. I'm part of this operation now and we have to find a way to work with the bank and delay the foreclosure. It's not just the ranch I'm thinking about. I'm also thinking about my job. We'll get through this, Chance. We'll find a way. We're not going to lose the ranch. We're not going to lose it."

Once again, Ryan seemed to be in complete control of the situation. The strength of character she showed him just now reminded Chance of one of the reasons he hired her. He wondered what he would do without her. In spite of the serious situation she just learned about, she managed to show him that big smile.

On her way out, Ryan stopped at the bedroom doorway and turned to look at Chance.

"I put your saddle blanket and your saddle back in the tack room. Oh... before I forget, I'll bring your six pack over and give it to Carmen—Sweetheart. One more thing—I think your cast is real pretty. Nice color."

Chance heard her laughing out loud as she was leaving. What was so damned funny? The pain medication started taking effect. For now, the pain in his leg was going away.

A load had been taken off Chance McKenna's mind.

Ryan Hollister knew about his other problem. It was a secret no longer.

THIRTY ONE

The Ponderosa Pine Savings and Loan Bank was located downtown on the main street.

The bank was one of the newest buildings in town. However, the architecture and construction did not fit with the rest of the buildings. It
didn't have that Southwestern architecture look and feel.

Next door to the bank was the Ponderosa Pine Realty Office. The
way it was attached to the bank made it look as though its construction
was an afterthought. Like someone decided a Realty Office was the
perfect addition to the bank. To absorb any foreclosures, perhaps.

~~~

Ryan walked into the bank and waited her turn.

When she was called, she told the teller she wanted to open a
checking account. The teller took her information. Ryan made an ini-

tial deposit of her payroll checks received since starting work at the ranch.

The teller handed Ryan the check book and receipt for the deposit.

"That should do it, Miss Hollister. Will there be anything else?"

"Umm... yes, Ma'am. I'd like to speak with a loan officer, if that's possible."

"That would be Mr. Lopez. Please, have a seat, Miss Hollister. I'll see if Mr. Lopez is available."

The teller disappeared into an adjoining office.

There was a nameplate attached to the wall outside the office door.

The teller returned moments later.

"Mr. Lopez will be with you shortly, Miss Hollister."

A few minutes later a well-groomed, well-dressed gentleman appearing to be in his early fifty's walked over to Ryan.

"Miss Hollister? How do you do? I'm Roger Lopez."

"How do you do, Mr. Lopez? Pleased to meet you."

They shook hands.

"Come with me, please," he said.

~~~

Mr. Lopez' office had the look of an office of someone who had made it to the top in his job.

Even though the office was large compared to most offices Ryan had been in, it felt claustrophobic to her.

The closed-in feeling and the stark surroundings reminded her of some of the reasons she had chosen her profession.

The outdoors.

The fresh air.

The freedom.

"Have a seat, Miss Hollister. How can I help you?"

"Well, Sir, I'm working for Mr. McKenna, on his ranch and I would like you to explain to me the foreclosure notice on the property."

"I've gone over all the details with Mr. McKenna, Miss Hollister."

"I'm sure you have, but I wish to keep this meeting with you private for the time being, Mr. Lopez, so whatever information you can give me would be appreciated."

Mr. Lopez said the loan on the property was the loan Chance McKenna's parents had taken out as a second mortgage and when they died there was an outstanding balance of seventy-three thousand dollars that included a significant inheritance tax added on top of the loan. He said Chance had not been able to pay the necessary monthly amount to keep the loan balance current.

"Therefore, the only recourse was for the bank to place the property in foreclosure, Miss Hollister."

"I understand, Mr. Lopez. My reason for coming in today is this... I wish to transfer an amount of money from my bank in Tulsa to the checking account I just opened and when the money arrives I will authorize your bank to apply the total amount to the loan balance."

"All right, Miss Hollister. I can set that up at this time," he said, opening a desk drawer and removing a folder of paperwork.

Mr. Lopez filled out the papers and Ryan signed them. Mr. Lopez said it would take a few days for the money to be transferred. He said he would call her to verify her approval before applying the money to the loan. Ryan asked by how much would the payment she was making extend the loan. Mr. Lopez told her the loan committee would have to consider the payment and make that decision.

Ryan removed the notes she had written down the night before and her trainer's license from her handbag and laid them on the desk in front of Mr. Lopez.

Mr. Lopez picked up the notes, read them hurriedly, then picked up Ryan's trainer's license and briefly looked at it. He made no comment about the notes or the license.

Ryan could see she needed to offer some additional information about her intention to race Midnight. She gave Mr. Lopez a brief description of Midnight's bloodlines. She mentioned some of Midnight's winnings would be used to pay on the loan.

"I'm impressed with your racing career, Miss Hollister," he said, handing the notes and license back to Ryan. "Have you raced that horse yet? The one you're talking about here? Has it won any races?"

"Not exactly, but—"

"You want to use the winnings of a horse that is unproven and untried as a racehorse to pay down the McKenna loan?" he said, interrupting with a sarcastic tone of voice.

"That's my plan, Sir. If you want to see a business plan I would be happy to bring one in an—"

"That won't be necessary, Miss Hollister. While I admire your plan to help Mr. McKenna keep his ranch, I must remind you the primary concern of the bank is the payoff of the loan and we will expect that payment to be made by whatever means you choose to make it. Is that clear, Miss Hollister?"

Mr Lopez began shuffling some papers on his desk in an attempt to appear as if he had more important matters to attend to. Apparently he didn't think very much of Ryan's plan to come up with the money to pay off the loan. His disinterest was obvious, both by his tone of voice and by his mannerisms which indicated he wanted to end their meeting.

Ryan was becoming increasingly more irritated with Mr. Lopez' superior attitude.

"I understand, Sir. I take it you're not really interested in anything I've said to you or showed you this morning, are you?"

Ryan picked up her notes and license and put them back into her handbag. Her eyes were fixed on his, waiting to hear his response.

"That's not the impression I want to leave with you, Miss Hollister. This is business. My interest is in securing payments on the loan to get it paid off. I've tried to make it clear to Mr. McKenna and now to you, this loan is currently delinquent. That's a serious situation. It's a very serious situation for Mr. McKenna's credit rating should he ever need financial assistance in the future. I'll accept the payment you are going to make and I'll let you know by how much it will extend the loan deadline—if, and when, it is approved. I cannot give you any guarantee at this time, Miss Hollister. I'll make a note to call you as soon as your money arrives from Tulsa."

"I would appreciate it if Mr. McKenna did not know of our meeting here today, Mr. Lopez. Please keep this meeting just between the two of us for the time being."

"I'll do that, Miss Hollister and—good luck with your horse," he said, in a more congenial tone of voice and with a forced smile. "Will there be anything else?"

"No, Sir. I won't take up any more of your time. I'll be expecting your call."

They shook hands.

Ryan walked out of the office.

Her business at the bank was finished. It did not go as she had hoped. Most of the excitement she had felt the night before was gone.

However, the wheels of Ryan's plan to save the ranch were beginning to turn. Now it was up to Mr. Lopez and the loan committee.

She was thinking about Mr. Lopez' curt and brusque manner. In his eyes he saw her as just another bank customer with a cash flow problem.

THIRTY TWO

All of a sudden, Ryan was faced with more responsibility than she ever had before. She could handle any problem to do with horses and horse ranching. The obligation she took upon herself to save the ranch was different. It was an obligation that affected her job and her self-esteem.

It was overwhelming.

~~~

"What is it, Liz? You look worried," Julie said, when Ryan entered the store.

"What am I going to do, Jules? We're likely to lose the ranch because of foreclosure. Midnight's not ready. Chance is on crutches. I just don't know if I can handle all this pressure, Jules."

"Wait a minute. Slow down. Chance is on crutches? Because of his accident? For how long?"

"For about three months. Can you believe that?"

"What's up with the foreclosure? That's serious, Liz. Real serious. Are you sure? What's that all about?"

"Chance told me he received a notice of foreclosure a few weeks before he hired me. He waited all this time to tell me about it, Jules. There's a balance due to keep the loan current, but he can't pay anything on it. It's a second mortgage his parents took out before they died. He's laid up for several months because of his stupid decision to try and put tack on Midnight by himself and now I have to run that ranch by myself. What am I going to do? I need to get started working with Midnight. He's my responsibility now. I went to the bank this morning and that Mr. Lopez was a real s.o.b.!"

Julie could see tears welling up in Ryan's eyes. She had seldom seen Ryan with tears in her eyes in all the years they knew each other. She had never seen Ryan so worried and troubled before. Ryan was usually in complete control of whatever situation she found herself in, but this time was different. She wasn't making a whole lot of sense. She was truly in need of some support and encouragement. Support and encouragement only Julie could give her.

"Take it easy, Honey. You'll think of something. You always do. Put those tears away and let's talk about this. Rationally. Yes, Chance made a bad decision to mess with that horse. Now, he's on those crutches, but you can't do anything about that. So, let's start with the bank. You say you went to the bank this morning? Who's Mr. Lopez? What happened there?

"Well, I'm transferring some money from my bank account back home. Mr. Lopez is the bank's chief loan officer. He didn't want to hear anything about my plan to pay off the loan or my plan to race Midnight. He said the money I'm transferring will probably make the loan balance current for an extended time, but it will be up to him and a loan committee to decide by how much time. He couldn't tell me any more than that. He didn't care. He just didn't give a damn, Jules."

"Okay. So, putting up some of your money will hopefully help. That's a good thing, right?. It's too bad it had to be your money, though."

"It's just until Midnight wins some races and then I'll tell Chance I expect it to be paid back. I asked Mr. Lopez to keep my visit to him between him and me. I don't want Chance to know anything about any of this yet."

"Well, it sounds like that pretty much takes care of the bank problem, Liz. At least for now. What are you going to do about Midnight? It won't be easy working with him. I mean, look what he did to Chance."

"I know. Chance told me Midnight's my responsibility from now on. He'll not interfere, so I need to get started right away. I need to get that horse broken and start him on race training. Time is running out. You know about the Quarter horse Fall Classic—the All American Futurity—right? It's only eight months from now. How can I get that horse on the track, winning races and qualified to run in the Futurity in only eight months?"

"I know about that race. You and your father always wanted to enter a horse. I remember that. You're thinking about running Midnight in that race?"

"Yes. I am. But he needs to win some local races around here first in order to qualify."

"Wow! You're right. There's a heck of a lot of stuff on your plate, Liz. Listen. You can do it. Just remember what your father told you and taught you and you'll get through this. You will. The ranch won't be lost. Okay? Don't let me see anymore tears in those blue eyes. Give your mother and father my love the next time you talk to them. Okay?"

"I will. Thanks, Jules. I just needed to vent."

They hugged. Julie gave Ryan a kiss on the cheek.

~~~

Ryan called home when she arrived back at the cabin. She had mixed feelings about telling her parents about Chance's accident. However, she did want them to know about her new responsibility on the ranch, so she would skip the details of the accident for now.

She wanted to tell her father about Midnight's bloodlines,

Her father answered his phone.

"Hi, daddy. How are you? How's mother?"

"We're both fine, Sweetheart," her mother answered, from her phone in the kitchen.

"I have more news for you. Some really good news. Some—not so good, but—"

"Is everything all right, Sweetheart?" her mother interrupted, sounding somewhat worried.

"Yes, mother. It'll be fine. Chance had an accident while working. Broke his leg, actually. He's on crutches for about three months. He put me in complete charge of the ranch until he's well again. That was the not-so-good news. Now, for the good news. It's about Midnight. I found his charts online. His dam, who is owned by a couple on a neighboring ranch, was bred from racing stock, but she was never on the track. Here's the really good news, you guys—his sire was an Easy Jet colt with winnings on the track. That means Midnight has racing bloodlines on both sides. What do you think?"

The news about Midnight's potential to race piqued her father's interest.

"What? An Easy Jet colt? I'd say ya've got a winner there, Baby Girl. Does Mr. McKenna know 'bout Midnight's background?"

"Umm... not yet, daddy, but I'm going to tell him soon. Chance told me I'm the one who will be breaking Midnight. By myself. That's the first thing I need to do. I need to get him under tack, daddy."

"You're right, Baby Girl an' ya can do it. I know ya can. You'll get that horse on the racetrack. I've no doubt 'bout that."

"Thanks, daddy. That means so much to me."

"That's great news about Midnight, Sweetheart. Thanks for sending all the pictures and videos," her mother said. "My—that Mr. McKenna sure is young-looking—and handsome, too."

"Mother. You sound just like Jules. She's been nagging me to get interested in Mr. McKenna ever since I got here."

"Elizabeth—leave her alone. She'll find her man when she's ready," her father said, speaking to her mother from across the room.

"Oh, by-the-way, mother, would you please send me my cue sticks?"

"Are ya playin' some pool out there, Baby Girl? Beatin' their butts, I'll bet," her father said. "Ya know, that picture o' Midnight is worth a thousand words. He certainly looks like a winner just standin' at halter. Good lookin' horse. Okay, Honey, your mom an' I need to go to town, so we'll say So Long for now. Keep up the good work an' keep us informed when ya break Midnight an' remember... ya can do it. Give Mr. McKenna our best. Thanks for callin'. Love ya, Honey."

"Yes, Sweetheart, tell Mr. McKenna we wish him well and let us know how it goes with Midnight," her mother said, "and good luck taking care of the ranch for Mr. McKenna while he's laid up. You can do it. I'll send your cue sticks. Thanks for calling. Goodbye for now, Honey. We love you."

"Thanks, mother. Goodbye. Goodbye, daddy. I love you both."

THIRTY THREE

The next several days were spent anxiously waiting for word from Mr. Lopez. Would the bank receive the money she transferred from Tulsa? Nervous tension was building. What if there was a problem with the transfer of the money?

Ryan tried to keep busy around the ranch. She didn't want Chance to see her anxiety for fear he would want to know what was wrong.

~~~

A phone call from Mr. Lopez three days later was the one Ryan was waiting for.

"Miss Hollister, I'm calling to let you know we have received the transfer of the money from your bank in Tulsa. So, as we discussed, I must ask you to verify your wish to have this money applied to the McKenna loan. Is that your wish, Miss Hollister?"

"Yes, Sir. That's my wish. You may apply the amount we discussed to Mr. McKenna's loan."

"I'll take care of it, Miss Hollister. As I mentioned to you, it will be up to the loan committee now. I will call you as soon as we review the loan details and make our decision. Goodbye."

"Thank you, Sir. Goodbye."

~~~

A couple days later, Ryan's cell phone Caller ID showed it was Mr. Lopez calling again.

"Hello. This is Ryan Hollister."

"Miss Hollister, this is Mr. Lopez calling to let you know the loan committee and I have reached a decision. Because of the amount of your payment, the loan will be extended for thirty-two weeks from the day we received the transfer of funds from your bank in Tulsa. There will be thirty-two weeks of time to come up with the remainder of the balance we discussed. If the balance is not paid in full by the end of thirty-two weeks we will reinstate the foreclosure process. Is that clear, Miss Hollister?"

"Yes, Sir, it is. I'll keep you informed. Thanks for calling. Goodbye, Sir."

"Goodbye, Miss Hollister."

Eight months.

That was all the time Ryan would have to break, race train and get Midnight on the track and qualified to run in the Fall Classic.

Not much time to work with an unproven horse, but it was better than having the bank come out and put a chain on the main gate in a couple of weeks.

THIRTY FOUR

Chance was sitting on the couch, wearing a pair of desert shorts, looking relaxed, but bored. He glanced up from the TV when Ryan entered the room.

"Hey there, Chance. How are you feeling? How's that leg doing? I see you've got it propped up on the coffee table."

"The leg's doin' all right. Those pain pills are workin'. Good stuff."

"Nice legs… for a guy," Ryan said, laughing, "I guess we both have a thing for the other one's legs."

"Yeah. I guess so," Chance said, with a big smile on his face. "What's up?"

"I brought you a few DVDs for your viewing pleasure. They're videos of some of my winning races."

"Thanks, Hollister. I'll watch 'em in a while. Daytime TV really sucks, except for ESPN. Yeah. I'll enjoy seein' some o' your horses run. How's everythin' outside? Any problems? How're the Gomez boys workin' out? I should be able to get out there in a few more days to give 'em a hand. I sure as hell miss bein' outside an' workin' with the horses."

"Don't worry about it, Chance. Don't rush it. Take your time with that leg so it can heal properly. Everything's good outside. The boys are doing a great job helping me with the chores and the horses. I asked them to put Dawn and her foal back in their corral. Dawn's wound is all healed. I'm going to go into town in a little while and pick up some tack I need to work with Midnight. Jules said it was in the store. Also, it's time to worm those horses. I'll pick up some worming medicine."

"Thanks for lookin' after Dawn an' thanks for doin' the wormin'. I hadn't gotten 'round to that yet. So... ya need to buy some extra tack to break that horse?"

"Yes. I'll be starting work with Midnight immediately. I need to get him broke. I want you to watch me do that, Chance, if you feel like it. You don't have to be there everyday, but I'd sure like you to see the method I use."

"Well... busted leg, or not... crutches, or not... I wouldn't miss that, Hollister. Are ya gonna work him in his paddock or in the ring?"

"The first thing to do is get him used to lunging. I'm guessing he's never been on the end of a lunge line. I'll do that in the ring every day before any other workout. After that, I'll work him in his paddock. It'll be easier on his legs, I think. I have a thirteen-step plan I'll use to break him. I used it to break all my horses and it works. It works every time."

"A thirteen-step plan to break a horse? Now, I've heard everything. This I gotta see, Hollister. I just learned somethin' new again. Let me know when to come out there."

"I'll give you a copy of the thirteen steps so you can follow along. You're going to enjoy it."

Ryan was gradually building up her courage on the inside to tell Chance what she had on her mind. The real reason for coming to see him.

"Chance, umm… listen. Before I go I have something to tell you. This is really important. It's very important, Chance, so let me say what I need to say and then we can discuss it together—I have a plan to save the ranch."

Chance raised his eyebrows.

"A Plan? Okay, Hollister. I'm listenin'. Tell me 'bout it."

"Well, after you told me about the financial difficulty the ranch was in I came up with this plan. I had money in my bank in Tulsa. I used some of it to pay on the loan and we got a—"

"Wait a minute, Hollister. Hang on. Ya did what? Ya did that without talkin' to me first?"

"Chance, you said you'd hear me out, so please, keep quiet, will you, until I've finished? Will you do that? I've transferred fifty thousand dollars from my bank account in Tulsa to pay on the loan. It was accepted by the bank and Mr. Lopez told me he and the loan committee would extend the loan for thirty-two weeks. That's eight months, Chance. That's it. It's not a lot of time, but it will let me get Midnight broken and—and here's the thing, Chance—it'll allow me some time to get him ready to run. I'm going to put Midnight on the track. Hopefully, his earnings will pay off the remainder of the loan and you'll be able—we'll be able—to keep the ranch. That's it, Chance. That's what I wanted to tell you. That's my plan."

Chance looked at her. Dumbfounded and speechless, wondering if he heard what he thought he just heard from his top hand. He kept shaking his head side-to-side. After some moments just looking at her, saying nothing, he spoke.

"Damn, Hollister! Did ya say fifty thousand dollars? Where'd ya get that kind o' money?"

"Yes. That's what I said and before you get your shorts in a twist, it's not a gift. It's a loan. It'll be paid back with earnings from Midnight's winnings, so don't feel indebted. It's not coming out of your pocket, Mr. McKenna. Now, I want to know—are you with me, or not? If you're not, then we can kiss this ranch goodbye. This is our last, best hope to save it. That's it. I want to know. I want to hear it from you. Are you with me, or not?"

Ryan was obviously both excited and agitated at the same time. There was anxiety in her voice. She was rushing her words.

"Wait a minute, Hollister. Take a breath. What ya've done with your money is done an' it can't be undone. I'll have to accept it. I don't like that ya went behind my back, but I'll accept it with my gratitude an' thanks, of course. Now, let's talk about that horse. D' ya think Midnight's good enough to race an' win? Ya're assumin' a hell of a lot here. Ya're assumin' that based on what?"

"Horse racing is never a sure thing, Chance, but Midnight's sire and dam both came from racing bloodlines. I looked at their charts online. That makes him an eligible candidate for the track. Yes, I feel that with the proper training—training I'll give him—he'll be a winner. But time is running out. There are only eight months remaining. Eight months... to get him ready for the All American Futurity this Fall. In September. Labor Day. Are you familiar with that race? It's the highest paid purse in Quarter horse racing. It's the crown. I want to get him ready and qualified to run in that race, Chance. Just remember my experience with horses on racetracks in Oklahoma when you're watching those videos. We can do this."

"Yeah. I know 'bout that race down there at Ruidoso Downs. So, what's next? Ya break him, then what? I don't have a facility here to train a racehorse. Ya're puttin' a whole lot o' faith in Midnight. Ya haven't even broke him yet an' ya're talkin' 'bout usin' his winnin's on a racetrack to pay off the loan? That's askin' a hell of a lot o' him, don't ya think?"

"How about me, Chance? Do you have any faith in me? I'm the one who has to train him. There's not a lot of time to do what I need to do. He should've been broken a long time ago and he should've already been in race training, but I can't dwell on what should've already been done. I need to concentrate on what needs to be done now. I'm getting a late start with him. I don't want to push him. I surely don't want him to break down with leg problems that would end whatever career he might've had. Will you help me?"

Chance was trying to compose himself after hearing everything Ryan said the past few minutes

"Whew! That was a hell of a lot o' information to process, Hollister. Of course, I have faith in ya. I've no doubt ya can do it. I'll help ya. I'm just sayin', what can I do?"

Chance pointed to the cast on his leg and the crutches leaning against the couch.

"I'll ask the boys to help me until your cast is removed. What I need now, Chance, is your moral support and your trust in me. I need that from you right now. It's important for me to know that it's you, me and Midnight against that Mr. Lopez and his bank. We can win this thing."

Chance looked at her, this time with a great big smile on his face.

"All right. I'm in. Ya know, ever since I introduced ya to that colt an' gave ya his papers I expected to be hearin' ya tell me this. It's really not a big surprise. I'll say this—beauty an' brains—ya've got both, Hollister. That's a potent combination."

They both laughed.

Ryan could not resist going to him and giving him a hug and a kiss on the cheek.

"Well then, Mr. McKenna, let's get started. I'll call Mr. Lopez and tell him to contact you from now on regarding the loan, the extension and anything else to do with the foreclosure business, but—and I want to be clear about this, Chance—I want you to keep me informed about what Lopez tells you. Do you hear me? I need you to keep me informed. I need to know what's going on with the bank."

"I hear ya, Hollister. I'll let ya know what's goin' on."

Ryan looked at Chance, winked and nodded. It was done. They were back on a level playing field again. No secrets between them.

There was one last bit of business Ryan needed to take care of. She looked at Chance with that little girl look on her face.

"Uhh… before I go, can I sign your cast? I think it's a tradition."

"Yeah. Sure. There's a pen there on the table."

Ryan picked up the pen and signed the cast.

Chance,
Get well soon
Your top hand,
Ryan

Chance watched her walk out of the room, looking back at him, waving and smiling.

Those tight-fitting jeans had a way of taking his mind off that broken leg.

Chance read what Ryan signed on his cast.

He brushed her name lightly with his fingertips.

"The ranch was in good hands," he thought, reaching for the DVDs Ryan left for him.

THIRTY FIVE

Ryan went to the main house the next day to give Chance the thirteen-step list after she finished with her part of the morning chores.

She let the boys finish up.

Chance was sitting at the dining table having breakfast. Carmen was at the sink washing some dishes.

"Good morning, everyone. Having breakfast, huh, Chance? Ham and eggs. Yummy."

"How about you, Miss Hollister? Would you like something to eat?" Carmen asked.

"No thanks, Carmen. I had breakfast earlier."

"Well then, Miss Hollister, how about a cup of coffee, maybe?"

"Thanks, Carmen. I'd like one."

Chance motioned for Ryan to take a chair.

Ryan fixed her coffee with the creamer on the table.

"Thanks again for what ya did for the loan. For me. For the ranch. I wasn't sure if I made my appreciation clear yesterday. Thanks, Hollister."

"It's okay, Chance. Let's concentrate on getting Midnight ready to do his part. Here's the list I'm going to use to break him. My thirteen steps."

Ryan handed Chance a printout of the thirteen steps.

Chance looked over the list. Ryan could tell he was not just hurriedly reading through it. He was intently reading each step. Some times with a serious look on his face. Other times with a smile. He did not look up until he finished reading the whole thing.

"Ya're serious 'bout this, aren't ya?"

"Yes. I am. What do you think?"

"I don't know quite what to think. This is the first time I've seen a list like this to break a horse. It's certainly thorough an' detailed, I'll say that."

"That's the way I do it, Chance. I broke all my horses that way. Using that list. It works."

"Ground drivin'? I don't have any ground drivin' harness 'round here. I've never done that."

"That's okay. That's the extra tack I said I needed. I picked it up yesterday at Jules' store."

"Tin cans hangin' on him? What's that all 'bout?"

"Well, if he can tolerate those cans hanging on him and banging on him and not be bothered by the cans or the noise, it will help take his mind off what's coming next. Me. On his back."

That brought a laugh from Chance.

"I guess so. I can see how everythin' ya have on this list might work to break a horse. Most o' the time, I just do it by trial an' error."

"Trial and error, huh? So… how many broken legs have you had in the past, Mr. McKenna?" she said, pausing, trying to hide a smile, then hurrying to apologize. "Sorry. I'm sorry. I wasn't—"

Chance could not help laughing out loud and shaking a finger at her.

"I know. I know. Tell me... what's up with the applesauce an' honey on the bit?"

Ryan explained she puts either unsweetened applesauce or honey on the bridle bit if there is a problem getting the horse to take the bit in its mouth. She would use one or the other of those treats on the bit the first couple of times she puts a bridle on him.

"I've never heard o' doin' that either, but I can see how it might work to get a horse to take the bit. I've said it before an' I'll say it again. Ya're an amazin' horse woman, Hollister. I'm impressed with this list an' all those treats. You're gonna spoil that damned horse, though. Ya know that, don't ya? I'll be watchin' ya as often as I'm able to hobble out there. I do have one more question. This last step. The one 'bout bein' bucked off. One o' us on crutches 'round here is enough."

"Well, if I get bucked off it won't be the first time I've been bucked off a horse and it probably won't be the last. The secret is getting right up and on its back to let the horse know who's in charge. Don't worry, Mr. McKenna, I'll be fine. Thanks for caring. Okay, I'm going to town to pick up some things I need. Alfredo and Juan have it under control out there. I'll be back soon."

Chance asked Carmen to bring him the DVDs from the coffee table in the family room.

Carmen put the videos on the table next to Ryan.

"I watched those videos an' I was really impressed with the way your horses ran those races. I really enjoyed watchin' 'em, Hollister. I was wonderin'... are the persons on each side o' ya in those winner's circles your parents? Your mother an' father?"

"They are. Those are mother and daddy, along with a few friends and my winning horses, of course."

"Your folks looked so proud to be there with ya. I'm sure your father misses ya on the ranch, Ryan. How could he not?"

"Thanks, Chance. I'm glad you enjoyed the videos. I'm looking forward to our winner's circle videos with Midnight. Okay. Finish your breakfast. I'll see you later."

Ryan picked up the DVDs, stood up and turned to leave.

"Wait. Come over here, Ryan."

Chance put his arms up to give her a hug. They put their arms around each other.

Chance looked into her eyes. He touched her lips with his fingertips then kissed her softly. They opened their eyes. No words were spoken. Words would have gotten in the way.

Ryan said Goodbye and went out to her truck.

Those feelings were welling up inside her again. Those overwhelming feelings she had for the man who just kissed her. The man inside the house. The man who was her boss.

THIRTY SIX

Midnight's first day in school, on the way to being broken, began in the exercise ring, on the end of a lunge line. He took to lunging right away. Ryan was careful to not overdue it. This was the first time Midnight let anyone work with him.

Ryan worked Midnight in the ring for about an hour. Midnight obeyed all her commands. Trotting, loping, galloping and changing his lead. He worked so well in the ring on the first morning, Ryan decided to take him to the paddock in the afternoon.

~~~

It was time to put a bridle on him.

At first, Midnight refused to let Ryan put the bit in his mouth, but the applesauce on the bit did the trick and soon there was no need to sweeten the bit with applesauce or honey. Ryan bridled Midnight several more times just to be sure he would tolerate it.

The first day's workout was finished.

Chance was so impressed with the way Ryan began Midnight's workouts. He got it all on video. This routine, those thirteen steps, was new to Chance McKenna. He was learning something again from his top hand.

"So, what do you think, Mr. McKenna?" Ryan asked, when she was finished for the day.

"I'm totally impressed, Hollister. Ya got him to lunge an' more than that, ya got him to take the bridle. I'm impressed. Congratulations. What's up for tomorrow?"

"Ground driving. I want to start early and work him for most of the day in the harness. Then, I'll see if he'll let me put a saddle on him. Maybe by day's end, he'll even tolerate those tin cans hanging on him."

"I can't wait for that. Well, today's work with him is all on video. Well done. I'm gonna call it a day. See ya in the mornin', Miss Hollister."

Ryan went to her cabin and thought about Midnight's first day of workouts. She was pleased with the way the day went. Ryan was more pleased she made Chance McKenna happy.

~~~

The second day's training began in early morning with Midnight working forty-five minutes on the lunge line.

It was time for the ground-driving step.

Midnight balked at first when Ryan put the harness on him, but with persistence and patience on her part and lots of apple and carrot treats, Midnight gave in.

Ryan was able to drive him around the pasture and control him with a pair of long reins while she walked behind him and called out verbal commands. Chance looked forward to the ground-driving step. He had never driven a horse using ground-driving harness. He was so proud of Ryan and the way she worked Midnight during this step.

"She knows what she's doin'."

Next, it was time to put a saddle blanket and saddle on Midnight's back.

After several tries, reaching back and throwing the saddle blanket and the saddle on the ground, Midnight tolerated them both after being given all the apples and carrots Ryan had with her.

Next, Midnight let Ryan tighten the girth strap around his belly.

That brought back memories for Chance. He glanced at his crutches propped against the fence.

Ryan put the saddle blanket and the saddle on Midnight then took them off several more times. All without incident.

Chance gave Ryan a thumbs up. She returned his smile.

Then, it was time to tie the tin cans on the saddle.

Midnight finally got used to those tin cans rattling around on him while Ryan drove him with the ground-driving harness.

By the end of the second day, Midnight was walking around his paddock, a saddle on his back and those tin cans banging on him while Ryan walked behind him, holding the reins in her hands and calling out commands to him.

It was early evening when the day ended. The sun was going down.

"All right, Chance. So far, so good. Tomorrow's the big day, though. The final test for Midnight."

"I know... an' for ya, too. Are ya ready for it?"

"Yes, I am. I think Midnight's ready. I'm so pleased with the way he progressed these first two days, Chance. In fact, he's working better than some of my horses back home. I can't wait for tomorrow."

"Neither can I. Congratulations on the ground drivin' an' puttin' a saddle on him. You're amazin', Hollister. I learned somethin' again today. I'm proud o' ya. Proud o' ya. I'll be here in the mornin' with the camera. Get a good night's sleep. G'night."

"Thank you, Chance. Good night."

THIRTY SEVEN

This was day three of Ryan's routine to break the stallion. It was the most important day.

The previous two days prepared Midnight for this one. This was the day Ryan would get on his back for the first time and attempt to ride him.

Her thirteen step plan was working.

Today was Midnight's final test before graduation.

Would he let Ryan get on his back? Would he stand still for a short time while she was just sitting in the saddle? Finally, would he let her ride him around the paddock?

~~~

"Good morning, Chance. I see you're ready to record this," Ryan said, walking to the pasture fence.

Chance turned to see Ryan carrying her workout saddle and those yellow leggings she bought for Midnight.

She was wearing a helmet instead of a Western hat.

Ryan was smiling ear to ear. She showed no fear or anxiety. She was calm. A lot more calm than Chance would be in the same situation. The crutches leaning against the fence beside him reminded Chance of his futile attempt to work with the stallion.

"G'mornin', Darlin'. Yeah. I'm ready to get it all on video. Are ya ready? How d' ya feel? Are ya sure ya wanna do this?"

"Yes. I'm sure. I feel great. I'm ready to go. I think Midnight's ready to go. At least, I'm hoping he is. Today is what the past two days were leading up to, Chance."

"I notice ya chose to wear a different hat today."

"I'm working with a horse that is—was—a wild stallion. I'm not taking any chances with him this morning."

"Good idea. I'll leave ya to it, then. I'm here if ya need me. I don't know how I could be of any assistance, in my condition, but I'm here if ya need me, nevertheless."

"You're here for that moral support I asked you for, remember? That's what I need from you today, Chance."

Ryan opened the gate and put her blanket and saddle on the ground.

She took the bridle over to Midnight. He took the bit and let Ryan put the bridle on him. She led him back to the fence in front of where Chance was standing.

She tied the reins around the fence rail.

She put the blanket and saddle on Midnight.

Even though Chance had seen Ryan working with Midnight the past two days, he was still amazed at how quiet Midnight was and how he tolerated the tack being put on him.

Ryan would begin today by getting on and off Midnight several times while keeping him standing still.

Trying to ride him around the pasture was the final step.

Ryan untied the reins from the fence rail and looked at Chance who gave her a thumbs up.

"All right. Here goes," she said.

Ryan put her left foot in the stirrup, took hold of the saddle horn with her left hand and lifted her five feet ten inch frame up and into the saddle.

Ryan held the reins in her right hand. Midnight turned his head slightly to see who was getting on his back. He stood still and didn't move. Ryan sat there holding on to the saddle horn with her left hand in case Midnight decided to make any sudden moves.

She rocked back and forth in the saddle a few times. Still no movement from Midnight, except to turn his head slightly to look back at her. After a few minutes she got off.

Ryan looked at Chance. She didn't say anything. She just gave him a thumbs up. Chance wanted to clap and cheer, but knew he had to suppress his excitement at what he just saw. Instead, he returned her thumbs up with both hands.

Ryan did this several more times. Getting on Midnight's back, then getting off. Each time the result was the same. Midnight just stood still and didn't move. When she got off the last time Ryan took some of the treats out of a sack tied on her saddle and gave them to Midnight.

"Okay, Chance. Now, it's time. Time for the big test. This is it. Put that camera on record."

"The camera's ready, Hollister. Be careful."

The result of all Ryan's work the past two days was about to be realized. This was the moment she had thought about ever since seeing Midnight for the first time in the barn. She gave Midnight one last handful of treats.

Ryan got on Midnight and took the reins in her right hand. She took hold of the saddle horn with her left hand. She made a clicking sound with her tongue. Midnight just stood still. She clicked again. No movement. He stood still. She clicked a third time. Midnight did not move. He only turned his head slightly to look back at her.

"Well, Midnight, are you gonna stand here all day? Let's go."

Ryan nudged Midnight in the belly with both knees and clicked again with her tongue.

The knees in the belly did the trick. Midnight reared, then bolted forward. Ryan leaned forward to get her balance. Midnight arched his back, jumping a foot, or so, with all four feet off the ground. He did this several times. He reared a couple of times, flailing his front legs in the air like a praying mantis. Ryan stayed with him. He bucked. He kicked his hind legs straight out. Ryan stayed with him.

She took her left hand off the saddle horn and waved it above her head the way rodeo riders do it.

"Yee ha!" she yelled.

Midnight continued to jump, rear, twist and buck. First, ahead in a straight line then, in tight circles. Rodeo style. Twisting and turning. Ryan stayed with him all the way. She continued to wave her left arm in the air.

"Yee ha! Midnight!"

Chance was speechless. He had never seen anything like it, except when watching rodeos on ESPN. He wanted to yell, too, but he knew he had to restrain himself. He had to be quiet. For now, he could only watch his top hand do her thing on the horse that put him on crutches. He was so proud of her. His video camera was recording every bit of the action.

"Stay with him, girl. Stay with him, Darlin'."

The jumping, rearing, twisting and bucking went on for several minutes longer.

Then, without any warning, Midnight decided to make an unexpected movement.

He swung his head and turned sharply. To the left. Ryan's body went the other way. To the right.

Ryan dropped the reins and landed on the ground. On her butt. She sat there, looking at Midnight. Chance thought he could hear her cussing under her breath.

When Midnight discovered his rider was no longer on his back he stood still, turned, looked at Ryan and gave a snort as if to say, 'That'll teach you to get on my back'.

"Damn. I knew this would happen," Chance said, calling out to her, "Are ya all right, Hollister? Are ya okay? Are ya hurt?"

"Only my pride, Chance. Only my pride. I'm fine. I'm good. Now, you're going to see what I meant when I said you should get right back on a horse if you're bucked off."

Chance got all that on video. Ryan being bucked off. All of it. He knew she would want to review it later.

Ryan got up and brushed herself off.

She walked over to Midnight.

Midnight put his muzzle down near Ryan's hand. She took hold of his ear. She gave it a pinch with her fingernails to get his attention.

Ryan pulled Midnight's head up.

"You're looking for treats, Midnight? After that maneuver you just pulled? Forget it. Now—look me in the eye. We're going to keep doing this until you get it right, so get used to it. Look me in the eye. That's it. You're going to let me get on your back again and we're going for a ride. Understood? If you keep fooling around, I'll have you fixed. Do you know what that means, Midnight? No mares in your future. Got it? Good! Now, let's get this done. Let's make Mr. McKenna proud."

After checking the blanket and saddle, Ryan made sure the girth strap was still tight. She took the reins and was back up on Midnight in a few seconds.

There was no tongue-clicking or coaxing this time. Instead, Ryan immediately got Midnight's attention by giving him the knees in his belly. Harder than before. Ryan kept poking him in his belly with her knees. Repeatedly. The jumping, rearing and bucking started again. More intense than before. This time, though, she was ready for Midnight's twists and turns.

Ryan called on all her experience and expertise working with bucking horses. She remembered all the advice she had received from her father.

She pulled back on the reins and stuck her knees into Midnight's belly again. Harder. He reared and arched his back. Ryan stayed with him.

With each successive twist, turn, jump and crow-hop leap, Midnight began to understand he was loosing the fight. All his clowning around slowed down. Barely off the ground now. He was almost standing still.

Ryan pulled back on the reins.

"Whoa, Midnight. Whoa. Whoa, boy."

Midnight stopped and just stood still. Ryan reached down and petted him on his neck. She let him stand quietly for a couple of minutes. Petting him. Talking softly to him.

Then, Ryan commanded Midnight to walk. She loosened the reins and clicked to him with her tongue using the same voice commands she used when teaching him to ground-drive.

"Git up," she said, clicking her tongue.

Midnight responded and walked in a large circle in the pasture. Ryan asked him to trot after a while and he responded. Then, a slow gallop. Midnight responded.

"She did it! By god, she broke that wild stallion!"

He could not contain himself any longer.

He let out a yell, a whistle and gave his top hand high fives. Ryan waved back and gave him a high five.

Her face was glowing. She knew he was pleased with what she just did. She knew she and that wild stallion had made Chance McKenna proud.

After slow galloping for a while around the pasture, Ryan slowed Midnight down and let him walk in that large circle for several minutes. First in one direction, then the other.

Chance looked on. He still did not believe what he just saw.

Ryan walked Midnight over to the fence where Chance was standing.

She got off.

She gave Midnight some treats and petted him all over. She removed her tack and the leggings and put his halter on.

She gave Midnight a pat on his flank. He galloped a short distance away and began grazing.

Ryan removed her helmet.

She looked at Chance with longing in her eyes.

She climbed over the fence and fell into his open arms. Chance pulled her close. He held her. They looked at each other. In Ryan's eyes Chance saw the desire she was feeling. She was shaking.

"Hold me, Chance. Hold me."

It wasn't fear from having just broken a horse that was causing her to shake in his arms. Ryan had broken hundreds of horses. No. It was that feeling of being in Chance McKenna's arms again. Chance pulled her closer. He could feel her heart beating. She looked up at him. Her eyes and her smile said it all.

Chance could not let that moment pass. He kissed her. Softly, then harder. She felt that same feeling she had felt when they kissed after their Dreamcatcher date. She was lost in his arms. She wanted that kiss to go on forever. Chance continued kissing her. He did not want it to end, either. The kiss continued. Finally, they ended their embrace, ever so slowly. Chance looked into her eyes. He smiled and spoke softly.

"Ya did it, Hollister. Ya broke 'im. Words can't express the pride I'm feelin' for ya at this moment. My top hand. Ya're the best. Congratulations to ya an' to Midnight for a job well done."

"Thank you, Chance. That meant so much to me."

What Ryan was thinking about, though, was that kiss she just received from Chance.

"Are ya sure ya're all right, after being bucked off? Does your butt hurt?"

"Yeah. I mean—No—Uhh... no, I'm fine, Chance. I'm good. Don't worry. Now, we've got to concentrate on training him to race. That's the next big test for him. We don't have a lot of time. I'll put tack on Midnight and ride him everyday until I'm comfortable with him, and he with me, and I know he's really ready to be ridden."

"Okay. Sounds good. I do have one question, though. Were ya talkin' to 'im after he bucked ya off? Before ya got back on 'im?"

"Yeah. I told him if he didn't behave, I'd have him fixed."

"Fixed."

"That's what I told him. I didn't have to explain it to him, Mr. McKenna. Do I have to explain it to you?"

They looked at each other and laughed heartily.

"Uhh... no, Hollister, ya don't have to explain it to me," Chance said, giving her a wink, "Take the rest o' the day off. We can talk 'bout Midnight's race trainin' later, in a day, or so. Don't worry. Well get him on the track. I'm gonna call the Hills an' tell 'em what ya did here today an' the other two days. I'm sure they'll wanna know. We can let 'em see the videos sometime so they'll know we weren't makin' it up. All three days are on the camera. We can look at it together sometime, too, if ya want."

"Thanks, Chance. I'd like to watch it with you sometime and talk about it together. Thanks for being here. I'll ask the boys to look after the chores and keep an eye on the horses and I'll ask them to put an extra scoop of grain in Midnight's bucket over there."

"I'll see ya in the mornin', Darlin'," Chance said, "an' again, my sincere congratulations."

Chance took up his crutches and headed for the house. Even though he was using crutches, Ryan noticed a lightness in his step. Almost a skip. She smiled. She and that wild stallion had pleased him. Chance McKenna had enjoyed this day.

Ryan was so happy it turned out well. She took one last look at Midnight, picked up her tack and headed for the tack room.

She was still delighting in the taste of that kiss.

~~~

When Ryan was back in her cabin she called her parents to tell them all about her success breaking Midnight. She knew her father would want to know how it went.

"Hello, mother. How are you? How's daddy? How's everything at home? I miss you."

"Hello Sweetheart. We're both fine. Everything's fine here. We miss you, too. Your father's on the other phone so we can all talk."

"Hi, Baby Girl. How's the job goin'?"

"Hello, daddy. The job's going really well. No problem running the ranch. It's really good experience for me. Chance is still on the crutches. He said I'm the best top hand he's ever had. I guess I'm qualified to be a top hand on a horse ranch now."

"I'm glad he knows a good thing when he sees it, Honey. I told ya ya'd be able to do the job," her father said.

"Mother. Daddy. Here's the reason I called—I have some really great news about Midnight. Remember I said he wasn't broke when Chance brought him home from a neighbor's ranch? Well, I broke him. I broke him. Just today. Just now. We just finished the three-day routine. Chance watched me go through my thirteen steps, daddy and I made him proud. We have videos of all three days and I'll email them to you. I'm going to put Midnight on the track. He needs to be racing."

"Honey, that's really great news. The best news a father could hear from his daughter. We wanna see the videos. I wanna hear how it went breakin' 'im an' how Mr. McKenna reacted. I knew ya could do it, Baby Girl."

"Sweetheart, that's wonderful. We're both so proud of you," her mother said.

"Thanks, mother. Thanks, daddy. You know, maybe I should tell you both what happened to Chance. The reason he's on those crutches, I mean. It's because he tried to put tack on Midnight when I wasn't around to help. Midnight kicked him and broke his leg. It was because of that accident Chance put me in charge of the ranch and told me Midnight was my responsibility. So, that's what happened to Chance. I thought you should know."

"Damn. That's too bad, Honey. About Chance, I mean. Is that horse so high strung he wouldn't let Chance touch him?" her father asked.

"No, Midnight's not high strung, daddy. The Hills, who sold Midnight to Chance, warned Chance Midnight would not tolerate being handled. Especially by a guy. I guess they thought it was Midnight's nature. Then, one day when I was in town, at Jules' store, Chance decided to try and put a saddle on Midnight, but when he tried to hook up the girth strap, Midnight decided he'd had enough so he kicked Chance. That's how the broken leg happened. Midnight just needed a certain touch and I was the one who gave it to him—thanks to you, daddy."

"Baby Girl, I'm so proud o' ya," her father said. "I'm more than proud o' ya. It sounds like Mr. McKenna is, too. Well, we hope Chance can get off those crutches soon an' the two o' ya can get down to business gettin' a racehorse on the track."

"Yes, Honey, thanks for telling us about Chance's accident," her mother said. "We were both wondering what happened. Please be careful with Midnight during his training. Tell Chance we hope his leg is well again soon."

"I will and mother, it's fine. There's no longer a problem working with Midnight. I'll make sure he'll be fine for anyone who rides him or works with him. I'll send the videos soon. Mother, daddy, I miss you and love you."

Ryan said Goodbye to her parents.

After a quick supper and a shower, Ryan went to bed.

She spent some restless moments, trying to go to sleep. Thinking about what she had accomplished with Midnight. Thinking especially how she had pleased Chance McKenna.

What Ryan Hollister was thinking about most, however, was that kiss at Midnight's pasture.

"I can't get that kiss out of my head. It was wonderful."

THIRTY EIGHT

It was Sunday afternoon. Julie was home. Ryan knew she was going to have to do some serious explaining when asking Julie to borrow candles and holders.

Julie was like a Pit Bull if the conversation showed even the slightest indication of going in the direction of discussing Ryan and her boss, Chance McKenna, as an item.

"Candles? Candle holders? What's going on, Liz? You having a dinner party? There's only one person you'd be cooking for and his initials are—Chance McKenna. Am I right?"

"I didn't say why I asked to borrow those things, or if I was having a dinner party, Jules. Maybe I have friends here in Ponderosa Pine you don't know about."

"Don't play games with me, Sweetie. So, you're cooking dinner for him. That's good. It's about time you showed Mr. McKenna some of your homemaking skills."

"Keep it up, Jules."

"Oh? It's not him? All right. Maybe you're so lonely out there in that cabin all by yourself, you've decided to have a dinner party for an imaginary friend. Like in that movie back when, with Jimmy Stewart? 'Harvey', I think it was called. Okay. Fine. I'm really worried about you, though. Mr. McKenna would love to come to your dinner party., Liz You know? You should ask him."

"Are you not listening? I didn't say who. I didn't say I was cooking anything for anybody. Slow down, Jules. You're frothing at the mouth. Maybe I'll tell you about it sometime, but not now. Do you have candles and holders I can borrow—or not?"

"Yes. I do. They'll be a gift, though. What're sisters for? You don't need to return them. How could you return half-burned candles anyway? Have a nice dinner, Liz and tell me all about it—sometime."

Julie went to a cupboard, took out two, white candle sticks still in their cellophane wrapping and two black, plastic holders.

That mischievous, impish grin was still on her face.

"Thanks, Jules and yes—I will tell you about it—sometime."

THIRTY NINE

Carmen told Ryan one of Chance McKenna's favorite meals was meatloaf, mashed potatoes and baked beans with biscuits.

Ryan picked up a couple six packs of Chance's favorite beer. She bought biscuits from Bishop's Grocery.

The meat loaf recipe was given to Ryan by her mother who got it from Ryan's grandmother.

Ryan wanted the dinner to be a surprise for Chance.

She asked Carmen to wait for a cell phone call in the afternoon when everything was ready for Chance to come to the cabin. Carmen was delighted and anxious to help with the surprise.

A table cloth was on the table. Ryan put a Country and Western CD in the music player. The candles were on the table and the table was set.

Ryan lit the candles and turned the light out in the kitchen.

Everything was ready for her very special guest.

Ryan called Carmen.

There was a knock on the cabin door.

Chance was standing there, holding his crutches, grinning like the cat that ate the canary.

"Chance. Come in."

Chance looked Ryan up and down. It was obvious he was happy to see her in the outfit he gave her.

"Hi, Darlin'. Ya wore it, an' there they are—those killer legs. Ya look beautiful."

Thanks, Chance. Please. Come in."

"It sure smells good in here, Darlin'. Ya cookin'? What're we cele-bratin'?"

"I wanted to show you how much I appreciated you being there every day when I was working with Midnight."

"This is really great. A home-cooked meal. What a treat. I'm ready for it."

They each enjoyed a beer and exchanged some lighthearted conversation while Ryan put everything on the table.

Dusk was settling over the area.

Inside the cabin the candles cast reflections that danced on the ceiling and the walls.

Ryan turned on the music player.

"Dinner's ready, Chance. Come. Sit down."

"A table cloth? Candle light? Music? Ya're totally surprisin' me, Miss Hollister. That meatloaf looks so good an' look at those baked beans. I'd say ya have at least one more hidden talent, Darlin'."

Ryan brought two cold cans of beer and poured them into their glasses.

During dinner they talked more about themselves and more about their early family lives.

Ryan could tell Chance was a lonely man on the inside. This despite his sometimes macho attitude.

He didn't have many friends, real friends, in Ponderosa Pine.

No friends outside of a few ranchers, all of whom were married and had families.

Ryan could feel his inner longing to be like them. To have someone of his own.

Someone waiting for him when he finished the chores at night. A wife and kids.

Ryan was beginning to see the real Chance McKenna.

It was time for Ryan to explain what they needed to do to begin Midnight's race training.

She opened two fresh cans of beer

"Okay, Chance, let's sit in the living room."

FORTY

C hance knew this would be an adventure for him but for Ryan it
would be just another race horse in training. One of hundreds she
had trained.

"We have to find a jockey, Chance. Do you know anyone who
would be able to give you a name? I could call the Jockey Club, I
guess. They usually keep a list of available riders."

"If you could do that, Hollister, it would prob'ly be the best way to
find someone. Guys I know 'round here mostly go the races and they
aren't that close to breeders and riders."

"Okay, I'll check with the Jockey Club. Now, for the part where
you can get involved, Chance. We need to choose our silks and colors
and get them registered with the New Mexico Racing Commission.
What do you think? What should be our colors?"

"Well, that seems like a pretty simple decision to me, Darlin'," he
said, pointing to his cast. "We should use your color for one. Yellow.

How about yellow, white an' black? Aren't there sometimes more than two colors on the jockey's silks?"

"Yeah, there can be more than two colors. That's great. I like those colors, Chance. Yellow. White. Black. You do have an eye for color. We can look online at some designs, okay? We can do it together. We're almost finished here."

Chance smiled to himself. He knew once Ryan started talking horse racing it was never finished.

"We'll need a training track here on the property. Two tracks, actually. A straight, quarter-mile, 440 yards, with a fine gravel surface. This will be for Midnight's sprinting time trials. We also need at least a one mile oval track marked off in 220 yards furlongs for his workouts. His endurance runs."

"Two tracks, huh? I'll take ya to a location 'bout a half-mile from the barn an' ya can see if that'll be okay for the tracks."

"Good. That about does it, Chance. We need to get started right away. The boys can help with some of it until your cast comes off. I'll call Tim Johnson to put shoes on Midnight and I'll ask Dr. Brown to come out and give us the OK."

"Whew! Ya sure are thorough, Miss Hollister. I suppose I shouldn't be, but once again I'm amazed at your understandin' o' horse racin'. Well, I'm ready to get started. I look forward to this. It's all new to me an' I understand there ain't a hell of a lot o' time to do all we just talked 'bout doin', but we'll get it done. Uhh—"

Chance hesitated. He directed his gaze to the floor.

"—Lopez' been buggin' me lately 'bout the loan extension date an' I'm tryin' to get him off my backside. We both know he's gettin' the payments on time with your help from that $50,000, Darlin'. I don't know what he's gripin' 'bout."

"Mr. Lopez has been calling you? It hasn't been that long since the extension was approved. What the devil does he want? Chance, I told you—please keep me informed about what the bank is telling you, okay? I need to be involved with this foreclosure thing. I need to know what's going on. Don't keep it from me. Okay? Promise? Don't keep anything about the loan from me, Chance."

"Okay. I didn't think ya needed to be gettin' upset 'bout this bank problem. I wanted ya to be able to concentrate on your job with Midnight. From now on, any word I hear from Lopez, I'll tell ya. Well, the time's gone by so fast, hasn't it? It's time I went back to the house, I guess—"

Chance hesitated momentarily, nervously fidgeting with his empty beer can.

"—unless ya want me to stay, Darlin'."

This was the moment Ryan knew she would have to face. The moment when it was time for Chance to leave.

The feelings inside her were saying, 'Ask him to stay', but she knew she couldn't give in. That persistent thought of him being her boss pushed those feelings aside again. Not only that, but she must concentrate on her job with Midnight and her plan to save the ranch.

"Chance. I'm a woman. A woman with needs, but I don't want to give in to them and spend the night with you only to wake up in the morning and realize I'd made the mistake of sleeping with the man I work for. I don't want romance to get in the way of our work relationship. I think we should keep it on that level. Especially now with all we need to do with Midnight. I hope you understand."

There was a pause before Chance answered.

"I do understand, Darlin'. Thanks for the dinner. It surely was a surprise. I'll see ya in the mornin'. We can get started on Midnight's race trainin'."

Chance set his beer can on the coffee table, put his hat on, picked up the crutches and hobbled to the door.

He opened the door and stepped outside.

Ryan walked slowly toward him.

Chance leaned his crutches against the door and took Ryan into his arms with a desire she had not felt from him before.

His mouth met hers. She gave up with a sigh. His arms felt so good wrapped around her. Soft, yet firm.

160

Then, she felt his hand on her breast. His finger tips caressed the nipple. The feeling was intense. She didn't resist. She couldn't resist.

There was a fire burning inside her. This was a brand new feeling she was experiencing with Chance McKenna. A feeling she had secretly dreamed about. She didn't want it to end.

His mouth pressed harder against hers.

In a heightened moment of passion, Ryan frantically struggled with the buttons on his shirt.

After some moments holding each other, Chance relaxed his arms.

"Chance—I'm sorry. I really do care for you, but I can't—I can't do this."

"All right then," he said, whispering in her ear, "I'm gonna say G'night. I don't know what brought this on suddenly tonight, but from now on I won't bother ya any more, Miss Hollister. Thanks again for the dinner."

Chance turned, put the crutches under his arms and started down the path to the house.

Ryan watched him walk away.

"Chance—I'll bring some of the meatloaf over tomorrow and give it to Carmen."

Chance McKenna didn't turn around. He didn't say anything.

He stopped momentarily, looked straight ahead then continued shuffling toward the house on those crutches.

"What happened just now? Am I having real feelings for him? Feelings that keep getting stronger. Did I just make sure it was never going to happen with Chance McKenna? Did I just step on any feelings he had for me? Why do romantic relationships have to be so difficult? I'll force myself to put any thought of a relationship with Chance McKenna out of my head."

Ryan made the decision at that moment to direct all her thoughts and all her efforts toward getting Midnight ready to race.

FORTY ONE

Ryan kept herself busy for a couple days following the dinner party. She needed to get started with Midnight's training. She rode Midnight for longer periods of time each day so she would not have to be concerned about running into Chance.

Chance spent his time in the main house watching TV.

~~~

It was about noon, Sunday.

Ryan just finished riding Midnight. She put him on the hot walker to cool down.

Ryan was putting her tack away when her cell phone rang.

"I was just thinking about you, Jules. When are you coming out here? We haven't talked in a few days."

"I know, Liz. Sorry. It's been one thing after another at the store. I'd like to come out today if that's okay."

"Yeah. Sure. That'll be fine. I'm really looking forward to having you finally see this place, Jules. Call me when you get to the main gate."

"Okay, Liz. See you soon."

Ryan took Midnight off the hot walker and put him in his paddock. She gave him some treats and waited for Julie's call.

Ryan was still thinking about the dinner party and how it ended. She had not seen Chance the past two days. That was how she wanted it, but she knew they would have to start working together soon. She needed to start Midnight's race training and Chance would need to be involved.

~~~

Julie was at the main gate. Ryan pressed the button on her remote control and watched Julie's van approaching in the driveway. She motioned for Julie to park along side the fence by Midnight's paddock.

"You were right, Liz. It's beautiful out here. The ponderosa pines, the smell in the air and—is that Midnight over there?" Julie asked, pointing to Midnight enjoying the grass in the pasture. "He's beautiful, but he looks like a whole lot of horse to me."

"He's my baby," Ryan said, with a grin and a nod in Midnight's direction.

"Your baby. Okay. So—talk to me, Sweetie. What's going on out here? How's the job? How did your dinner party turn out? How's Mr. McKenna?" Julie said, asking a number of questions, hoping to get an answer to at least one of them.

Julie listened to Ryan telling how she broke Midnight and how Chance was there the whole time. Julie wanted to hear more. She could see Ryan was reliving those three days and her words had nothing to do with being on Midnight's back. No. Ryan was talking only about Chance McKenna being there with her.

This was Julie's opportunity to find out all she could about the relationship between Ryan and Chance. Was it going anywhere? Julie dug deeper.

"Chance was with you when you broke Midnight? Is he still on those crutches? Are you two spending any time together? Away from the horses, I mean."

Ryan began starring into space. She was off in one of her daydream worlds again. Julie recognized this and decided to let Ryan tell her story.

"When Chance gave me that outfit, I almost lost it. It was the nicest present any man ever gave me and our date—at the Dreamcatcher? It was wonderful, Jules. You know that. I told you all about it. When Chance kissed me that night, those kisses were like no kisses I ever had."

This is good. She's going to spill it all again. Maybe something new this time.

"I went into the kitchen and when I left he kissed me. He kissed me," Ryan continued, still staring into space. "He kissed me out here. Right here. At the paddock. After I broke Midnight."

Well, at least they've been doing a lot of kissing. Is there anything more going on, I wonder?

"Chance kissed me goodnight after dinner—before he left the cabin and—he touched me."

Oh my, this is getting real interesting. I'd better bring her out of this trance.

Julie snapped her fingers in front of Ryan's face. Ryan turned to look at her.

"Wait a minute. Wait a minute, Liz. He touched you? Is this the dinner party were talking about here?"

"Yes."

"Finally. The truth. I knew it all along. Tell me—he touched you? Where did he touch you?"

Ryan came back to the full reality of the moment and realized she better not get too specific. Julie didn't need to hear all the juicy, little details.

"I mean—he moved me. Hasn't a man ever moved you, Jules?"

"Well—I guess not—but, if that's how it makes you feel, I'm certainly looking forward to it," Julie said, with that devilish grin on her face. "You know, Liz, it's obvious to me you've got the hots for this guy. Why can't you admit it?"

"I'm not having feelings for him. How many times do I have to tell you that?"

"No feelings? You just spent fifteen minutes starring into space, talking about him."

"Jules—I've told you... Midnight's race training and the foreclosure problem are first and foremost on my mind."

Julie pointed to Midnight eating grass in the paddock a short distance away.

"You broke that wild stallion over there, but you can't handle your feelings for Chance McKenna? We've been best friends since—since forever. Right? I know you, Ryan Hollister, almost better than I know myself, so I'm going to say this—you've got some real serious relationship issues when it comes to Chance McKenna, Sweetie and you need to deal with them."

"There's a ranch to run here, Jules, and it's in trouble. Okay? I do not have time for romance with Chance McKenna, or anyone else, for that matter. Besides, I've told you, I work for him. He's my boss."

Julie looked at Ryan for a few moments, thinking how was the best way to say what was on her mind without offending her friend.

"Your boss? You're trying to sell that same old excuse again, Liz? You wore that excuse out a long time ago and I'm not hearing it anymore. Why can't you admit it? You're falling in love with him."

"Stop trying to put words in my mouth, Jules. How about you? What's going on in your love life? Huh? Who's Bobby, Jules? The guy you were with that night in the Dreamcatcher. Who's he and what's going on with him? Huh?"

"Bobby—Bobby's a guy who comes into the store now and then to buy feed. He works on one of the ranches. We go out once in a while. He's just a good friend—but not that kind of friend."

"Can we please change the subject, Jules?"

Ryan did not look at Julie. She just turned away and sighed deeply.

A sideways look out of the corner of her eye told Julie she had better shut up and leave well enough alone.

"I'm sorry, Liz. I don't mean to be pushy."

"I know—but you are, Jules. You are."

"I just want you to have someone in your life to love, Liz—someone besides a horse."

"Someday—love will happen with someone, Jules. It will. But right now I can't afford to have any distractions. Romantic, or otherwise. I need to concentrate on my job. Now that you're here, help me give Midnight a bath. Park your van up there by the cabin and I'll meet you at the barn. When we're finished, I'll show you the cabin and we'll have a couple of cold ones, all right?"

"Wait a minute. You want me to do what? You're going to give that horse a bath?"

"No, Jules. We—you and I—are going to give that horse a bath."

"If I would have known I was coming out here to give a horse— that horse—a bath, I would have probably stayed home and watched the Home Shopping Channel. All right, Liz. It's been a long time since I've messed with a horse. He's not going to put me on crutches, is he?"

"No, he won't put you on crutches. I had a long talk with him about that."

"You talked to him about that. Okay. Well, then, let's do it—"

Julie looked at her friend, hesitated, then decided to say something she had been wanting to say to Ryan for some time, but always gave in to her otherwise overbearing questions and comments, even though she really meant nothing by them. She took Ryan's hand.

"—but first, one more thing, Liz—I promise not to mention you and Chance McKenna again—in the same breath."

"Jules—"

"I mean that. If the two of you are meant to be together, it'll happen. Without my interference. Without my nagging. I promise. I won't talk about him and you being involved again. I promise. I'm still here for you, though, as always. I love you, Liz."

"I love you, too, Jules. Thanks for understanding and caring."

"All right, then. I'll meet you at the barn. I'm looking forward to giving that horse over there a bath and I'm really looking forward to those refreshments when we're finished."

They both laughed and gave each other a hug.

Ryan was obviously relieved to hear Julie's promise and she knew her friend would stick by her words.

FORTY TWO

A few days passed since the dinner party. Chance realized he needed to show Ryan the location he had in mind for the training track location.

They both realized from now on they must keep their relationship strictly on a working basis. No romance. They both knew it would be difficult. They had feelings for each other, but saving the ranch was the most important task ahead of them.

It would be especially difficult for Ryan. She was aware those feelings inside her would rise up from time to time. She knew eventually she would have to deal with them.

For now, she needed to get started with Midnight's race training. The clock was ticking.

Ryan and Chance met at the barn. There were a few uncomfortable, awkward moments. They looked at each other. This was their first encounter since the dinner party.

"Mornin'," Chance said.

"Hi, Chance. Thanks for coming out. I'm excited to see the training location you have in mind."

Chance tossed the tractor keys to Ryan.

~~~

The location Chance had in mind was about a half mile from the barn.

There were ponderosa pine trees everywhere. Thick underbrush covered the ground.

Soon, they drove into a large, open space, approximately one-half mile in diameter.

"This is it," Chance said, with a sweeping wave of his hand.

"It looks perfect, Chance. I'm really excited."

"Have a look 'round. Shade would be nice, Hollister. Why don't ya park this thing over there, under that tree?"

"Sorry," she said, looking at him with a sheepish grin on her face.

Ryan moved the tractor to a shady spot under a nearby ponderosa pine tree, stopped the engine and got off.

"I won't be long."

"Take whatever time ya need."

~~~

There was enough area to allow for the long oval track and the short sprint track.

Ryan walked over a large part of the grounds. There were no fallen trees or tree trunks to worry about. It was a natural clearing. She did not find any large rocks in the area either.

Chance waited patiently on the tractor.

As he watched Ryan scouting the area Chance could not help but think about how lucky he was to have her working for him. There was no man he knew who could come close to knowing what she knew about racehorse training or horse racing. Even a couple of the locals who considered themselves to be knowledgeable when it came to

169

training racehorses would have a difficult time keeping up with her. Chance McKenna had no doubts about Ryan's ability to train Midnight.

After forty-five minutes scouting the area Ryan walked to the tractor. A big smile was on her face.

"What?" Chance asked.

"It's perfect, Chance. It's a perfect place. Not too far from the barn. Perfect. Nice and level. We'll have to find a way to clear the underbrush away for both tracks, but it looks good. I'm really excited. You know, we should have some fine gravel brought in and put down on the tracks after they're cleared. With some dirt on top. Is that possible?"

"Of course, that's possible, but it'll take a hell of a lot o' gravel, Ryan. D' ya need gravel on that one-mile oval?"

"It would be nice, but—no. For now—no. We'll just need to clear the grass off it. That's all. If we can put gravel and dirt on the 440 yard one that will be just fine. Also, can we clear a path from here to the barn? I want to be able to ride Midnight back to the barn after his workouts, as part of his cooling down."

"Yeah. We can do that. We can put gravel down on the short track when the clearin's done. This tractor has a front scoop attachment we can use. I'll have Juan do the clearin'. Ya'll need to be out here to show him what ya want done. How 'bout first thing in the mornin'?"

"Good. That's good. Let's get started right away, Chance. I wondered if this day would come. Actually starting to lay out a training area for a racehorse here on the ranch. I can't wait to get started."

"Ya know? I'm kind o' excited, too, Hollister. Trainin' a racehorse on this ranch was somethin' I never considered doin'."

At that moment there was a mutual goal they could work on together.

It would be a demanding time for both of them. There was a lot of work to be done. It would take all Ryan's will power to keep their time together on a strictly working relationship.

FORTY THREE

Six weeks had passed since the accident. It was time for Chance to keep his first appointment with Dr. Alquist.

Ryan wanted to continue with Midnight's morning workouts, but the appointment with Dr. Alquist today was more important.

Ryan was as eager for Chance to be off those crutches as he was. She had confidence in Alfredo's handling and riding ability. She asked Alfredo to continue working Midnight on the oval track while she took Chance to the clinic.

"Are you ready for your appointment with Dr. Alquist, Chance?" she said, when Chance opened the front door of the main house.

"I'm ready. Let's go."

"I'm sure you'll get a good report," she said, on the way to her truck.

"Yeah. I hope so. The leg feels good. Maybe she'll take the cast off," he said jokingly.

Nurse Higgins was waiting for them in the waiting room area when Ryan and Chance arrived.

"Nurse Higgins, this is Miss Hollister. Ryan, meet Nurse Higgins," Chance said, when they entered the front door.

The two women shook hands.

"Please, wait here, Miss Hollister," Nurse Higgins said, "This is just a routine checkup and shouldn't take long."

Nurse Higgins and Chance walked down the hall to the patient examination room.

"I see you're getting around a lot better on those crutches, Mr. McKenna."

"Thanks for remindin' me, Nurse," he said, grinning.

When they entered the examination room, Nurse Higgins took Chance's vitals.

Soon, there was a soft knock on the door and Dr. Alquist came into the room.

"Hello, Mr. McKenna. How's the leg feeling? I take it there have been none of the symptoms on the list I gave you?"

"Hi, Doctor. The leg feels fine. No symptoms. I'm just lookin' forward to the day when this cast comes off."

"Well, let's take an X-ray. Nurse Higgins will go with you to the lab."

When the X-rays were developed the film showed a nearly healed fracture. Dr. Alquist told Chance to continue as he had been doing and asked him to make an appointment in six more weeks.

"Is there any way we can speed this up, Doctor?"

"I'm afraid not. We have to let the healing process take its course. You're half way there though, Mr. McKenna."

Some more of Dr. Alquist's humor to lighten the moment.

"Do I get to have any more o' those pain pills?"

"Do you need them? I don't want you to become addicted."

"I guess not, Doctor. I was just kiddin'. They sure did the job, though."

Dr. Alquist told Chance if everything looked good in six weeks she would recommend removing the cast at that time.

They walked to the front of the Clinic where Ryan sat patiently waiting. Chance introduced them.

"Hello, Miss Hollister. I'm happy to meet you."

"I'm happy to meet you too, Doctor. You did a wonderful job on Chance's leg. We appreciate it. Carmen and I have been keeping him honest during his recovery."

"Thank you, Miss Hollister. If you ever need a physician, I'm here for you."

They said their goodbyes.

Ryan and Chance stopped at Bishop's Grocery store before returning to the ranch.

FORTY FOUR

The twelve-week appointment date with Dr. Alquist arrived. Chance asked Carmen to take him to the Clinic this time. Chance told Ryan it would be better for her to remain at the ranch and continue with Midnight's workouts. Ryan agreed and wished Chance good luck with his appointment.

X-rays showed the leg was healed well enough to allow Chance to have the cast removed and a boot put on the leg and foot. Dr. Alquist referred him to an orthopedist, Dr. Franklin, at Albuquerque General Hospital in Albuquerque.

"Don't do any aggressive horseback riding from now on, Mr. McKenna," Dr. Alquist said, jokingly.

"I won't, Doctor. Thank ya for everythin'," Chance said, laughing.

~~~

Dr. Franklin removed the cast and put a boot on the leg and foot. Dr. Franklin told Chance he would need to wear the boot for about one month when he was not in bed. Dr. Franklin told Chance he could put weight on his right leg, but he should use a cane when walking until the boot was removed.

Wearing the boot and using a cane would not be a problem. At least Chance could walk around again like a normal human being.

~~~

"I thought you probably went to the hospital when you didn't come home after a couple of hours. I'm really happy to see you're walking around without those crutches. Tell me about the visit to the hospital."

Chance told Ryan all about the visit to Dr. Alquist and the visit with Dr. Franklin at the hospital. He told her he would have to wear the boot and use a cane for about a month whenever he was walking.

"I can deal with this boot an' cane for four weeks. 'Specially after wearin' that cast an' bein' on those crutches for three months. No problem," he said, as they walked to the house, "How's everything around here, Ryan. How'd Midnight do today?"

"Alfredo was checking Midnight's time. He did really well. I'm about ready to take him to a racetrack. We can talk about that later."

Ryan helped Carmen cook supper for the three of them.

~~~

After one month wearing the boot, it was time to go back to see Dr. Franklin.

Ryan took Chance to the hospital in Albuquerque for this visit.

FORTY FIVE

It was a great day for Chance McKenna. No more cast! No more crutches! No more boot! No more cane!

"You drive, Chance," Ryan said, handing the keys to Chance.

"Wow! This is a great day, Darlin'. Leg's healed. Able to drive again. I don't know if I can handle all this excitement!" Chance exclaimed, obviously in high spirits.

They looked at each other for a few moments, then burst into much needed laughter together.

Ryan knew she would enjoy the ride home.

~~~

It was noon when Ryan and Chance arrived back in Ponderosa Pine.

Time for a lunch break.

"Let's go to the Dreamcatcher for lunch. What d' ya say, Hollister? My treat for puttin' up with my condition the past three months."

Chance gave her a big grin and a wink.

Ryan was inwardly excited. Some leisure time alone with Chance. Away from the ranch. Away from the horses.

It would not be a date. Only a quick lunch, then back to the ranch. Ryan would suppress any memories of their date. It would not be easy. Also, this would be their first real time alone since the dinner party.

"Yes. I'd like that, Chance. Sounds great. Let's celebrate the day."

When Chance pulled into the parking lot at the Dreamcatcher, he recognized a familiar pickup truck.

~~~

Ryan and Chance walked into the Dreamcatcher.

Chance gave a quick glance and waved to a couple sitting in one of the booths. He promptly put a finger to his lips signaling the couple not to say anything.

Hawkeye looked up from taking inventory of the well drinks when Chance and Ryan walked in.

"Hey, ya guys. How're y'all doin'? Haven't seen y'all for a while," Hawkeye said.

"We're doin' good, Hawkeye," Chance said.

"Nice to see you, Hawkeye. We're doing well. How are you? How's Linda?" Ryan asked.

"Linda's good. I'm good. Thanks. I see ya're off the crutches, Mac. Heard 'bout ya're accident. Ya gonna get back on that horse again?" Hawkeye said, looking at Ryan and winking.

"No, Hawkeye, I'm not. I'll let my top hand ride 'im. Ya know, Hawkeye, Ryan broke that s.o.b. an' now he's tame as a puppy, but I'm not 'bout to try an' get on 'im again," Chance said, putting his arm around Ryan.

Ryan and Chance used this as an excuse to give each other one of their special looks. Ryan felt those feelings inside her beginning to come alive.

"Learned your lesson, huh, Mac? Okay. What're ya guys gonna have? I'm guessin' ya didn't come in here to play pool."

"Ya guessed right, Hawkeye. We're just gonna have some lunch an' a couple o' beers, then back to work," Chance said.

Hawkeye took their lunch order and poured their beers.

"Bring your beer, Ryan. I have a surprise for ya," Chance said, leading the way to the couple having lunch in a booth on the far wall.

Tina and Derrik Hill were a couple in their late twenties. Both were Ponderosa Pine natives and were married after graduation from high school. They worked and saved enough to buy their property as well as some stock. Mostly horses.

They bred one of their mares, Away She Goes, to an Easy Jet stallion owned by a friend. Midnight was the result of that breeding. It was not possible for them to put Midnight on the track. They discovered his disposition prevented them from doing anything with him, so they decided to sell him to Chance with the hope Chance could do something with him.

"Ryan, I'd like ya to meet Tina an' Derrik Hill. Tina. Derrik. This is Ryan Hollister, my top hand."

"Oh, this is a surprise, Chance. Tina. Derrik. I'm so happy to finally meet both of you. Chance told me so much about you," Ryan said, extending her hand to both of them.

They all shook hands.

"Thanks, Miss Hollister," Derrik said, "Chance called to tell us you'd broke that colt. We're really anxious to hear everything ya did to break him."

"Yes, we are, Miss Hollister," Tina said, "and we think the nickname you gave him—Midnight—was perfect."

"Thanks so much and please, guys, call me Ryan. It just so happens we have a surprise for you guys," Ryan said, looking at Chance and smiling.

Chance reached into his jeans pocket and handed his cell phone to Derrik.

Derrik and Tina watched the videos of Ryan's three-day workout to break Midnight. They watched the videos twice. They also watched some of Midnight's workout sessions on the training tracks.

When Tina and Derrik finished watching the videos they offered their congratulations to Ryan for the work she had done with Midnight. They said they had hoped someone would be able to break him and put him on the racetrack.

Chance told them he will send them the videos by email. Ryan told them about her intention to get Midnight qualified to run in the All American Futurity. They couldn't believe it and wished Ryan and Chance the best of luck in that race.

"Those are amazin' videos," Derrik said,."Ya should put 'em up on YouTube. No kiddin', Ryan. They would be a lot o' help to a lot o' horse people."

"Thanks, Derrik. Maybe I will do that."

"I see he did buck ya off once," Derrik said.

"Yeah. Well, that's part of the job of breaking a horse, Derrik. That wasn't my first rodeo, so to speak," Ryan said, looking at Chance, who was grinning ear-to-ear.

That was good for a hearty laugh from all of them.

"What d' ya think o' that ground drivin', Derrik?" Chance said.

"That was awesome. I'd never seen it done. Heard o' it, though. I hope ya know what ya've got here, Mac," Derrik said, looking at Ryan and smiling.

"Don't worry. I know," Chance said, putting his arm around Ryan again and looking at her with that special look in his eyes, "an' I'm damn proud o' her."

Ryan saw the look she had seen before when they were holding each other. She wished they were alone together at that moment. She wanted a kiss from Chance McKenna.

"Ya know, that colt was tough for Tina an' me to manage, even as a weanlin'," Derrik said. "We thought it was 'cause we took 'im off his mother's tit when he was four months old."

That brought laughter from all of them.

"You did a great job with him, Ryan," Tina said.

"Well, we're happy to see ya're off those crutches, Mac. Will ya be gettin' on Midnight's back now that he's broke?" Derrik asked, winking at Ryan.

"No, Derrik, I won't. Why does everyone keep askin' me that?"

More laughter.

"Congratulations again an' good luck puttin' 'im on the track, Miss Hollister. We know ya can do it," Derrik said, turning to Ryan.

"Thanks, guys. I'd like to see his dam sometime," Ryan said.

"Anytime, Ryan," Derrik said, "Away She Goes has a much quieter disposition. You're more than welcome to come over to see her. Anytime."

"We'd love for you guys to come to Ruidoso Downs for the race," Ryan said, "The more the merrier—in the winner's circle."

They all laughed again and gave each other high fives.

"We'll let ya know if we can make it, Ryan. Thanks for askin'," Derrik said.

Chance said they should get together some time for a night out.

Ryan and Chance said Goodbye to the Hills.

It was an enjoyable lunch for Ryan and Chance.

It was a very special alone time for the two of them.

They headed back to the ranch.

FORTY SIX

Spring in Ponderosa Pine. Even though it had been only a few months since the bank approved the loan extension, that did not lessen the badgering Chance was receiving from Mr. Lopez. The telephone calls continued.

Keeping to his word, Chance kept Ryan informed. She was not happy about Mr. Lopez' hounding her and Chance, but she had a job to do and she put Mr. Lopez' badgering out of her mind. Chance was always there to comfort her.

"We need to enter Midnight in one of the local fairground races, Chance," she said, after one of his workout days. "We need to get him officially time-qualified. His time on the short track here at the ranch is not improving that much. I want to see how he does on a real track in a real race. First though, we need to find a jockey. We can't put that off any longer."

"All right. What d' we need to do?

"I was going to contact the Jockey Club, Chance, but I've got a lot of paperwork to submit to the Racing Commission. So much to do. Will you see if you can find someone who knows a jockey? I'll check on time-trial events and what local races are being run near here. We don't want to trailer Midnight all over the State. There's not time to make long trips to and from a racetrack."

"All right. I'll make some phone calls. There're a couple o' guys 'round here who follow Quarter horse racin' in the area. I'll call 'em."

Ryan spoke to the Quarter horse racing authority in the county and was informed of several Quarter horse races upcoming. A couple of them were on local fairground tracks. The fairground races would be used for Midnight's official time trials.

Chance talked to a local rancher who told him there was a jockey who was looking for a mount. His name was Hector Sanchez. He was young and had not ridden that many races. Chance and Ryan were both skeptical, but they were running out of time and needed to get Midnight qualified to race.

Ryan and Chance met with him at the ranch. Ryan made sure his license was current.

They took Hector out to Midnight's paddock.

Ryan put tack on Midnight and asked Hector to ride him around the paddock for a while. The young jockey seemed hesitant at times, almost afraid, to give voice commands to Midnight.

After a half-hour riding, Ryan told Hector that was enough.

Ryan offered him the mount for Midnight's time trials. She had him sign the contract and told him he would be informed when and where the races would be held.

"I didn't have a comfortable feeling about him, Chance. He seemed tentative and uncertain. Almost scared at times," Ryan said, after the meeting with Hector. "Let's put him on Midnight for the time trials and see if he can do the job. If he can't, I'll let him go."

"I don't know that much 'bout hirin' jockeys, but I'm with ya. I didn't feel that good 'bout him either, but what choice do we have? Like ya said, we're runnin' out o' time here."

Ryan made sure all the paperwork requirements had been taken care of to satisfy the New Mexico Racing Commission.

She and Chance went online together and selected their silks. Yellow, white and black. Midnight's head cover and saddle blanket were in the same colors and design as the jockey's silks.

"Midnight will be the most beautiful horse in the field," Ryan said, showing the things to Chance when they arrived by United Parcel.

Ryan and Chance went to Julie's store and bought matching outfits. Of course, the colors were yellow, white and black. Pale yellow Western shirts with white trim, white neckerchiefs, black slacks, matching black Western hats and black boots. They decided to wear those outfits at all Midnight's races.

Ryan ordered a new racing bridle and racing saddle for Midnight.

She also asked Julie to order some horse cookie treats from Mrs. Pastures Horse Cookies in California. The product contained, among other ingredients, oats and molasses. Ryan knew Midnight liked the taste of molasses. She added some to his grain from time to time. Midnight also liked to lick the molasses off a wooden spoon.

Chance offered full-time, permanent employment to the Gomez brothers. Both were happy and excited to be a part of operations at the ranch. They eagerly accepted employment. They had earned it and came highly recommended by Ryan.

The eldest of the brothers, Alfredo, was especially good with Midnight. Ryan had complete trust and confidence in Alfredo. She told him he would be Midnight's personal handler from now on at the ranch and at the racetrack. Feeding Midnight. Grooming him. Riding him during his workouts.

~~~

Time trials were required before Ryan could enter Midnight in several Grade One Futurity races to get him nominated to race in the Fall Classic at Ruidoso Downs.

Only five months remained before the All American Futurity.

Time was not on Ryan's side.

Chance and Ryan took Midnight to a local racetrack for his official time trials.

Hector Sanchez was retained as Midnight's mount for the first set of time trials and the second set of time trials.

Midnight's time at both time trials qualified him to run in a sanctioned race.

"I'm so happy. Midnight will be able to run in a sanctioned race. He's going to qualify to run in the Fall Classic, Chance. I just know it. I'm so excited."

"I can see that, Hollister. I'm excited, too. His time trials did go well an' Hector rode him without any problems."

"He did. We'll let Hector ride Midnight in Midnight's maiden race. That race is very important to me, Chance. Let's hope Hector can bring Midnight across the wire as the winner."

"All we can do is hope, Hollister."

Ryan did not let up on Midnight's workouts after his successful time trials. She realized she got a late start with him and decided to work him at the ranch as long as she could.

~~~

Midnight's maiden race would be a sanctioned race run at The Downs at Albuquerque Racetrack. It was a Futurity race which meant it was a qualifying race for the All American Futurity Fall Classic.

Hector showed he was capable of riding Midnight during Midnight's time trials, but Ryan still had a lingering doubt about his ability to ride Midnight in a real race. Midnight's maiden race.

Chance told Ryan he would support her, but the final decisions regarding the jockey for Midnight's races would be hers to make.

FORTY SEVEN

It was an exciting day. The day Ryan looked forward to after so many weeks of training and workouts. The day Midnight would be taken to the track where he would run his maiden race.

All Ryan's training and effort the past few months prepared him for this day. Even though she had experienced many days like this with her horses back home, this was a special day. There was so much at stake in this race.

Not just Midnight winning his maiden race, but more important, there were the bank's threats ever present in Ryan's mind. This race would prove, or disprove, her plan to save the ranch.

Chance drove his truck with Midnight in the two-horse trailer. There was a sleeper at the front of the trailer. Alfredo rode with Chance and would sleep in the trailer the two nights Midnight would be at the track.

Ryan drove her truck. She would bring Midnight's hay, grain and tack to the track. She also made sure she had a bag of his favorite treats. Mrs. Pastures Horse Cookies.

Alfredo stayed in the barn with Midnight to feed, groom, and look after him the two days before the race.

Ryan and Chance made arrangements to meet Hector at the barn area a couple of hours prior to race time on the second day.

Hector Sanchez was at the track both days. He was responsible for riding Midnight during the morning workouts and reporting any problems to Ryan.

~~~

Midnight's maiden race day. Ryan spent a restless night. However, she managed to get a few hours sleep.

After a hurried breakfast, she put on the outfit she and Chance picked out at Julie's store. She was anxious to see Chance wearing his.

Juan would remain at the ranch to look after the horses. He had a feeding and watering routine worked out and it was not too much for him to do the chores by himself for one day. He felt disappointed he wouldn't get to see Midnight's first race, but Chance told him something would be worked out for future races and Juan would be able to go along.

A knock on Ryan's door told her Chance was outside. She opened the door and drew in a breath.

"Chance. My! You look so handsome."

"Darlin', ya look stunnin' too, in that outfit."

"Thanks. I probably shouldn't bring this up, but our matching outfits reminds me of our date—at the Dreamcatcher—wearing our other matching outfits."

"Yeah, I was thinkin' the same thing back when we were tryin' 'em on at Julie's store. Ya sure look beautiful. Uhh... ya ready, Darlin'?"

"As ready as I'll ever be. This is the day we've been waiting for, Chance. My stomach's turning flip-flops. I'm really nervous. You know, I've been through so many race days at home—maiden races for my horses, I mean—but there's something different about this one."

"I know. It's my first race, but I'm feelin' a bit nervous myself. I wonder if Midnight's nervous."

"No, I don't think he is. My real concern is our jockey, Chance. I guess a lot of my nerves are about wondering how Hector's going to do on Midnight. Is he ready to ride in this race? He did okay in the time trial races, but this one's different. It's Midnight's maiden race. It's also a qualifying race for the Fall Classic. I'd be lying if I said I wasn't concerned and nervous."

"Well, we're gonna find out soon enough. Are those things for Midnight over there?"

"Yes. His head cover, saddle blanket and leggings," she said, picking them up from the couch.

"Okay. Let's go."

Chance and Ryan headed to the racetrack.

The Downs at Albuquerque Racetrack and Casino was located in the city limits of Albuquerque, New Mexico. It was a high energy venue for live horse racing, slots, table games and an upscale restaurant.

~~~

Ryan and Chance walked to the barn.

"How'd Midnight do with his feed last night and this morning, Alfredo?" Ryan asked, when they entered the barn.

"He did good, Miss Hollister. He ate everything."

"Did you exercise him last night?"

"Yes, Ma'am. He did just fine. I jogged him and galloped him like you told me to do. He felt good. No heavy breathing. I rubbed his legs down after I took him off the hot walker."

"That's great, Alfredo. Good job. Here's the saddle blanket and the tack."

"I really like the colors you and Mr. McKenna picked out, Miss Hollister. Both of you look real nice."

"Why, thank you, Alfredo. That was sweet. Mr. McKenna and I are very happy with our colors."

~~~

Chance stayed with Ryan while she put the tack on Midnight. Hector stood by and waited for Ryan to give him his riding instructions.

Chance was feeling his pride for his top hand. This was the first time he was able to see what goes on in the paddock area before a horse race.

Chance McKenna was so impressed with the way Ryan took charge.

Ryan gave Hector his riding instructions, gave him a leg up on Midnight and wished him good luck in the race.

Ryan and Chance returned to the grandstands.

FORTY EIGHT

There was a field of ten horses in the race. Midnight drew post position number seven off the rail, putting him on the far outside of the field.

Ryan and Chance were disappointed with Midnight's position, but there was nothing they could do about it.

Midnight showed no anxiety when he was loaded into the gate. Ryan had schooled him well. He walked right in and stood still with Hector Sanchez in the irons.

~~~

Moments later, the field broke from the gate.

Ryan watched the race through her binoculars.

When the field approached the finish line, Midnight was in second place.

"What in hell is he doing?" Ryan yelled, above the crowd noise, "Why'd he—"

Ryan's words were lost in the din of the crowd.

"What's the matter?" Chance asked, hearing only part of what Ryan was saying.

"C'mon. Let's go to the barn. I need to talk to him," she said, taking Chance by the arm.

They hurriedly pushed their way through the crowd in the grandstands with Ryan leading the way.

~~~

"I should never 've let Hector ride this race, Chance," Ryan said, trying to control her anger as they approached the barn.

"I know. We talked 'bout it when we hired him, remember? We had no other choice at the time, Ryan. What's wrong? What d' ya see?"

Alfredo was removing Midnight's tack and getting him ready for his cool down. Hector was waiting for Ryan and Chance.

"I watched the race with my binoculars, Hector," Ryan said, hurrying up to him, "Midnight was in full gallop at the end. Why did you pull up before reaching the finish line, Hector?"

"I don't know, Miss Hollister. I thought the horse next to me was farther back."

"You thought. Even if that horse was farther back that's no reason to pull up. You lost that race, Hector."

Ryan's voice was rising with each word.

"Midnight's maiden race. The most important race of his career. He could've won it. You lost it. Turn in—"

"Wait a minute, Ryan. Easy," Chance said, interrupting her and taking hold of her arm, trying to calm her down.

"I'll handle this, Chance. Just—back off," Ryan said, with a glaring look at Chance, pulling away from him.

"Okay. All right. Fine," Chance said, throwing up his hands. "You handle it then, Hollister. I'm goin' over to the Casino."

Chance walked away.

"Chance! Wait!"

Chance did not respond. He did not look back.

Ryan turned to Hector. Business with him was the most important issue to deal with at the moment.

"You're off Midnight, Hector. "I'll deposit your earnings for today's ride to your account. Turn in your silks."

Hector left the barn area and went to his car.

Ryan went over to Alfredo who was walking Midnight for his cool down.

"Mr. McKenna will come for you and Midnight in the morning, Alfredo. Take care of Midnight tonight."

"I'm real sorry, Ma'am. I'll look after Midnight. Don't you worry none."

~~~

Chance was not home when Ryan drove up to the cabin. He was probably still at the Casino. Going to a bar was not like him. In all the months she had worked at the ranch, Ryan knew Chance never went to bars downtown. He always kept beer in the refrigerator.

Ryan could not get the negative thoughts out of her head. She realized she should have been more considerate of Chance's feelings at the barn.

How could this day have ended so badly? All the effort and work Chance and I put into preparing Midnight for his maiden race was for nothing. In the end it came down to my choice of a rider for the race and that choice proved to be the wrong one. Hector Sanchez was not qualified to ride in that race.

Ryan began questioning her ability. Her reputation was at stake after today. Only on very rare occasions did her horses at home lose their maiden races.

Ryan was devastated and heartbroken. There was no one she could talk to or lean on at this moment. Her father's words the day she left home to come out to Ponderosa Pine drifted into and out of her head. She had let her father down. If ever she needed her father it was now.

Thoughts of what could have gone wrong ran wildly through her head.

Did she push Midnight too hard? Does he have what it takes to be a winner on the racetrack despite his bloodlines and his lineage? Ryan wondered what more she could have done to prepare him for his maiden race.

She kept whispering Chance's name. She wanted him with her more than ever at that moment.

Her thoughts were of him and their Dreamcatcher date and thoughts of him and the dinner party.

Conflicting thoughts.

The Dreamcatcher was such a wonderful memory.

The dinner party was a regretful memory that haunted her often.

Ryan regretted many times her words to Chance the night of the dinner party. Why did she push him away? She needed Chance. She wanted him to be with her now. Holding her in her bed.

She cried herself to sleep.

~~~

Ryan woke up very early after a restless night. Her head was full of a hundred thoughts.

She failed in her plan to save the ranch. She failed in her attempt to get Midnight trained to race. She failed to realize her feelings for Chance McKenna.

Ryan knew sooner or later she would have to come to terms with those failures.

For now, though, Ryan Hollister needed to be alone.

FORTY NINE

Chance McKenna had a hangover. He cleaned up and went into the kitchen where Carmen was already fixing his breakfast.

"You don't look so good, Mr. McKenna. You feeling alright?"

"Yeah. I'm fine, Carmen. Just a headache. That's all. Alfredo an' Midnight are still at the track. I'll be goin' to pick 'em up after breakfast."

"How did Midnight do, Mr. McKenna?"

"He, uhh... he lost, Carmen. Finished second."

"Oh. I'm sorry. But second is not too bad, no?" she said, as if to make it sound better.

Chance ate his breakfast hurriedly.

On the way to the barn he noticed Ryan's truck was gone. Juan was already busy with the morning chores.

"G'mornin', Juan. Miss Hollister's truck is gone. Did ya see her this mornin'?"

"Uhh... no, Mr. McKenna. I didn't see Miss Hollister."

"I'm goin' over to the track an' pick up your brother an' Midnight, Juan. Take care o' things 'round here."

"How'd Midnight do, Mr. McKenna? Did he win his first race?"

"He finished in second place."

"I'm sorry, Mr. McKenna. I know you and Miss Hollister wanted him to win his first race."

"Yeah. We did. Call if ya need me, Juan. We'll be back soon."

Chance wanted to get to the track and pick up Alfredo and Midnight. It was already mid-morning.

Obviously, Ryan was not in the cabin so why go there. He decided to call Ryan before leaving. There was no answer. Chance left a message in her mailbox.

~~~

Alfredo was waiting when Chance arrived at the barn.

"G'morning, Mr. McKenna. I already fed Midnight and walked him."

"Thanks, Alfredo. Let's get 'im loaded."

Chance hooked the trailer to the truck. They put Midnight inside along with the tack and some leftover hay and grain.

"We need to stop at the feed store on the way home," Chance said.

~~~

Julie was on the front porch arranging several roll-around clothes hangers.

It was a warm, sunny day and the clothing display on the porch would attract customers.

"Hi, Mr. McKenna. Who's that with you?"

"Uhh... this is Alfredo, Miss Scott. He and his brother 've been workin' for us on the ranch."

Alfredo came over and shook hands with Julie.

"Is that Midnight in the trailer? How'd he do yesterday, Mr. McKenna?"

"He didn't win. Came in second."

"I'm really sorry, Mr. McKenna. It was his maiden race, wasn't it? I know Ryan was hoping he would win that race."

"Thanks. Uhh... we need some feed, but first—I'm really concerned 'bout Ryan. She was really upset yesterday after the race. We had some words an' I left. Her truck wasn't at the ranch this mornin'. Have ya heard from her?"

"No, she hasn't called me, Mr. McKenna. I'm sure everything's okay, though. Maybe she's gone to the grocery store."

"Ryan never leaves the ranch without tellin' me or the boys where she's goin'. Juan stayed at the ranch yesterday an' he's not seen her this mornin'. I tried callin' her twice with no luck. Only her voice mail. I should've stayed with her at the track. I just don't—"

"Wait a minute, Mr. McKenna. Let me try."

Julie listened to Ryan's number ringing then going to the mailbox. Julie left a message.

"Don't worry, Mr. McKenna. I'm sure she's alright," Julie said, trying to offer some comfort. "I'll keep trying to reach her."

"Thanks, Miss Scott. Let's get the feed in the truck now."

~~~

Chance expected to see Ryan's truck when he pulled up to the barn. Her truck was no where in sight.

Chance and Alfredo unloaded Midnight and Alfredo put Midnight in his paddock.

Juan helped Chance put the hay and grain away.

Chance busied himself the rest of the morning with chores.

During lunch he tried to appear calm and made small talk with Carmen. There was no need to involve her.

~~~

Chance was in the tack room after lunch when the annunciator horn in the breezeway sounded. Someone was at the main gate.

A young man's face appeared on the monitor screen.

He was well-groomed and looked to be in his late twenties or early thirties.

Chance's immediate reaction was to assume the visitor had some information about Ryan.

"Can I help ya?" Chance asked, anxiously speaking into the intercom.

"Yes, Sir. I'm Mr. Morris. Rob Morris. I'm looking for Miss Ryan Hollister. I was told she might be here."

"Rob Morris? That name rings a bell. Where've I heard it?"

Chance pressed the remote control to open the gate.

~~~

Rob Morris drove up to the barn area in a late model Lexus. He stepped out of the car. He was casually dressed in slacks, a turtle neck sweater and a sport coat.

"I'm Chance McKenna. Ya're lookin' for Ryan?"

"Yes, Sir. I am. I'm out this way from Tulsa. On business. I decided to stop and see Ryan—if that's possible."

"Rob Morris, ya say?"

"Yes, Sir. Miss Hollister and I knew each other back in Tulsa."

Suddenly, Chance recalled the name. This was the 'Rob Morris' Ryan had mentioned on their date at the Dreamcatcher.

"What was Rob Morris doing here? How did he get this address?"

"Sooo—ya're the boyfriend? Ryan's not here."

Rob Morris let the question about him being the boyfriend slip by unanswered.

"I'd appreciate if you would let her know I was here, Mr. McKenna."

"I'll do that, Morris. That gate'll be open when ya get out there. G'day."

The two men stood starring at each other for a few seconds, sizing each other up as rivals who were interested in the same woman. If they had horns, like the males of many species in the wild, they would probably have been butting heads to establish their territory and make their claim for the female. Ryan Hollister.

"Thank you, Mr. McKenna. Good day to you, Sir."

Chance watched him drive away.

"Ryan told me 'bout the two o' them. What in hell was he doin' here? He never did say how he got this address."

Chance's cell phone signaled an incoming call.

"Hello. Mr. McKenna? This is Mr. Stewart calling from Ponderosa Pine Realty. How do you do, Sir?"

"Ponderosa Pine Reality?"

"Yes, Sir. We've been talking with Mr. Lopez about the loan on your property, Mr. McKenna. Mr. Lopez and I both feel the need to speak with you regarding the payments on the loan balance. It's my understanding there are payments to be made on the loan balance be-fore the extension ending date. Looking at your record of payments it appears you may be having trouble meeting those payments. If so, would you mind if I came out to the ranch to discuss an all-cash offer we've received from a buyer interested in your property an—"

"Hold on, Stewart. You're not welcome to come out here. I'm deal-ing with Lopez an' the bank, not Ponderosa Pine Realty. This is McKenna property an' it'll remain so from now on. Understood? Do not call me again, Stewart."

A few minutes later, his cell phone signaled another call. Could this finally be the call Chance was waiting for? Information about Ryan.

Chance took the phone out of his pocket.

"What d' ya want, Lopez an' why am I gettin' a call from Ponderosa Pine Realty?"

Chance McKenna's patience was wearing thin.

"Mr. McKenna. How are you? I haven't received any word from you or Miss Hollister for some time. How's it going with your race-horse?" Mr. Lopez asked, trying to calm the irritation he was hearing in Chance's voice.

"We're busy out here, Lopez an' we'll make another payment in a couple o' days. I just had a phone call from a Mr. Stewart at Ponderosa Pine Realty. Answer my question, Lopez. Why was Stewart callin' me?"

"Mr. Stewart and I've been talking abou—"

"Get this straight, Lopez—you've been receiving payments from us an' so far they've been on time. There's still a couple o' months 'til the end o' the extension period. You an' Stewart have no business hasslin' me or Miss Hollister. Ya got that?"

"Yes, Sir. I got that. Just make sure you make those remaining payments on time, or the loan will be in default and you know what comes next, Mr. McKenna. Good day, Sir."

~~~

Chance McKenna was annoyed and irritated. His concern for Ryan's whereabouts was mounting. Where was she?

The day's events put Chance in a mood best described as angry and bitter.

It was late afternoon. Ryan's truck was still gone. There had not been a call from her, or from Julie.

Something was terribly wrong.

Chance called Julie.

They spent some time discussing Ryan's departure. Both wondered if she had an accident somewhere and if not, why was she not letting one of them know? At least, why was Ryan not calling her friend, Julie?

"All right, Mr. McKenna. I'll try to reach Ryan again. If I can't, I'll call her parents."

"Wait. I don't think we should involve her parents, Miss Scott. Not yet, anyway."

"Well, maybe you're right. Okay. I'll call Ryan right now. I'll get back to you, Mr. McKenna. Try not to worry."

"Before ya go, Miss Scott, d' ya know a guy by the name o' Rob Morris?"

Julie's end of the line went silent for a few moments.

"Uhh... Rob Morris? Why do you ask, Mr. McKenna?"

"He showed up at the ranch this afternoon. Askin' to see Ryan."

"Rob came out there? Ryan used to date him, Mr. McKenna. She called it off at least a year ago, I think. Maybe more. I can't imagine why Rob Morris would come out to Ponderosa Pine."

"He mentioned somethin' 'bout it bein' a business trip."

"Well, like I said, let me see if I can reach Ryan, Mr. McKenna. I'll keep trying. Please. Try not to worry."

"Thank ya, Miss Scott. I'll be waitin' to hear from ya."

FIFTY

A flashing, neon sign up ahead signaled a vacancy at a roadside motel. It was a welcome sight.

Ryan had been driving since early morning.

She turned into the parking lot and parked in front of the rental office. She sat in her truck for a few minutes.

Should she get a room for the night or turn around and try to make the drive back to the ranch?

Her nodding head and drooping eyelids answered that question.

~~~

Before lying down for the night's sleep she so desperately needed, Ryan sat on the bed in the motel room for the better part of an hour thinking seriously about why she had ended up here.

She learned from her father early on never to give up on what she started.

Her father's parting words when she left home haunted her now.

'Just give it a hundred percent like ya always do.'

"I'm not a quitter. I can't give up. It wasn't Midnight's fault he lost his maiden race. It was my fault. I should have realized I needed to find another jockey for that race and maybe, just maybe, Midnight needed more workout time."

Ryan realized most of all she owed it to her father to not give up.

She realized she owed it to Chance McKenna.

She needed to finish the job she started with Midnight. The ranch had to be saved. That was the goal from the start. That was the plan.

It was time to let someone know where she was.

Ryan turned her cell phone on.

Her mailbox was full.

~~~

It was early evening. Julie was trying to busy herself at the store for a few hours longer rather than sitting at home worrying about her friend.

Ryan was on Julie's mind. She wondered why Ryan did what she did. Leaving the ranch. Telling no one. That behavior was unlike anything Ryan ever did in the past.

Julie's cell phone rang.

"Liz! What the heck is going on? Are you alright?"

"I'm okay, Jules. I'm—I'm in a motel."

"A motel? What the heck are you doing in a motel, Liz? Where are you?"

"Uhh... just across the Texas line, I think."

"What? You're in Texas? What are you doing in Texas, Liz? What's going on?"

"How's Chance? Have you talked to him?"

"Yes, I've talked to him. He's worried sick, Liz. He's been trying to call you. Both of us have been leaving messages. What the devil were you thinking?"

"I don't know, Jules. I don't know. I just had to get away for some time alone. Midnight lost his maiden race."

"I know. Chance told me. Don't blame yourself, Liz. Some of your horses have lost their maiden races before, haven't they? Don't blame yourself."

"I should've tried to find a different jockey. Is Chance pissed, you think?"

"Well, I don't know if he's pissed. He's terribly worried, though. We both are. You need to get back here and make it right with him."

"I'll leave tomorrow, Jules. Tell Chance I'll call him in the morning and—don't say a word about where I am. Okay?"

"I won't, Liz. I won't say anything, but there's something else you need to know before you hang up—"

Julie hesitated for a moment.

"—Rob came out to the ranch today."

There was a very long pause on Ryan's end of the phone.

"Liz? You there? Hello."

"Rob—came to the ranch?" Ryan asked, her voice barely audible.

"Yeah. He did. Chance asked me if I knew him. You and Chance can talk about that. I don't want to get in the middle of it. That is strictly between the two of you. Just get your butt back here, Liz and be sure to call Chance in the morning. Do you hear me?"

"Yeah, Jules. I will."

"Love you."

"Love you, too, Jules. Bye."

Ryan undressed and went to bed.

Sleep came quickly.

FIFTY ONE

Chance was becoming more alarmed with each passing hour. He helped Alfredo and Juan with the morning chores.

His cell phone rang.

It was Ryan.

Neither one said a word. It was a waiting game to see who would speak first. Chance decided it was Ryan's dime.

He waited for her to say something.

Ryan spoke. There was a slight quiver in her voice.

"Chance?"

"What're ya up to, Hollister—an' ya'd better come up with a good answer?"

"I uhh... I just needed some time to—to clear my head, Chance. Time to make a decision about what to do—what to do about Midnight, I mean."

"Clear your head? What the hell does that mean? I've never had a hired hand up an' walk out before without a word—the way ya did. D' ya wanna keep your job here, or not?"

Ryan wanted to hold off answering any questions until she was face-to-face with Chance McKenna. No sense getting into an argument over the phone.

"Yes, Chance. I want to keep my job. I'll explain everything when I get back."

"When'll that be?"

"I'll be back tomorrow morning."

"You'd better be. We have some serious issues to talk about."

Chance hung up abruptly.

Ryan could only guess his state of mind and what Chance meant when he said 'serious issues'. Were the issues about her leaving or could they also be about Rob Morris?

Ryan called her mother.

"Hello, Sweetheart. How are you? Your father's outside."

"That's okay, mother. I'm fine. I really wanted to talk to you. Rob came to the ranch. I wasn't home. He talked tao Chance. How did Rob get the address, mother?"

"Honey, I'm so sorry. He got the address from me. He kept—"

"You gave it to him, mother? Why?"

"I know I shouldn't have, Ryan, but he continued badgering me for it. He said he had business out that way and wanted to see you. Honey, I know it was a mistake giving your address to him. You said Mr. McKenna talked to him?"

"Yes."

"I'm sorry. Was there a problem between you and Mr. McKenna over it?"

Ryan did not want to complicate the situation by telling her mother she left the ranch.

"No. No problem, mother. It's fine. I think Chance took care of it. Well, I have to go, mother. Tell daddy 'Hello' for me. I miss you and love you both. Goodbye."

"We love you and miss you, too, Sweetheart. Goodbye."

Now, along with trying to explain her reason for leaving the ranch, Ryan would also have to explain Rob Morris' arrival at the ranch to Chance McKenna.

She tried watching a few hours on TV before having something to eat at the 24-hour diner next to the motel.

Ryan asked the front desk for a three-thirty a.m. wake up call. She would try to get five hours sleep. Not much, but if she left at that time of the morning she should be back at the ranch by mid-day.

~~~

The call from the desk woke Ryan at three-thirty the following morning.

She showered and gathered what few items she had brought with her.

The diner next door was packed with early morning travelers.

A vending machine in the motel lobby provided breakfast in the form of a cup of coffee, a cold meat sandwich and a couple bags of snacks.

Ryan checked out of the motel.

She was on her way back to Ponderosa Pine.

~~~

It was morning on the third day of Ryan's departure from the ranch.

Chance was expecting Ryan to be back before noon. He had no idea where she was when she called last night so he had no idea how long it would take her to get back to the ranch. He thought he should have asked her where she was.

He decided to wait for her in the cabin.

Chance read the note Ryan taped to the outside of the cabin door.

Chance, I'm sorry

He tried the door.

"Why would she leave the door unlocked?"

There was nothing out of place in the living room or the kitchen to suggest Ryan had ever left the cabin.

Even though a feeling of embarrassment came over him, Chance went into the bedroom.

Nothing appeared to be out of place there, either.

The yellow rose he gave her on the night of their Dreamcatcher date was pressed between two sheets of saran wrap on top of the dresser. The bed was made. He opened the closet doors to check for missing clothes.

The outfit he gave her was on hangers.

It brought back memories of their Dreamcatcher date. Memories of a time when he enjoyed the happiest, most enjoyable, moments he had ever spent with a woman.

"How'd our relationship get from that time to this time?"

Chance went back to the living room and sat down on the couch.

"Looks like she never planned on takin' off for good."

His thoughts were confused.

"Why'd she decide to leave? What was the real reason? Why'd Rob Morris come to the ranch?"

The sound of Ryan's truck interrupted his muddled thoughts.

~~~

Ryan walked slowly to the open door of the cabin and knocked softly.

"Chance?"

Chance stood up from the couch and turned to face her.

They stood looking at each other in silence for several awkward moments.

"I'm sorry, Chance. I—"

"Damn, Hollister. Sorry won't cut it. Ya scared the livin' hell out o' me! Ya've been gone for three days. No word. Nothin'. I didn't know if ya were gone for good, or—if ya were lyin' in a ditch somewhere. Where'd ya go?"

The genuine concern in his voice told Ryan she had to make this right with him.

She motioned to the couch, "Let's sit down and I'll explain everything, Chance."

"Don't ever leave again, Hollister—or, if ya do, just keep on goin'. Don't put me through this again."

At first the words came with some difficulty, but Ryan's confidence in herself and what she needed to do to finish the job she started with Midnight took over.

Ryan had spent the better part of the drive from the motel thinking about this meeting with Chance McKenna and what it was she wanted to say.

"It wasn't about you, Chance. Or the job. It was about me. I'd put so much time and effort into training Midnight and I was devastated when he lost his maiden race. Heartbroken. It was all my fault. From hiring the wrong jockey to realizing later Midnight wasn't ready yet to run that race. He wasn't fully ready."

"Ya spent a hell of a lot o' time with that horse, Hollister. If he wasn't ready to run that race why didn't ya say so?"

"I don't know, Chance. I don't know."

Chance looked at her and just shook his head.

"Where's that ambition, that drive, that desire ya showed me when ya came askin' for the job? That attitude was one o' the main reasons I hired ya, Hollister. Are ya givin' up on this job?"

"No. I'm not giving up. I have a fifty thousand dollar investment in this job, in this ranch and in Midnight, Mr. McKenna. Don't forget that."

"How can I forget it? I didn't ask ya for that fifty thousand dollars, Hollister. Don't guilt-trip me."

The level of their voices was rising. The words between them were becoming more heated. This was what Ryan hoped would not happen.

She decided her soft-spoken words would not get her through the rest of the conversation with Chance McKenna.

"You're right, you didn't ask me for the money, Mr. McKenna, but where would you be right now if I hadn't put it on the loan? The fact is, I'm invested in this plan to save your bacon, as well as my job and I'll see it through to the end. That means continuing work with Midnight and giving him the training I should've given him before sending him out to run his maiden and yes, it means finding a rider who is qualified to ride him. That's what I have invested here, Mr. McKenna and I will finish the job. If you prefer, I'll leave when I've finished the job and I'll go back to Tulsa."

Ryan waited for Chance to reply to what she just said. He seemed more than taken aback by her suggestion to go back home. Would he show her some forgiveness for having left?

"Suit yourself, Hollister. If ya wanna leave when your job with that horse is finished, that's up to you. But finish the job first, then ya can go back to your boyfriend."

Chance stood up from the couch and went to the door. Ryan followed him.

So, just as Ryan thought. The other 'serious issue' on Chance McKenna's mind was Rob Morris. Ryan knew that whatever else was bothering Chance, she had to make it clear to him Rob Morris was not part of her suggestion to go back to Tulsa.

"I heard Rob came out here. Let's be clear about this once and for all, Mr. McKenna. I don't know why he came to the ranch and I could care less. I do know he badgered my mother until she gave in and gave him this address, but I told you before—there is no relationship between Rob Morris and me. It's over. Do you understand that, Mr. McKenna? It's over!" Ryan exclaimed, trying hard to control the level of her voice.

More deafening silence between them.

"What're ya gonna do to get Midnight ready to run more races—an' win, Hollister?"

"I have a plan to work Midnight's hind end a bit more. I think that's the main reason he gave up at the end of his maiden race. He just didn't have the muscle power he needed in his back end to finish, and win, that race."

"Well, do whatever ya need to do with him. Get him winnin' some races so I can get Lopez off my ass."

"Lopez has been calling?'

"Just finish the job with Midnight, Hollister! Finish it!" Chance said loudly, on his way out the door.

That was the end of the conversation between them.

The past hour was a blur. The past three days were a blur.

Ryan felt an empty feeling in the pit of her stomach.

Beneath all the emotional turmoil of the conversation just now with Chance McKenna, Ryan realized those feelings for him were still lingering inside her.

"I wanted us to feel our arms around each other. I wanted us to comfort each other. I wanted us to tell each other it would be all right. It can't end this way, but I have a job to do and that job comes first."

FIFTY TWO

The day following her return to the ranch began with Ryan going to Midnight's pasture to check on him.

Midnight greeted Ryan with the whinny she had become accustomed to expecting from him. She climbed over the fence and walked to where Midnight was standing. She had some of his favorite treats in her hand. Carrots and a couple of his very favorite snacks. Mrs. Pastures Horse Cookies. By now, Midnight knew Ryan always had special treats for him.

"Hello, Midnight. Hello, boy. I've missed you," she said, softly, giving him the treats and petting him.

Midnight stood still, letting Ryan check all four of his legs.

"Hello, Miss Hollister. Welcome home. Are you all right? Everyone was really worried. Midnight's doing just fine," Alfredo said, walking up to Ryan.

"Hi, Alfredo. I'm fine. Have you been riding him?"

"Yes, Ma'am. I've been exercising him every morning and looking after his feed."

"He looks great. How's Juan? I haven't seen him yet."

"Juan's fine, Miss Hollister. I think he's out behind the barn."

"I've been thinking a lot the past several days about why Midnight had a rough outing at his maiden race," Ryan said, as they walked back to the fence. "He needed more time to strengthen his hind end, Alfredo. I think he ran out of steam at the end of the sprint."

"What more can we do, Miss Hollister?"

Ryan had her back to him and didn't see Chance approaching the pasture.

"G'mornin', y'all."

Ryan turned around. She faced Chance. The tone of Chance's voice was matter of fact and not directed to either Alfredo or Ryan, as if it was just a polite, general, first greeting of the day spoken to anyone within hearing distance.

Ryan forced a smile, turned away from Chance and looked at Midnight.

"Good morning, Mr. McKenna," Alfredo said, then he turned to Ryan, "I'm going back to the barn and help Juan with the morning chores, Miss Hollister."

"Thanks, Alfredo. Good job. Talk to you later."

Ryan turned to face Chance. She spoke in a strictly business-like monotone. Emotionless. There was not going to be any small talk between her and Chance McKenna.

"I need to spend more time working on Midnight's back end. I have an idea. Is there a small rise or knoll somewhere near the training track location?"

"What d' ya mean? A rise. A knoll."

"Like the one behind the house only a lot smaller. Not as high and not as steep as that one."

"There's a medium-sized hill with a fairly gentle slope not too far away from the track. Ya can take a look at it. What d' ya have in mind?"

"If it's not too steep, I'll gallop Midnight from the bottom to the top several times every morning before his workouts on the oval track. I had an area similar to that at home. It helped my horses a lot. I'm anxious to try it with him. I'm sure it's what he needs."

"Ya're sure 'bout that, Hollister? If it's somethin' ya did with ya're horses at home, why didn't ya try it on Midnight before puttin' him in his maiden race?"

Ryan did not answer the question. She turned away and continued looking at Midnight.

"If there's an area like that, here on the ranch, I want to see it, Mr. McKenna. Let's have a look—we don't have the time to stand around arguing about it. Let's go."

"I didn't realize we were arguin', Hollister. Wait here. I'll get the truck."

~~~

The short trip was made in silence. Ryan stared out her passenger side window.

Chance stopped the truck near the oval track and pointed to a slight rise in the ground about a half-mile away.

"I think the ground between here an' there is okay to drive over. I'll get ya a bit closer."

The knoll area was perfect for what Ryan had in mind. Exactly what she wanted, in fact. It was similar to the area she had at home. Not too steep and not too high.

After suffering the terrible depression she felt after Midnight lost his maiden race, Ryan was once more experiencing the feelings she had when first beginning his training several months ago. This time she had complete confidence in herself and in Midnight.

For once, Ryan's thoughts were not of Chance McKenna. Her thoughts were of Midnight and winning the All American Futurity.

~~~

Ryan worked Midnight on that slope each day before his workouts on the one-mile oval track.

Ryan called Dr. Brown and asked him if she could increase the protein added to Midnight's grain. Dr. Brown gave his okay and asked Ryan to check Midnight for muscle cramps during his workouts.

The results were beginning to show. Midnight was gaining strength in his hind quarters. Ryan could feel it when she was on his back. Midnight labored slightly at first, galloping up that slope, but after a week of daily exercises he showed signs of increased stamina and strength in his hind legs. It also showed when Ryan galloped him around the one-mile oval. Midnight's speed was increasing. Ryan could not have been more pleased.

Ryan decided to conduct these workouts by herself. She knew Alfredo wanted to be riding Midnight, but this was an important workout regimen and it needed a seasoned rider and trainer to be on Midnight's back.

Alfredo understood. He accepted the responsibility of minding the stopwatch during Midnight's oval track workouts and his sprint workouts.

Chance was not at these workouts everyday, but when he did come, he acknowledged to himself Ryan had the right idea to get Midnight ready for the big race. Chance could see the difference in the horse's speed and his gait.

Dr. Brown came out to the ranch and pronounced Midnight fit to race. Ryan called Tim Johnson to trim Midnight's feet and put new shoes on him.

~~~

It was time to find a jockey who had experience and time riding in and winning, Quarter horse races.

Ryan took it upon herself to search for a rider. She didn't want Chance to be involved this time in case it didn't work out. She didn't want to spend any more one-on-one time with Chance McKenna than she had to. Not yet.

Ryan contacted the local Quarter Horse Jockey Club. She was introduced to a jockey currently without a mount. He came highly recommended by owners and trainers who knew him. He had a winning record on several horses and was available to ride. His name was Roberto Vasquez. He was in his late twenties.

Roberto made a favorable impression on Ryan when they met at the Jockey Club. She told Roberto about Midnight's maiden race loss. She told him she knew Midnight was more than capable of winning any race he ran.

Ryan showed Roberto some photos of Midnight and also a video Chance had made of his workouts on the oval track. Roberto said he was anxious to try out as Midnight's mount.

Ryan asked Roberto to come to the ranch and meet with her and Chance.

"Is he the one this time, Hollister?" Chance asked, when hearing about Roberto.

"You can judge for yourself after we meet with him, Mr. McKenna."

FIFTY THREE

Ryan gave Midnight a bath and put him in his paddock. She wanted him to look his best. She stayed with him to make sure he didn't lie down and roll like horses want to do after they have been washed.

Her cell phone rang.

It was Roberto calling from the main gate.

Ryan waited for Roberto outside the barn.

"Good morning, Roberto," she said, when he stepped out of his car.

"Good morning, Miss Hollister. Happy to see you again. Real nice place here."

"Yes. It is. Thanks for coming out. Let's go meet Mr. McKenna."

Chance answered the front door.

Ryan introduced him to Roberto.

The three of them walked out to Midnight's paddock.

On the way, Ryan talked about the future plans for Midnight's racing career including getting him qualified to run in the All American

Futurity. Roberto said he had always wanted a chance to ride in and win, that race.

"Wow!" Roberto said, when they reached Midnight's pasture.

"Beautiful, isn't he?" Ryan said.

"He sure is, Ma'am. Is it possible for me to ride him? Now?"

"That's exactly what Mr. McKenna and I had in mind, Roberto," she said, including Chance in her response. "You can ride in the truck with Mr. McKenna. I'll ride Midnight over to the training area."

Chance chatted with Roberto while they waited for Ryan to bring Midnight to the barn area. She put her workout saddle on him. Ryan told Roberto he could use her saddle.

Chance and Roberto followed Ryan and Midnight.

Roberto's jaw dropped again when he saw the training area.

"You've got your own track, Mr. McKenna."

"Yeah, we do, Roberto."

Ryan got down off Midnight and stood beside him.

Chance explained to Roberto the training area had been adequate until now, but there was more he and Ryan wanted to do to it.

Ryan's gaze was intently on Chance when he mentioned the intentions he and she had for the training area. It sounded like he was about to be as involved as he was in the past.

Ryan smiled at Chance.

Chance returned her smile.

That was the first time they looked into each others eyes since Ryan returned to the ranch.

The look caused a weak feeling in Ryan's knees. She quickly pushed it aside.

~~~

Ryan and Chance watched for an hour as Roberto took charge and showed he had just what it took to command Midnight to do what he wanted Midnight to do. Walking. Trotting. Galloping.

Ryan could no longer contain her enthusiasm.

216

At one point, as Roberto and Midnight were rounding the home turn on the oval track, she let out a shriek and took hold of Chance's arm.

"My god! He's great in the saddle, Chance. I'm so happy."

"I get that, Hollister. I'm still learnin' this racehorse business, but I think ya made the right decision this time. I think we can get this job done. I approve your use of the exercise knoll and your choice of a jockey."

Was Chance McKenna showing signs of mellowing after the words they had the day of her return to the ranch? Was he ready to work with Ryan again during her effort to get Midnight and a new jockey ready for the big race?

Ryan was still not able to completely forget the words they had the day she returned to the ranch. Not that she was one who carried a grudge, but she made a commitment to herself that day and she intended to keep it.

Ryan decided to take it slow this time.

"Chance—we'll get it done. Midnight will run his race at Ruidoso Downs—and he'll win—with Roberto on his back."

"I believe ya, Hollister."

Roberto's workout session ended with Ryan letting Roberto ride Midnight back to the barn.

Ryan and Chance followed in the truck.

There was conversation between them this time. Conversation about the morning so far and especially about what was going to happen soon with Roberto riding Midnight.

Ryan removed her workout tack. She put Midnight on the hot walker for his cool down.

Ryan introduced Roberto to Alfredo and Juan. She asked the boys to put Midnight back in his paddock after his cool down.

While the three boys were chatting, Ryan walked over to Chance.

"Let's ask Roberto to join us for lunch, Chance. All right? Would you ask him?"

"Yeah. Good idea."

Ryan motioned Roberto to join her and Chance.

"Roberto, Miss Hollister and I would like you to have lunch with us."

"Thanks, Mr. McKenna. Ma'am. I'd like that. Thanks," Roberto said, smiling from ear-to-ear.

Roberto said Goodbye to Alfredo and Juan.

~~~

Ryan, Chance and Roberto sat down at the kitchen table. They talked about the morning while Carmen fixed sandwiches and drinks.

The three of them discussed at length Roberto's riding experience and his winning races. Ryan took the lead in the conversation. She would make sure Chance was included in all her decisions. Chance was showing a renewed interest in Midnight's performance after his workouts on the knoll and after seeing Roberto riding him just now.

"You looked real good in the irons this morning, Roberto," Ryan said, "It was obvious you and Midnight were working as a team. Both Mr. McKenna and I were very impressed with the way you handled Midnight. So, here's the plan. We want to get Midnight ready to run in the Fall Classic at Ruidoso Downs. The Futurity."

Roberto was smiling and rocking in his chair, anticipating what coming next.

"That means Midnight needs to win some qualifying races before then. Mr. McKenna and I would like you to be Midnight's mount for all his races. Are you interested, Roberto?"

"I sure am. I'm ready to ride him. I'll bring him across the wire in every race he runs from now on. He's a winner. I can tell. Midnight and I won't let you down."

Ryan and Chance looked at each other with big smiles on their faces.

Ryan offered Roberto the contract. He looked it over then eagerly signed it, remarking again his confidence in himself and Midnight, saying together they would be a winning team.

Ryan and Chance walked Roberto to his car.

Ryan told Roberto she would be in touch with him regarding a schedule of qualifying races.

"Well, Mr. McKenna. What do you think?" Ryan asked, as they watched Roberto's car heading toward the main gate.

"What d' I think? I think he'll get the job done. You're right, Hollister. He looked damn good on Midnight."

"Chance, I wish he would've—"

"Enough, Hollister. Enough. I know what you're thinkin'. That race was in the past. Just forget 'bout it an' let's move on. This time'll be different. We've got the horse. We've got the jockey. We're gonna win this thing."

"All right, Chance. Thanks for your support today," she said, hearing the sincerity in his voice.

Ryan tried not to show Chance McKenna the longing in her eyes. A reflection of the desire she was feeling inside.

Chance returned to the house.

On the way to the cabin, Ryan thought, "The weeks ahead will be difficult, but I must stay focused."

FIFTY FOUR

Summer was turning into Fall. Roberto came to the ranch every day to work with Midnight.

Ryan and Chance were both excited about what was becoming a habit with Midnight.

After Ryan worked on getting Midnight's back end in shape on that knoll and after Roberto started riding him, Midnight began finishing first in all his local races.

Midnight was winning those races by a half length to three quarters length over the horses in second place.

A couple of the races were futurity races which qualified Midnight to run in time trial races ahead of the Fall Classic.

Ryan was overjoyed. It was all coming together.

Chance was beginning to express his attention toward Ryan in ways he had done in the past. She accepted this attention, but for now she did not want to encourage him by acknowledging those moments.

It was extremely difficult for her, but Ryan reminded herself of her commitment to the job in front of her. She realized she must focus now more than ever on the Fall Classic.

Once again, Ryan decided she must put her feelings for Chance McKenna out of her thoughts. At least until after Midnight's race at Ruidoso Downs.

A large portion of the loan balance was paid off using some of Midnight's winnings at the local racetracks, but not all of it.

It was the end of August already and Mr. Lopez was becoming increasingly antagonistic regarding the remainder of the payments due, even though he was receiving all the payments due until now. He continually reminded Chance the eight months extension date on the loan was fast approaching and warned Chance the foreclosure would be reinstated if the deadline was not met.

Chance kept Ryan informed of all the conversations with Mr. Lopez as she requested.

"I'm dealin' with Lopez. He's gettin' pay offs on the loan continually as a result o' Midnight's earnings, as ya know. I'm in this battle with ya, Hollister. Fightin' it along with ya. We'll win this thing in spite o' Mr. Lopez an' his bank."

"Thanks, Chance. I know we will. You, I, Midnight and Roberto will win this thing. The ranch will be saved, Mr. McKenna."

Chance looked at Ryan and spoke her name the way he had done so often in the past. Softly. Almost a whisper.

"Ryan... I—"

Ryan saw in Chance's eyes and heard in his voice at that moment all the desire she had seen and heard so many times before. Those feelings inside her were bubbling up to the surface again. Like a volcano about to erupt.

"Chance... we—"

"I know, Darlin'. I know."

FIFTY FIVE

August. The All American Futurity was just a couple of weeks away. Midnight clinched his spot in the Fall Classic when he won two sanctioned races at The Downs at Albuquerque Racetrack. The same racetrack where he lost his maiden race.

How the tables had turned for Midnight in just a couple of months. Thanks to Ryan's extended training routine and Roberto's outstanding riding skills.

Midnight was ready. Roberto was ready. Ryan and Chance were ready. Excitement was building for all of them.

Chance's changed attitude toward Ryan was becoming more affectionate with each passing day. Ryan accepted this attention from Chance. She looked forward to it. She knew, however, she must keep her thoughts on the big race. It was almost here. After that, Ryan realized she would need to deal with her feelings for Chance McKenna. Feelings that were becoming stronger and more intense.

On this day, after doing the morning chores together, Ryan approached Chance.

"Chance, I want my parents to come out for the race. I want them to meet you."

"That's a great idea, Darlin'. Fine by me. I was gonna suggest ya call 'em. I'd like to meet 'em. In fact, they could stay in the guest room."

"Are you sure?"

"Yeah. That room's never used. Carmen keeps it clean. Ya can offer it to 'em when ya call 'em. Yeah. Good idea, Darlin'."

~~~

Ryan called her parents that evening after supper. This would be the first time she called home since talking with her mother about Rob Morris coming to the ranch.

"Mother? How are you? How's daddy?"

"Sweetheart. It's so good to hear your voice. It's been awhile. We're fine here. Everything's good. I'll let you talk to your father in a minute. He's outside right now—Brian, come in, it's Ryan on the phone—"

"Be right there, Elizabeth."

"—So, how's it going, Honey?" her mother continued. "We were becoming a bit worried. Not hearing from you. Your father said you were probably busy with Midnight."

"I'm sorry, mother. I'm fine. I'm okay. Chance is fine. We've been so busy. I have some really great news. A surprise, actually. I'll wait until daddy is on the line to tell you. Everything's good here, mother. Chance and I are getting ready to sell some of the yearlings at the yearling sale. The weather's turning. We're a bit higher up here so it starts getting cooler sooner."

"I'm happy to hear about the sales. Are you going or is Mr. McKenna going by himself? Oh—and how's Julie?"

"Jules is fine, mother. Umm—I'm not going to the yearling sales. In fact, neither is Chance. We're letting two of the hands go in our place. We trust them and they'll have all the information they need from me. Chance and I are very busy getting everything ready for the surprise I men—"

"Hey, Baby Girl. How're ya doin'?" her father interrupted. "Really good to hear your voice. We haven't talked for awhile. How are ya? How's that race horse doin'?"

"Hi, daddy. I was telling mother, we're all good out here. Midnight's just fine, daddy. He's doin' great. He's been winning some local races and he won a couple of sanctioned races that qualified him to run in the—are you guys sitting down?—the Fall Classic. Midnight ran in this year's All American Futurity trials and he's qualified to run in the Futurity. Chance and I took him down to Ruidoso a couple of days ago. We left him down there. He's going to run in the Fall Classic, you guys."

There were some moments of silence on the line.

"Hello. Mother? Daddy? Are you there?"

"Baby Girl, are ya kiddin' me?" her father said. "Ya got that horse trained an' qualified to run at Ruidoso Downs? By god—ya're our daughter an' we're so proud o' ya, Honey."

"Yes, we are, Sweetheart. What a surprise. Such good news. Please tell us more if you can," her mother said.

"Well, there's not too much more to tell. I did make a very bad choice of jockey for Midnight's maiden race. He lost that race. Came in second by a head. I let that jockey go and was able to find one who was older and more experienced riding Quarter horses. I accept full responsibility for Midnight's maiden race loss, including not enough preparation and training, but that's in the past and this new jockey is great with Midnight. Midnight has the heart to run. He loves to run."

"I know it's what ya want every time one o' your horses runs," her father said. "Winnin' its maiden race, I mean, but sometimes they don't win their maiden. Right? So, just forget that race, Honey an' concentrate on the next one. It's great Midnight's been winnin' his races an' I'm glad ya found a qualified jockey. That's wonderful news."

"Yes, daddy. We're all so excited and here's the other part of the surprise I wanted to tell you guys. Chance and I want to know if you can get away for a few days. We want you to come out for the race at Ruidoso. Can you do that? Can you come out? We really want you to come. Chance wants to meet you. Jules wants to see you, too. You can visit her store. What do you think? Can you come out? I really miss you guys."

"We miss ya, too. That would be great. I'm sure we can arrange to get out there. I hired a couple o' hands—like ya an' I talked 'bout that time, Honey—remember? They can take care o' this place," her father said, with a chuckle.

"Yes, daddy. I remember our conversation about my replacements," Ryan said, laughing.

"Great news, Honey. What d' ya say, Elizabeth? Ya wanna go?"

"Of course I want to go, Brian. We'll come out, Sweetheart. We'll be there. We wouldn't miss it and we're both looking forward to seeing you and meeting Mr. McKenna and seeing where you live and seeing Julie and her store. We're both very excited about this news."

"Mother. Daddy. I'm so happy. I'm so looking forward to seeing both of you. I miss you both so much. This is great. Okay, I'll Email you the details and how to get here. You'll be driving, right, daddy?"

"Yeah. Of course. We'll drive."

"One more thing—Chance wants me to tell you there's a spare room available in the main house. You're welcome to stay at the ranch."

"That's gracious of him, Honey, but I think we should stay in a motel. Is there a motel in town?" her mother asked.

"Uhh... yes. There's a Motel 6 and there's a local Bed and Breakfast owned by the Wilson's. Both those places are in town, mother and they are probably online."

"Fine. We'll check on them. Thank Mr. McKenna for offering us a place to stay," her mother said.

"Yeah. Thank him for us," her father said.

"Okay. I'll tell Chance. I'll send the info on the address and how to get to the ranch. It's been so good hearing your voices."

"Same here, Baby Girl. Your mom an' I are lookin' forward to seein' ya an' meetin' your boss," her father said, "an' seein' your lay-out there. We're lookin' forward to seein' that horse run."

"We're anxious about seeing you, Honey. This has been a wonderful surprise," her mother said. "We're looking forward to the trip. Tell Mr. McKenna we look forward to meeting him and give our love to Julie."

"I will, mother. Thank you. Thank you, daddy."

"Bye, Sweetheart. We miss you and love you very much," her mother said.

"So long, Baby Girl. Love ya," her father said.

"Bye, mother. Bye, daddy. I miss you and love you both. See you soon."

FIFTY SIX

This was the day Ryan's parents were due to arrive at McKenna ranch. They went online before leaving Tulsa and made reservations at Wilson's Bed and Breakfast for their stay in Ponderosa Pine. They decided it would be better to support a local business.

~~~

Ryan and Chance were waiting for them when her parents drove up to the main house.

Ryan and her parents hugged each other for several minutes. There were kisses. There were tears. It was a wonderful and happy reunion of parents and daughter after nearly one year apart.

Time for the introductions.

"Mother. Daddy. I'd like you to meet Chance McKenna. Chance, my mother and father. Elizabeth and Brian Hollister."

"It's my pleasure, Mr. an' Mrs. Hollister. Welcome to McKenna ranch. I'm so happy to finally meet the two o' ya. Ryan's told me so much 'bout ya an' where she grew up. Ya have a wonderful daughter. By-the-way, ya can call me Mac."

"Thanks, Mac. No need to be formal here. Just call me Brian. Elizabeth an' I are so happy to be here an' to finally meet ya, Mac. We're so proud o' Ryan an' we're happy to be here for the big race. Congratulations to ya both. Ryan an' I often wanted to have a horse in that race an' now ya kids'll be able to enjoy the experience. I know Ryan's got 'im ready to run—an' win."

"Brian and I are so happy to be here, Chance. You can call me Elizabeth. You have a beautiful property. Congratulations on your horse, Midnight. We were so sorry to hear about your accident. Is the leg all right now?"

"Thanks, Elizabeth. Thanks, Brian. I'm good. The leg's fine an' yeah—Midnight's gonna win that race. He has to win it."

Ryan looked into Chance's eyes. She saw that look. It touched her. She smiled.

"I like all the trees 'round here. Ya got a real nice place, Mac. If ya don't mind me askin', how much land is it?"

"A hundred acres, Brian," Chance said, motioning with his arms, "The trees are Ponderosa Pines."

"You should smell the trees early in the morning," Ryan added. "It smells so good around here."

"It is a beautiful place, Chance," Ryan's mother said.

"Thanks, Elizabeth. We think so. Uhh… we took Midnight down to Ruidoso a couple o' days ago. One o' our hands is with 'im. You'll be able to see 'im down there, Brian."

"Yeah. Ryan mentioned that. I'm lookin' forward to seein' 'im, Mac. Can't wait."

"C'mon. I'll show ya the barn," Chance said.

~~~

"Nice barn, Mac. Twelve stalls, huh?," Ryan's father said.

"Yeah. I've only had twelve horses in here once in three years. Due to some bad weather. Most o' the time there're four or five mares in here when it's foalin' season."

"I see ya've got automatic water bowls in all the stalls," Ryan's father said.

"They sure cut down on time to do chores, Brian. You see there're small doors on the stalls also, so feedin' alfalfa an' grain is real easy from the breezeway. Now, if someone could come up with an automatic stall cleaner—"

That brought a laugh from all of them.

"We have those automatic water dishes, too. Great idea 'bout the stall cleaner, Mac. I think we all hate muckin' out stalls."

They walked through the breezeway and went into the tack room.

Ryan winked at Chance. She reached for the switch and turned on the music system.

"Damn! Are ya kiddin' me, Mac? Classical music?"

"I like that. Mozart, isn't it?" Ryan's mother said.

"Yeah, it's a Mozart symphony, Elizabeth. Ryan had the same reaction the first time she heard it, Brian. The horses like it, though," Chance said, laughing.

"Would ya folks like to see the trainin' area?" Chance asked.

"Yeah, I would, Mac," Brian said.

"You go with Chance, daddy. I'll show mother the cabin."

FIFTY SEVEN

W hen her father and Chance returned from the training track area, Ryan's father remarked, "I was tellin' Mac, Baby Girl, ya got a real nice place back there to train a racehorse."

"I know, daddy. There's more we'd like to do back there."

While Ryan's mother showed Brian around the cabin, Chance took Ryan aside. He suggested they take Ryan's parents to dinner at the Dreamcatcher.

"Mother. Daddy. Chance and I would like to take you to dinner at a favorite place of ours," Ryan said, when the four of them were together in the living room.

"We really appreciate that, kids, but—"

"No buts, Brian," Chance said. "Y'all are comin' to dinner—on us."

The Dreamcatcher would bring back memories. Wonderful memories. Ryan was looking forward to this evening.

~~~

Ryan's parents followed her and Chance to the Dreamcatcher.

The Friday night crowd was already starting to gather as evidenced by the number of vehicles in the parking lot.

Once inside, the four of them headed to the bar where Hawkeye and Linda were tending customers.

"Mother. Daddy. I'd like you to meet Jake Hennessy and Linda Silvernail. This is Jake's place. We all call him 'Hawkeye'," Ryan said. "Linda. Hawkeye. My mother and father. Elizabeth and Brian Hollister."

After the handshakes and hugs, Hawkeye asked Ryan and Chance where they had been the past couple months. Chance said Midnight's training and racing took all their time.

"How's that horse doin' on the track, Mac?" Hawkeye asked.

"He's doin' great an' winnin'," Chance said.

"Mr. Hollister, I understand ya taught your daughter the art o' playin' pool. 'Specially that awesome massé shot. Is that right?" Hawkeye asked.

"Well—yeah, Hawkeye. I'm to blame for that," Brian said, laughing and winking at Ryan. "Ryan not only showed a keen interest in the horses, but she also showed remarkable skills on our pool table at home from a very early age. She picked up on that massé shot like she'd been doin' it all along. That shot won her a lot o' games an' a lot o' trophies. Right, Sweetheart?"

"It did, daddy," Ryan said, giving Chance a big grin.

"Yeah," Chance said, chuckling. "Everyone who was in here that night knew somethin' happened back in that pool room."

"So—is pool part of the plan for tonight, guys?" Hawkeye asked.

"No, not tonight, Hawkeye. We're just gonna have some drinks an' some o' that famous barbecue an'—maybe a dance, or two, later," Chance said, looking at Ryan again with that special look in his eyes.

Ryan realized she was staring at Chance. Wanting him at that moment. She recovered her thoughts in time to avoid her mother's glance.

"We have a question for you and Linda, Hawkeye," Ryan said. "Can you and Linda make it to Ruidoso Downs for Midnight's race this year in the Futurity? We'd love to have the two of you join us—in the winner's circle."

That brought another round of laughter from everyone.

Hawkeye said he and Linda appreciated being asked, but there was no one else to watch the bar and restaurant if both of them were away. He asked Ryan and Chance to be sure and get a video of the race and also the awards ceremony. There was more laughter and joking among them.

Hawkeye told them to sit down. He said the waitress would be right over to take their orders.

Chance took Ryan's father back to the pool room to show him where Ryan made her game-winning massé shot.

Ryan and her mother went to a booth and sat down.

"I didn't want to bring this up in the cabin, Honey," Ryan's mother said, "but—now that we have a moment alone again, I want to apologize in person. I'm really sorry I let Rob talk me into giving him your address. I'm really sorry if it caused a problem for you, or for Mr. McKenna."

"Mother, we talked about this. It's okay. Nothing came of it. If Rob shows up again, I'll make it unmistakably clear to him I'm not in the least bit interested in a relationship. Don't worry, mother."

Ryan's mother was not known for putting on a face accented with a devilish grin. This was, however, a special one-on-one alone time between mother and daughter. There was something Elizabeth Hollister wanted to say to her daughter. This was the perfect time.

"Mr. McKenna would be quite a catch, Honey. I noticed how he looks at you," Ryan's mother said, smiling, with a twinkle in her eyes.

Ryan remained silent, looking around the room, pretending she didn't hear her mother's comment.

"Sooo—are you two—you know—", her mother continued, raising her eyebrows.

After a few moments, Ryan turned and looked at her mother, "Mother. Really!"

Chance and Brian returned from the pool room just in time to prevent an embarrassing moment for Ryan.

"That's a nice pool room, Baby Girl. Nice tables. I wish I could've been here that night to see your winnin' shot in that third game. No offense, Mac," Ryan's father said, laughing.

"None taken, Brian. I wish ya could've seen your daughter's winnin' shot, too. It was amazin'. She's amazin'."

More laughter.

Chance's last remark did not go unnoticed by Ryan's mother, who winked and smiled at Ryan.

Cindy approached their booth carrying a pitcher of beer.

"Hello you two. Nice to see you again. It's been awhile. How've you been?" she asked, smiling at Ryan and Chance.

"We're good, Cindy. Thanks. These are my parents. Elizabeth and Brian Hollister. They're out here from Tulsa. Mother. Daddy. This is Cindy. Hawkeye's number one waitress."

"I'm happy to meet you, Mr. and Mrs. Hollister. Welcome to Ponderosa Pine. Welcome to the Dreamcatcher."

Handshakes all around.

"Hawkeye wanted to send over a complimentary pitcher," Cindy said, partly filling their glasses then setting the pitcher on the table. "Is everyone ready to order?"

Based on Chance's recommendation, it was barbecued steaks with all the side dishes for all of them.

Time for the toasts. Chance did the honors.

"Elizabeth and Brian, Ryan an' I are so happy y'all could join us for a few days an' I'm more than happy ya're here. 'Specially after Ryan told me so much 'bout the two o' ya. Again, our heartfelt welcome."

Everyone raised and touched their glasses.

Chance turned to Ryan.

"To my top hand, Ryan. You're the best."

Ryan's parents put their glasses down and clapped softly. Ryan could see the pride in their eyes and on their faces.

They all raised and touched their glasses again.

Ryan felt that feeling welling up deep inside. Tears came to her eyes, but she managed to hide them. Especially from her mother.

All those memories of her date night with Chance McKenna were coming back. She was looking forward to the dancing she knew would be happening after dinner. She longed for that time to come. To be in Chance McKenna's arms again. Her thoughts were interrupted by the sound of her father's voice.

"Sweetheart, I have to say it again. Your mom an' I are so very proud o' ya an' what ya've done with that stallion. You an' Mac. Both o' ya. So very proud an' anxious to see 'im race."

"Yes, Honey. We're both so proud of you and Chance," her mother said.

"Thanks to the both o' ya for such a wonderful an' talented daughter, Mr. an' Mrs. Hollister," Chance said. "Ryan deserves all the credit workin' with Midnight. I'm just an eager student learnin' the race horse business."

"Ya've got the best teacher ya could have, Mac."

More conversation followed during dinner.

After dinner they waited for the band to begin the first set.

Country Express was the same group that was playing when Ryan and Chance were on their date.

Ryan's parents waited for a slow song from the band.

They went to the dance floor.

Chance stood up and extended his hand to Ryan. He didn't have to say anything. Ryan stood up, took his hand and followed him to the dance floor, which by this time was crowded.

"Ryan and Chance," the leader Sean spoke softly into the mic.

Chance touched his hat and gave a thumbs up.

"Wow. He remembered," Ryan said.

Chance put his arms around Ryan's waist and pulled her close. A smile was on his lips and in his eyes Ryan saw that look. She felt her knees going weak. She laid her head on his chest and closed her eyes. Just as on their date night, she was oblivious to all others on the dance floor. She was in the moment.

Ryan Hollister was in Chance McKenna's arms again.

A second slow song followed. Ryan and Chance remained on the dance floor.

Ryan's parents returned to the booth.

Ryan's mother's undivided attention was on her daughter and Chance dancing. There was a look of joy on her face.

"They make a handsome couple, don't they, Brian?"

"Elizabeth. What're ya thinkin'?"

Elizabeth just looked at Brian and smiled with a mischievous look on her face, not answering.

Chance and Ryan returned to the booth after the second dance, holding hands.

Chance caught a glimpse of Ryan's mother trying to hide a yawn.

Everyone decided to call it a night.

Brian and Elizabeth said goodnight to Ryan and Chance, thanked them for dinner and went back to Wilson's Bed and Breakfast.

Chance and Ryan stopped by the bar to thank Hawkeye for the drinks and said goodnight to him and Linda.

On the way home, Ryan knew she and Chance were once again feeling what they felt for each other during those months past.

FIFTY EIGHT

Fall Classic race day. It was early morning. Final preparations were underway for the drive to Ruidoso Downs.

Alfredo and Roberto were already at the race track. They were responsible for feeding and caring for Midnight and holding his morning workouts. Ryan had complete trust in both of them.

Chance told Juan he must stay behind. Juan understood and was pleased to know he was being placed in complete charge of the ranch and the horses for a couple of days. He had gained the trust of Chance and Ryan months ago.

Ryan made reservations at a local Ruidoso Downs motel for her parents to spend the night after the race.

Ryan and Chance wore their matching outfits. Ryan's parents exclaimed how handsome they both looked. Ryan's mother was especially forward with her praise and compliments and Ryan took notice, giving her mother a nod, a smile and a wink.

Ryan packed Midnight's racing tack and some treats for him.

Ruidoso, New Mexico was several hours driving time from Albuquerque. Only Julie and her friend Bobby and Derrik and Tina Hill would be able to make the drive to the track. For everyone else it was too far to drive and would take up too much time away from work.

The Hills made arrangements with a local neighbor to watch their ranch. Julie left Rosalynn in charge of the store.

They all met for an early morning breakfast at a diner in Ponderosa Pine.

This was a happy and joyful occasion for Ryan's parents. It was about three years since they saw Julie. Elizabeth and Brian often thought of Julie as a daughter because she and Ryan were so close.

The breakfast also provided an opportunity for Elizabeth and Brian to meet the Hills. There was talk between Brian and Derrik regarding a breeding of one of the Hollister stallions with Midnight's dam, Away She Goes.

Breakfast was over. It was time to go.

"Listen up, everyone," Chance said, when they left the diner. "There's a rest stop at 'bout the half-way point for leg stretchin', usin' restrooms, etc."

"My parents enjoyed that, Chance. I'm so happy we all decided to have breakfast together before leaving."

"Yeah. I think ya're father an' Derrik got on really well. I can see a foal comin' out o' that meetin'," Chance said, laughing.

"Chance—I wish we were driving down together," Ryan said, on the way to their trucks.

"So do I, Darlin'. So do I," Chance said, taking Ryan's hand, in full view of Ryan's mother who was smiling ear-to-ear.

"If anyone has a problem on the way, let me know with a cell phone call," Chance said. "All right, y'all, let's go. Follow me. We'll meet at the rest stop."

The five-vehicle caravan headed to Ruidoso Downs with Chance in the lead.

Ruidoso Downs race track was located a short distance from the town of Ruidoso, New Mexico. There was a casino with a bar and restaurant on the track property.

Chance led the way to the owner's and trainer's access and parking area on the backside of the track.

Roberto and Alfredo were waiting for them outside the barn.

Ryan introduced everyone.

"All right. Mother. Daddy. You've been waiting for this. Let's go inside and meet Midnight."

Ryan proudly lead the way to the barn.

They approached Midnight's stall. He let out a soft whinny just as he had done so many times before when he saw Ryan walking toward him. Chance was quick to confirm this was the case every time Midnight saw Ryan.

Everyone laughed.

"Hello, boy. These are for you," Ryan said, taking a couple of Mrs. Pastures Horse Cookies out of her pocket and giving them to Midnight, standing with his head outside the stall door.

"Midnight prob'ly greets Ryan with that whinny 'cause he knows she's got treats in her hand," Chance said.

Alfredo opened Midnight's stall door. Ryan entered the stall and motioned to her father to come inside.

"I want you to meet someone, Midnight," Ryan said, speaking into Midnight's ear.

Brian Hollister stood looking at Midnight in silence for a few moments, stroking his neck and withers and feeling his front legs.

"Damn! That is one fine lookin' piece o' horse flesh, Baby Girl. Ya're right. He looks like a winner to me," Brian said, grinning at Ryan. "Mac, ya got yourself a race horse here."

"I told you, daddy," Ryan said, with a big grin on her face.

"Yeah. He's some kind o' animal, Brian. He's gonna win that race today," Chance said, looking at Ryan with that look in his eyes.

Ryan momentarily lost control. She was unable to put aside what she was feeling at that moment. Not on this day. She returned the look. It was a special moment for the two of them. Moments shared with their eyes that were coming more frequently lately.

"He's gorgeous, Honey," Ryan's mother said, "I love his color and it's obvious why you chose his nickname as you did."

"It sure fits 'im, Baby Girl," her father replied.

They stayed with Midnight for a while longer, talking and making a fuss over him. Ryan had never seen her father show so much interest in a horse before. She knew he was seeing all the qualities and potential in Midnight she had seen in him that first day Chance showed her the stallion.

Everyone left the barn and went to the grandstand and the owner's boxes to relax until time for the big race.

~~~

There were eight horses, including Midnight, who were qualified to run in the All American Futurity. Two of the horses were fillies. A bit unusual for this race. There were two horses that were previously scratched.

The shared purse was two million, six hundred thousand dollars with one million, three-hundred thousand dollars going to the winner.

Weather at the track was clear. The condition of the track was fast. This was Midnight's kind of track.

~~~

Finally, it was time for Ryan to go to the paddock area.

Chance decided to remain in the grandstand with Ryan's mother, Julie, Bobby and Tina Hill . He wanted this day and this race to be about Ryan.

Ryan's father and Derrik went to the paddock area with her.

Alfredo led Midnight from the barn to the paddock area and was waiting for Ryan.

"Do you want to put the tack on him, daddy?" Ryan said, when they approached Midnight.

"This is your time, Baby Girl. It's your race."

"Thanks, daddy. I love you."

Alfredo helped Ryan with the tack while Roberto looked on, anxiously waiting to mount up.

"Midnight looks real good in your colors, Honey," Ryan's father said.

"I agree, Miss Hollister," Derrik said, "Your choice o' colors was great."

"Thanks. Chance and I love our colors."

The call was given for riders up.

Before giving Roberto a leg up, Ryan gave him his riding instructions.

"Let Midnight run his race, Roberto, just like you always do. Let him have his head. Show him the whip, if you have to, but don't use it."

"I understand, Miss Hollister. I'll let Midnight run his race."

Ryan's father was so proud of Ryan as he watched her and listened to her give her jockey his riding instructions. He had witnessed this before at races he and Ryan had gone to in Oklahoma. This race was different. A lot different. Brian Hollister was beaming with pride for his daughter. Brian Hollister had never felt this way before.

Derrik and Ryan's father returned to their box seats in the grandstand.

Ryan remained with Midnight and Roberto, along with Alfredo, waiting for the post parade from the paddock area out to the track.

~~~

Time for the running of the main event arrived. Everyone in the McKenna box seats was on their feet.

The bugler sounded the call to post.

The horses left the paddock area in single file in the order of their post positions.

Midnight was number two in line.

The track announcer's voice came over the loudspeaker.

"Ladies and gentlemen. That was the call to post for the richest Quarter horse race in America. The prestigious All American Futurity for two year olds. This is race number twelve on the card with a purse of two million, six hundred fifty thousand dollars," the track announcer said.

When the field of eight horses entered the track from the paddock area in front of the grandstand there was a thunderous applause from everyone in the grandstand.

Midnight's odds showed him to be the favorite.

Alfredo was leading Midnight with Roberto aboard. Ryan was walking along side, beaming with pride as she looked toward the grandstand to see her parents, Julie and Bobby, Tina and Derrik waving and cheering for her and Midnight.

Ryan saw Chance give her a thumbs up and a high five.

At that moment, she wanted to be in his arms, holding her, telling her it was going to be all right. Suddenly, she felt those feelings for him deep inside her. Burning. She wanted the two of them walking beside Midnight.

Chance blew Ryan a kiss.

Ryan placed her fingers on her lips and blew a kiss to Chance.

The gesture probably went unnoticed by everyone in the McKenna box seats except for Chance McKenna. He smiled, waved to his top hand and gave her another thumbs up.

Ryan had never experienced this much joy at a race with her horses at home. This was a once in a lifetime moment. This was what she wanted from the day Chance gave her the opportunity to work with Midnight on her own. This was the race for which she had trained Midnight. Now, it was just moments away.

One final good luck wish from Ryan to Roberto. She left the track and went up to her box seat in the grandstand to watch the race.

Alfredo continued on with Midnight, leading him to the starting gate along with the other horses.

Midnight was prancing, bobbing his head, as if to say, 'Yeah. I'm ready for this race'.

The track announcer's voice announced the loading of the field into the starting gate. The two fillies in the race were Petite Fleur in post position four and Tom Boy in post position seven. Midnight drew post position number two. Ryan and Chance were very pleased with his gate number.

Midnight loaded quietly into the gate when it was his turn. He was his usual calm self. He stood still with Roberto aboard and waited for the bell.

"Ya looked real good walking with Midnight out there on the track, Baby Girl," her father said. "That horse looks ready to win this thing."

"Thanks, daddy. Thanks so much. This is what Chance and I have worked for the past eight months. I know he's going to do it. Did you notice how calm he was when they entered the track from the pad-dock? He's always good-natured in all his races. The crowd doesn't bother him."

Ryan turned to the group.

"Don't forget, you guys. Midnight's name is 'Flyin' High' and he's in gate number two. You guys know his colors, so make sure you're yelling for the right horse. Okay?"

Everyone shouted, "Yea! Flyin' High! Yellow. Black. White!"

They all clapped, cheered and gave each other high fives.

The track announcer called the crowd's attention to the starting gate.

All the horses were loaded.

Ryan glanced at Chance standing beside her. That look was in his eyes. It was all Ryan could do to control her emotions. She smiled at him, affectionately and thanked him for the kiss. Chance reached for her hand, took it and squeezed it gently.

"Don't worry, Darlin'. He's gonna win it."

Post positions for the race:

1. Eat My Dust, on the rail
2. Flyin' High
3. Bold Aggressor
4. Petite Fleur
5. *My Turn*
6. Willy Nilly
7. Tom Boy
8. Wishin', on the outside

Everyone in the McKenna box seats was on their feet. Ryan had her binoculars focused on Midnight. He was calm in the gate.

The culmination of all her efforts and Chance's efforts was just seconds away.

The bell sounded.

The gates opened.

The field of eight horses bolted forward and began their sprint to the finish line, 440 yards away.

The Track Announcer's voice came over the loudspeaker with the call.

"They'r-r-r-re running in the Grade One All American Futurity—"

"—Petite Fleur broke out of the gate first with Flyin' High second, Eat My Dust third on the rail with Bold Aggressor, My Turn, Willy Nilly, Tom Boy and Wishin' making up the rest of the pack."

"They're at the half-way mark. Petite Fleur still in the lead followed by Flyin' High in second, Eat My Dust third and Bold Aggressor fourth—with the rest of the field following."

Roberto reached down, petted Midnight's neck and spoke to the stallion, "C'mon, Midnight—let's go get 'em, boy."

Midnight responded with a burst of speed and energy Roberto had not felt from the stallion in any of his races before.

The track announcer continued, "Eat My Dust dropping back, Flyin' High coming on strong now, neck 'n neck with Petite Fleur for the lead, Bold Aggressor second, and My Turn third."

"Go, Midnight! Go, boy! Go!" Ryan yelled, along with the others in the McKenna box seats.

"It's Flyin' High in the lead by half a length," the track announcer continued.

Everyone in the grandstands went wild. Screaming and yelling Midnight's name.

"They're at the wire—it's Flyin' High crossing the finish line three-quarters of a length ahead of Petite Fleur with My Turn third and Bold Aggressor fourth—and it's Flyin' High, winner of this year's All American Futurity!" the track announcer concluded, amidst thunderous applause from the grandstands.

Midnight won the Fall Classic by just over three-quarters length.

Ryan and Chance were in each others arms. Everyone was hugging each other. It was an ecstatic and joyful moment for those in the McKenna box seats.

Ryan wanted Chance to hold her. He held her tightly.

"Ya did it, Darlin'. Ya did it. Ya've made me so damn proud. I can't tell ya—"

"Oh, Chance. Chance—we did it together. You and I and Midnight —and let's not forget Roberto."

Chance and Ryan held each other tightly for what seemed like minutes, not hearing the roaring and applauding crowd in the grandstands around them. Ryan and Chance were in their own world. Oblivious to everyone else.

Chance leaned down and kissed her. Ryan had secretly waited for this moment for so many months.

Their private moment ended.

"That filly, Petite Fleur, sure gave Midnight a run for his money, didn't she?" Chance said.

Everyone laughed.

"Yeah, but you know, we gals let you guys win all the time just to keep you quiet," Ryan replied, winking at the other ladies in the group, which brought more cheers from everyone."

Midnight's winning time was twenty-one point one seconds. It was almost a track record for the Fall Classic.

Time to leave their box seats in the grandstand and head to the winner's circle.

"C'mon, Everybody. Let's get down there," Ryan said.

The McKenna party left their box seats and hurried to the infield.

Roberto rode Midnight in a circle in front of the grandstand so all in the crowd could see him then headed to the winner's circle.

Midnight's prancing and head bobbing on the way to the infield was majestic. It was as if he knew what he had just done.

Ryan's parents looked so proud to be there with their daughter.

Presentation of the trophy and taking the group photos followed. It was a joyous occasion.

Ryan was aware Chance could not take his eyes off her.

They smiled and shared their special look with each other.

FIFTY NINE

Alfredo stayed with Midnight after the race, walking him, rubbing him down and feeding him. Alfredo was sorrowful he had to miss the party, but he understood his responsibility was to look after Midnight.

Ryan and Chance took Ryan's parents, Julie and Bobby, Tina and Derrik and Roberto to a dinner party at the Billy the Kid Bar and Grill at Ruidoso Downs.

When the drinks arrived at the table, Chance stood up, his glass in hand.

"It's too bad they don't allow horses in this room. Here's to Midnight."

Laughter, cheers and a round of applause followed. Everyone raised their glass.

"I wanna make a toast to ya, Ryan. When ya showed up at the main gate that mornin' a year ago ya were not the sex I expected to see lookin' back at me from the call box," Chance said, waiting for the laughter to subside before continuing. So many good things've happened at McKenna ranch durin' the past nine months because o' ya. Ya took a wild stallion an' turned 'im into a winnin' race horse. Ya saw his potential for racin' immediately, when I didn't have a clue. Ya broke 'im, worked with 'im an' got 'im to where he is today. I tried to put a saddle on 'im—once—an' I found out that was like tryin' to put a pair o' socks on a rooster," again loud laughter from everyone interrupted Chance. "Sooo, I wanna say publicly—I don't know what I would've done if ya hadn't o' showed up that mornin'. We're all here today because o' ya an' Midnight. My deepest appreciation an' gratitude. Please. Everyone. Raise your glasses. To Ryan Hollister—my top hand. Ryan, ya're the best."

Ryan could not help looking at her mother who was beaming. Tears were in her mother's eyes. Even her father's eyes were a bit moist.

There were tears in most eyes in the room as they applauded and cheered and raised their glasses to Ryan.

Ryan herself was trying to hold back the tears, but she couldn't. She looked up at Chance with such a longing in her eyes. She wanted him so badly at that moment.

Chance had more toasts to make.

"Elizabeth an' Brian, ya deserve to be recognized as the ones who nurtured Ryan through her early years an' gave her the opportunity an' encouragement to pursue her love o' horses an' I might add, her love o' pool. Thank ya for bein' her parents. Thank ya for bein' here. To Elizabeth an' Brian Hollister."

More laughter, cheers and applause. Everyone raised their glasses.

"Also, I wanna recognize an' thank Tina an' Derrik Hill for sellin' Midnight to me an' lettin' me take him off their hands. Thanks, guys. This race was as much for the two o' ya as it was for Ryan an' me."

All in the room gave a thumbs up to the Hills.

"There's one more person in the room I must mention," Chance said, looking in Julie's direction. "Her name is Julie Scott."

Julie tried to scoot down in her chair, but she couldn't escape everyone's eyes looking her way.

"Miss Scott," Chance continued, "if ya hadn't o' called your friend that mornin' I put an ad on your bulletin board, we wouldn't be here today. Would we? Thank ya, Miss Scott, for makin' that call to Ryan."

Applause broke out.

Julie's face turned bright red. She smiled at Chance and nodded. She looked at Ryan who gave her a big smile.

"Finally, there are two more—actually three more—I wanna toast. The jockey who rode this race, Roberto Vasquez, for a job well done. We're lucky to have ya ridin' Midnight for us, Roberto."

Loud applause for Midnight's jockey.

"Also, to the Gomez brothers who work for us on the ranch. Alfredo, who's out in the barn with Midnight an' Juan, who had to stay on the ranch to take care o' things back there. Ryan an' I could not manage the ranch without 'em. Thanks to y'all."

Everyone raised their glasses and gave loud cheers and applause.

Chance nodded and took his seat.

The party continued with dinner and conversation.

Chance was sitting at the head of the table. Ryan was sitting to his right.

They could not keep their eyes off each other throughout the dinner. What would have been uncomfortable staring between two other people was for Ryan and Chance an intense sign of the deep feelings they were having for each other at that very special moment.

They expressed those feelings for each other through their eyes.

Ryan's past year on McKenna ranch flashed briefly through her mind.

Her dream was coming true.

Have I fallen in love with him? Could Jules see it all along? Should I finally admit it to myself? I want him.

A tidal wave of passion coursed through her body.

I want him.

SIXTY

Chance had a new sign made of wrought iron letters above the main gate. New wrought iron posts held the wrought iron cross-beam where the letters were attached.

The letters read:

McKenna Racing Stables

A sign was made and located on the grassy knoll outside the main gate. There was a photograph of Midnight behind plate glass

An inscription beside the photograph read:

McKenna Racing Stables
Ponderosa Pine, N.M.
Home of Flyin' High
a.k.a. Midnight
All American Futurity Winner

Ryan was thrilled.

"We can add 'Standing as Top Sire' to the sign when Midnight is standing at stud," she said.

"That's a great idea, Darlin'. What d' ya think 'bout a stud fee for 'im when the time comes?"

"I'm thinking we can start at thirty thousand and if his first crop of foals does well, we'll increase it to fifty thousand. Maybe more. We'll have to wait and see. He is an unknown after all. We'll see how he does."

"Are ya serious?"

"He just won the Fall Classic, Chance and he has the bloodlines to back it up."

"Wow! I'm thinkin' we oughta start his stud service tomorrow," Chance said, bringing laughter to both of them.

~~~

The mortgage loan was paid off from Midnight's Fall Classic winnings.

Mr. Lopez and Ponderosa Pine Savings and Loan Bank eagerly signed the deed of the ranch over to Chance McKenna.

Mr. Lopez wished Chance and Ryan much success in the future.

Chance changed the operation of the ranch to a stable of racing Quarter horses.

Midnight won several more races. He would be retired to stud the following year.

Chance asked Ryan to take charge of the racing side of the business. Ryan could not be more excited. She was living her dream, but— there was a part of her dream still unfulfilled.

~~~

Sunsets on McKenna ranch were special.

Serene. Peaceful.

A time to ponder the day just ending and speculate about what the new day would bring.

Chance would often put tack on Sunny and ride off by himself to watch the sun go down.

His thoughts would always come back to how much Ryan had done for the ranch since coming to work for him twelve months earlier. He owed her a debt of gratitude he would never be able to repay.

Chance knew how he felt about Ryan. He wondered if she ever thought about the times they had spent together in the past. Did she think about those times the way he was thinking about them now?

Chance recalled their date at the Dreamcatcher and the kisses they shared after the date. He thought about the affectionate moments and all the kisses they shared since then. He knew Ryan wanted to keep their relationship on a business level. She had let him know that in no uncertain terms at the dinner party and afterward, except for a few fleeting moments lately.

"What d' ya think, Lady?" Chance said, petting the dog sitting beside him who was his companion on this ride like she was on all his rides. "Am I barkin' up the wrong tree?"

Lady responded with a soft, exhaled moan, indicating her concern for her master's feelings.

Chance missed Ryan on those sunset rides.

He missed her terribly.

What would it take to bring her back?

SIXTY ONE

Chance was excited to see Ryan's truck parked in front of the cabin.

"Hi, Chance. I was just thinking about you. I made some selections from two of the sale catalogs and wanted to show them to you."

"That's good, Darlin'. Great. I'll take a look at 'em later. Uhh... I'm stoppin' by to ask a favor. Well, not a favor, really. I guess ya could call it a request. I know ya've been busy with the upcomin' sales an' all an' that's good, but I'm thinkin'—maybe we need some time off for a change. To relax. Away from work. Just the two o' us. What d' ya say?"

"Chance—"

"Now, wait. I know how ya feel 'bout us spendin' time alone together an' I've tried to respect that. I just thought it would be good if we could enjoy an afternoon together. There's this place on the ranch I wanna take ya to. For a picnic. That seems pretty safe to me. It's not— it won't be—a date. What d' you say?"

"A picnic? Well, that does sound like fun, Chance. Okay," she said, wondering if this was what she was hoping for. Dreaming about for so long. Time alone with him again. "Where are we going?"

"You'll see. It's a special place. Ya've never been there before or if ya had been there ya would've said somethin' 'bout it."

Thoughts of their date at the Dreamcatcher entered Ryan's mind. Unlike that time, Chance seemed more sure of himself now. She wanted to spend time alone with him. Just the two of them. This is what she thought about for so long.

"All right. I'll go on a picnic with you. When and what should I bring?"

"How's this comin' weekend? Sunday? I'll come to the cabin a little before noon. We'll have to horseback to the place. Too far to walk. We can't drive to it, either. If ya could bring the sandwiches an' some fixin's, I'll bring the drinks and somethin' to sit on. How's that?"

"It sounds great. I'm looking forward to Sunday. Thanks, Chance."

Ryan watched Chance walk the path back to the house. When he reached the side door of the house he turned and waved. He must have suspected she would be watching.

Ryan waved back.

It had been so long since the day of the dinner party.

Would this be the special time alone with Chance McKenna she had hoped for all those weeks?

SIXTY TWO

Excitement was building the past couple of days and as much as Ryan wanted to keep her emotions in check, she could not help thinking about the picnic coming up on the weekend. Just like the dinner party, she wanted this to be a special occasion for the two of them.

~~~

Sunday morning.

There was a knock on Ryan's open door.

"Hi, Darlin'. Ya ready?"

"Yes, Chance. I'm very much looking forward to this," she called out, from the bedroom.

"Ya look beautiful, Darlin'," he said, when she entered the living room.

"Thanks, Chance. I'm ready."

Ryan picked up the backpack with the things she was bringing.

The temperature was kind today. Low seventies. Clear. Lot's of sunshine.

They went to the barn area. Chance had already tied his favorite mare, Sunny, to a corral rail. Ryan went to Midnight's paddock and led him to the barn area.

"I've never seen Sunny outside her paddock and I've never seen you riding her, Chance."

"Yeah. I guess ya've always been somewhere else when I rode her. I usually ride her in the evenin's. She's my favorite. I'm gonna breed her next season for the first time."

"What stallion do you have in mind for her?"

Chance gave Ryan that boyish grin she had seen so many times before. She knew which stallion he was thinking about. Let Sunny and Midnight enjoy their first time with each other.

They joked and laughed about the picnic date while they put the tack on the horses. For now, they were both relaxed.

They mounted the horses.

"This way," Chance said.

Ryan followed on Midnight.

Lady accompanied them on this ride.

~~~

There were trees and undergrowth on the way and Ryan understood why they were riding the horses. The ponderosa pine trees were thick in some areas.

They eventually came upon a clearing.

Ryan let out a gasp and a shout.

There in front of them was a medium-sized pond, several hundred feet in diameter, completely surrounded by Ponderosa Pine trees.

The water was a bluish-green color reflected from the sky above and the trees surrounding the pond. It was crystal clear, revealing the bottom.

"Chance, this place is awesome. It's beautiful. I never knew about it. I'm so thrilled you brought me here."

"My dad proposed to my mom here. They would ride over here often. Like I said, it's a special place. The pond is fed from an underground spring. None o' the other ranches I know of has a pond like this one. It adds that much more value to the property. Ya know, Darlin', we should come here an' go skinny-dippin'—when the weather warms up again."

The comment about Chance's parent's engagement at the pond did not go past Ryan, but she gave it no further thought at the time except to wonder if Chance got some of his occasional sensitivity from his father.

As for the skinny-dipping comment, Ryan thought she should probably wait for a more fortuitous time to respond. Instead, she gave him a girlish grin and nodded in agreement.

"It surely is a magical place, Chance."

They tied Sunny and Midnight to two nearby trees.

The picnic items were unpacked.

Chance brought a mat and a cooler containing the drinks. He unrolled the mat and placed it in a shady spot on the ground.

They sat down.

"I have a surprise for you, Chance. I have your favorite sandwiches here," Ryan said, reaching into her backpack.

"Turkey bologna? With cheddar cheese slices?"

"Yes—and some ham and Swiss cheese ones, too and look—"

Ryan opened the cooler with the potato salad and some lettuce and tomato slices inside.

"This lunch looks so good, Darlin'. My favorite sandwiches an' fresh, home made potato salad. What more could a guy ask for?"

A kiss from my top hand would be nice.

Chance opened the cooler he brought and took out a couple plastic bottles of spring water and a six-pack of Sprite and placed them on the mat.

Chance raised his can of Sprite.

256

"A toast to ya, Darlin' an' to secluded places. Thanks for bein' here."

"Chance. Thank you. You did find a way to surprise me again. I love it here. Thanks for bringing me."

During lunch they chatted about all that had happened during the past year and about the future of the ranch and how it was changing.

Absent from their conversation, perhaps purposely on both their parts, was the role they would play in each others future lives. Ryan and Chance both chose not to go there and avoided that subject.

The picnic was a relaxing time for the two of them, though. A much needed time alone together. Away from the day-to-day operation of the ranch. Away from work and the horses.

Ryan noticed a subtle uneasiness in Chance while they were eating and chatting.

Being nervous was not one of Chance McKenna's character traits. Ryan recalled the way he stood at her door the day he asked her for their first date. A little boy, somewhat frightened, with an anxious look on his face. That was anxiety more than nerves. These were real nerves showing. Maybe it was because the two of them were completely alone again after many weeks. In a secluded place. With no outside distractions.

"The sun's gonna set pretty soon. We should prob'ly head back."

"I had such a good time, Chance. Thanks for bringing me here. I can understand why this is such a special place. I want to come here again sometime."

"I'm glad ya like it here. I'm happy ya were able to see it."

"After today, the pond will be our special place, Chance and yes—let's plan on coming here next summer for some skinny-dippin'. All right?" she said, looking at him with that coy, little girl look on her face.

Chance wasn't sure he heard her say that, but he didn't want to ask Ryan to repeat it in case she might say she was just kidding. He gave her a big grin instead.

"Yeah. I'm really lookin' forward to Summer in that case, Miss Hollister," he replied, giving her a wink.

They picked up all their things and went to where the horses were tied.

Chance whistled. Lady came running.

"I have an idea. Why don't we ride back to the barn by a different way? There's an old gate near here that's never used. Wanna go back that way?" Chance said, pointing in a direction leading away from the pond.

"Sure. It'll be a chance for me to see more of the property."

When they were on the horses Chance led the way.

~~~

Soon, they came upon a wooden gate barely visible through the underbrush.

"Just as I thought. I'll pull some o' those weeds an' brush away," Chance said, getting off Sunny.

He hand the reins to Ryan.

"Is that Ponderosa Pine Road?" she asked, pointing to a road on the other side of the chain link fence.

"Yeah," he said, removing underbrush and pushing the gate open. "C'mon through. I'll cover the gate up again so it's not visible from the road. I prob'ly should replace it with chain link."

They rode the short distance on Ponderosa Pine Road to the main gate.

SIXTY THREE

They stopped the horses at the main gate and looked at each other for a brief moment.

Ryan shrugged her shoulders ever so slightly and raised an eyebrow.

"Wanna get down—for a minute?" Chance said.

They got off the horses and tied Sunny and Midnight to the main gate.

Chance removed the cooler from his saddle. He took Ryan's hand and led her to the grassy knoll where Midnight's sign was located.

Chance opened the cooler and removed a bottle of champagne and two champagne glasses. He set them on top of Midnight's sign, then took a corkscrew out of his jeans pocket and popped the cork.

Ryan's jaw dropped.

"Champagne? Real glasses?"

Finally, some nerves started to show again. Chance seemed to be reaching for an answer.

"Well—it's to celebrate your first visit to the pond today, Darlin'."

"We're celebrating my first visit to the pond? Here? At the main gate? We've already been to the pond, Chance."

Chance poured champagne into the glasses. He toasted Ryan again as he had done many times before and thanked her for all she had done for him and the ranch.

They continued to look at each other briefly, in an awkward moment of silence. Chance's gaze shifted from Ryan's eyes to the ground then back to her eyes.

"Darlin'—there's, uhh... somethin' I wanna say—"

"What is it, Chance?" she asked, beginning to feel a bit nervous and anxious herself

Chance took her hands in his. He knelt down on one knee.

He hesitated a moment longer, took a deep breath and gazed into her eyes.

A look of total surprise came over Ryan's face. Her eyes widened. She drew n a breath.

"Chance. What—what is this? What are you doing?"

His words came slowly. Softly.

"Darlin', you're constantly on my mind when we aren't workin' together. I wonder where ya are an' what ya're doin'. Alone, recently—watchin' the sunsets—I tried to compare their beauty with yours. There was no comparison. There's more beauty in you than all the sunsets that've ever been."

Ryan let out a gasp. She could not believe she was hearing those words from Chance McKenna. They were intoxicating. She was being swept away by an irresistible flood of emotion for the man kneeling in front of her.

Did I just hear those beautiful words coming from Chance McKenna? Those feelings again. What's happening to me?

Chance smiled, continuing to look up at her. She could feel his hands shaking ever so slightly. He continued to speak with an increasing self-assurance.

"I've fallen in love with ya, Darlin'. I never expected it to happen. I don't know how it happened or when it happened, but—it happened."

Ryan, still wide-eyed, opened her mouth to speak. Chance squeezed her hands gently. He shook his head slightly side-to-side as if to ask her to hold back the words he knew she was about to say.

"Wait, Darlin'. Let me—let me get all o' this out before I lose my nerve. I know what you're thinkin'. I know what you're gonna say. Well, I wanna change that. You're the one. The one I've been waitin' for. You're beautiful, intelligent, charmin' an' ambitious. Ya have an adorable little girl quality an' a spirit I've never seen before. I've just been driftin' for a long time. No real purpose to my life. Ya turned my life around. Oh—I know there was a rough time, or two, between us, but—we overcame those times an' I wanna be a part o' your dream, Darlin'. Right here. On this ranch."

Ryan could feel the intense emotion building inside her. It was uncontrollable. She could not hold it back. Tears welled up in her eyes.

Chance let go her hands, reached into his shirt pocket and removed a black, velvet-covered jewelry case. He opened it to reveal a brilliant, sparkling, diamond ring.

He held the open case in his hands and presented it to her.

"I love ya, Ryan Elizabeth Hollister. Will ya marry me?"

The tears had been building as Chance was speaking, but now they were gushing. Ryan tried to hold them back. She tried swallowing. Hard. It didn't help. The tears kept coming.

During all the time he had worked with her, Chance had never seen tears in Ryan's eyes. She always showed that ambitious determination on the outside. She never showed the feminine, inner side that is sometimes a vulnerable part of every woman. But she was showing that vulnerability now. Those were real tears flowing.

Ryan looked down at him through the tears.

"Yes, Chance. Yes. I'll marry you."

Ryan's face was radiant. Beaming. Joy overwhelmed her.

Ryan held out her hand. Chance removed the ring from the case and placed it on her finger. She managed a tearful smile.

Chance stood up, put his arms around her and held her close.

"Darlin'... top hands don't cry," he whispered softly, brushing the tears from her cheeks with his fingertips.

"Sometimes they do, if their boss just proposed to them," she said, with the hint of a smile, "Then... they cry happy tears."

Chance held her face in his hands, bent down and kissed her softly. Ryan put her arms around him and pulled herself against him.

The kiss continued until both of them were out of breath. Each one could feel the desire, the passion, building inside them.

Ryan looked into his eyes. She wanted to tell Chance how she really felt. Once and for all. All those feelings bottled up inside her all those weeks came pouring out.

"Chance—I tried to deny my feelings for you for such a long time. I tried to push them out of my head, out of my heart, with the excuse you were my boss. I love you, Chance. I love you so much. I know we've been together, working, but—I've missed being close to you all those weeks and months. Darling, I'm so sorry I pushed you away. It was never about you. I had to prove something to myself an'—"

"I know. I know. Ya don't have to explain. That was the past. This is the future, Sweetheart. Our future. Together."

"It's the most beautiful engagement ring I've ever seen," she said, admiring the ring. "It's gorgeous. That was such a beautiful proposal, Chance. Today is the happiest day of my life."

Ryan looked again at the ring finger on her left hand to make sure there was really a ring there and she wasn't in one of her day-dreaming moments.

She moved her hand into a sliver of sunlight shinning through the trees. The reflection burst into a thousand tiny sparkles of multi-colored light. A miniature fireworks on her finger!

"Mother and daddy will be so happy for us, Chance. I can't wait to tell them and all our friends. I'm so happy and—I wish your mother and father could share this, too."

"Thanks, Darlin'. I know they would've been as proud o' ya as I am an' they would've loved ya as much as I do."

Holding the ring up, with a smile on her face, she said, "Wait til Jules sees this."

Ryan's voice was barely above a whisper.

"Will you stay the night—in the cabin?"

Chance nodded.

"I'll let Carmen know where I am."

They headed to the barn on horseback. Chance held Ryan's hand.

Ryan smiled at her love riding beside her. She glanced at the sign above the main gate.

McKenna Racing Stables

Her dream was fulfilled.

The Beginning...

Another romance by Valerie West...

Jessica Caldwell was facing not only an immediate crisis, but also feelings for a past love. Will she overcome the danger and will she recover the love she had given up years ago?

Please visit
https://www.valeriewestromance.com

Another romance by Valerie West...

Arabella Beaucaire met a love who changed her life, but they lived in different worlds. Will the feelings coming from her heart be strong enough to reconcile the differences between them?

Please visit
https://www.valeriewestromance.com

Another romance by Valerie West...

Cynthia Pruit was devoted to her life as a dancer but she yearned for a relationship. When he joined the dance company her life changed. Will she be able to have both her career and the relationship she longed for?

Please visit
https://www.valeriewestromance.com

Made in the USA
Middletown, DE
02 January 2018